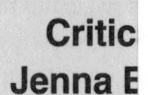

Critic
Jenna B

THE DEVIL INSIDE

Nominated for the 2007 *Romantic Times* Reviewer's
Choice Award for Best Urban Fantasy
Finalist for Love Romances and More Café's Best of
2007 Award for Best Book All Around

that reaches out and grabs your attention. Ms. Black has created a spine-chilling new series." —FreshFiction.com

"An outstanding beginning to a new supernatural series! The book starts out with action and only gets faster. I never noticed the story to slow down at all. The plot slowly unfolds to reveal that more is going on than anyone can possibly guess. I sincerely believe the author to have a major winner on her hands with Morgan Kingsley. Five stars." —*Huntress Reviews*

WATCHERS IN THE NIGHT

"Clever plotting and terrific supporting characters elevate this novel into a first-rate romantic thriller."
—*Romantic Times Book Reviews*

"Jenna Black has crafted a fine story with *Watchers in the Night*. She supplies deft handling of plot, characters, and genre, and I enjoyed the novel tremendously. I see many more fascinating novels coming from this author in the future!"
—Heather Graham, *New York Times* bestselling author of *Kiss of Darkness*

"You'll want to bare your throat to Jenna Black's enthralling heroes. This cleverly plotted romantic tale will leave you hungry for more!"
—Sabrina Jeffries, *New York Times* bestselling author of *Only a Duke Will Do*

"Grabs you from the very beginning and doesn't let you go until the very end. Even then, you're hoping for more. Peopled with an intriguing supporting cast, and a plotline that twists and turns like a maze, Ms. Black does a wonderful job creating a world where you're never sure what's going to happen." —Vivi Anna, author of *Hell Kat*

SECRETS IN THE SHADOWS

"Paranormal romance at its finest! Black writes the kind of hero I want to date!"
—Gena Showalter, author of *The Nymph King*

SHADOWS ON THE SOUL

"Dark, magical and deliciously brooding, just how I like them!" —Gena Showalter, author of *The Nymph King*

THE DEVIL'S
DUE

JENNA BLACK

A DELL SPECTRA BOOK

THE DEVIL'S DUE
A Dell Spectra Book / December 2008

Published by Bantam Dell
A Division of Random House, Inc.
New York, New York

Dell is a registered trademark of Random House, Inc., and
the Dell colophon, Spectra, and the portrayal of a boxed "s" are
trademarks of Random House, Inc.

ISBN 978-0-440-24492-9

Printed in the United States of America
Published simultaneously in Canada

www.bantamdell.com

OPM   10 9 8 7 6 5 4 3 2 1

To the Heart of Carolina Romance Writers.
I can't tell you how much your
unfailing support has meant to me.

Acknowledgments

Thanks first to Anne Groell, my fabulous editor, who saved me from leaving a plot hole big enough to drive a truck into. Editors are worth their weight in gold! Thanks also to my agent, Miriam Kriss. I don't know what I'd do without your enthusiasm and savvy. And last but certainly not least, thanks to all the readers out there who have dropped me a line to tell me you enjoy my books. It makes my day every time!

THE DEVIL'S DUE

Chapter 1

It was my first time in the office in more than a week. Somehow, my actual paying job as an exorcist didn't seem so satisfying these days. Finding out that exorcizing demons doesn't actually kill them had robbed me of my joie de vivre. Of course, being possessed by the king of the demons myself had something to do with it, too.

Still, harboring the demon king and trying to protect him from his brother, Dougal, the would-be usurper of the demon throne, didn't pay the bills, and I had a lot of them piling up. It had been less than two months since my house had burned to the ground with all my worldly possessions inside, and my insurance company had yet to begin showering me with largesse.

I was seriously behind in my paperwork, and was disappointed to discover that the Paperwork Fairy hadn't taken care of everything during my absence. With something between a sigh and a groan, I dropped into my chair and turned on my computer. While I waited for the dinosaur to muster the energy to boot up, I checked my phone messages. There were a bunch from the U.S. Exorcism Board reminding me that (a) I was late paying my dues, and (b) I was late filing the paperwork on my last three exorcisms. There were also the usual calls from telemarketers who were desperate for me to change long-distance phone companies, but I was much more interested in the three messages—each one more urgent than the last—from a woman who identified herself as Claudia Brewster. She didn't say what she wanted, but I made an educated guess that she had a loved one who'd been possessed by an illegal demon.

I frowned as I took down her number, because it was local. In Philadelphia and the surrounding area, I'm almost always contacted by the court system when there's an illegal or rogue demon in custody, and I hadn't heard anything. It wasn't unusual for me to be hired by distraught family members (not to brag or anything, but I have the best record of any exorcist in the U.S.), but those were usually out-of-state cases.

I called the daytime number Ms. Brewster left and got her secretary. Ms. Brewster was in a meeting, but the secretary took a message and said I should receive a call back within a couple of hours. I hung up, and my shoulders slumped. So much for my reprieve from the dreaded paperwork.

My computer had finally roused itself from its slumber, so I began slogging my way through my backlog. As you might have guessed by now, this wasn't my favorite part of my job, and I had to work hard to resist the lure of a rousing game of Spider Solitaire.

About an hour later, I was feeling conspicuously virtuous about my productivity—and about my willpower—when there came a tentative rap on my office door. I wasn't expecting anyone, and, as far as I knew, no one knew I was here. I pulled my bag from the desk drawer and grabbed my Taser. Hey, better safe than sorry, right?

"Come in," I beckoned, holding the Taser, now armed and ready, in my lap, where my desk would hide it from view.

The door opened, and a lovely forty-something woman walked in. Dressed in a dark blue pinstriped pants suit that looked like it had been made exactly to her measurements, she screamed conservative corporate America. That image was enhanced by the blond hair fastened in a well-sprayed French twist and a makeup job that was supposed to make her look like she wasn't wearing any. She'd have fit right in as the token female in a boardroom full of old fogies.

I took a wild guess as to who my visitor might be. "Ms. Brewster?" I asked, wondering why she hadn't bothered to call first. Paranoia—which was my constant and very reasonable state of mind these days— created any number of unpalatable suggestions, so instead of standing up and offering to shake hands, I remained seated with my Taser at the ready.

"Please, call me Claudia," she said with a brittle-looking smile as she closed the door behind her.

"Claudia," I agreed, taking an instant dislike to her for no good reason. "I usually meet with clients by appointment only, and I'm very busy at the moment." I idly tapped a couple keys on my keyboard, turning my face to the screen while keeping a watch on her out of the corner of my eye. "I can fit you in tomorrow at..." I pretended to scrutinize a calendar. "Three o'clock. Will that work for you?" I turned to face her once more, putting on my blandest smile.

Claudia licked her lips and shifted her grip on the designer pocketbook that hung from her shoulder. It was only then that I noticed how she clutched the strap of that bag as if it were a lifeline.

"Please, Ms. Kingsley," she said, and she sounded

like she might be on the verge of tears. "I've been trying to reach you for a week, and I'm . . . Well, I'm desperate."

My opinion of her softened, and I realized my initial dislike had been a result of her looking like she had her shit together—in deep contrast to myself. But no power suit and fancy makeup could camouflage her misery for long, and I felt a surge of kinship.

"You can call me Morgan," I said, and I let my curiosity get the better of me. "Please, have a seat." I indicated the pair of chairs in front of my desk, and, with a sigh of relief, she sat in the one on the right and put her bag on the one on the left. I folded my hands on the desk in front of me, leaving the Taser on my lap, where I could easily reach it if necessary.

"What can I do for you, Claudia?"

She took a deep breath as if steeling herself for a mighty effort. Strain showed in the tightness in the corners of her eyes, and she wet her lips again. "I don't know where else to turn," she said, giving me a pleading look.

"Okay," I said slowly, then gestured for her to continue when she seemed to stall out.

"I'm in desperate need of your . . . services."

People were often reluctant and uncomfortable when they hired me. For reasons that escaped me, they often found having a loved one possessed to be a source of embarrassment. However, Claudia was taking it to the extreme with this strange hesitancy. I'd been sympathetic for about sixty seconds, which I think is a personal record. I decided it was high time to revert to my usual bluntness.

"Just spit it out already," I said, with more than a touch of impatience. "You want me to exorcize a demon."

A hint of fire flared in her eyes, and it seemed like

my prickly bedside manner had steadied her some. "Yes. But of course it's not quite that simple or I'd have gone through more traditional channels."

She crossed her legs, her foot jiggling restlessly. "It's about my son, Tommy." She grimaced. "Tom," she corrected herself, and I had to suppress a smile.

"You think your son is possessed."

She shook her head. "I *know* he's possessed." She seemed to notice her jiggling foot and stopped herself with what looked like a concerted effort. "He was possessed while his father and I were on vacation."

I still didn't get why she was here. "It's a police matter at this point," I told her. "Once they take him into custody, I can come to the containment center and make an official diagnosis." I held up a hand to forestall her attempt to interrupt. "I'm not saying I don't believe you—it's just that we have to follow standard procedures. After I diagnose him—"

"Ms. Kingsley," she cut in, "let me get right to the crux of the matter. All the evidence except for common sense says that my son is a willing host."

"A willing host," I repeated stupidly. I'd pictured Tommy Brewster as a petulant teenager, but he had to be at least twenty-one to be a legal host. I nudged my estimation of Claudia's age up a few years.

She nodded. "They've got the signed forms and everything. But there is no way in hell my son volunteered to host a demon."

And to think I'd believed she had her shit together! I thought I was the queen of denial, but it looked like there was a new contender to the throne. "You do understand the process of registering to be a legal demon host, don't you?" I asked.

She made an impatient tsking sound. "Of course I do, but—"

I counted off the points on my fingers. "He had to

sign the documents before witnesses. In a courtroom. On videotape. And after he'd been interviewed by a shrink to establish competency. Are you seriously trying to tell me he did all that against his will? And that no one noticed?"

She pressed her lips tightly together. "I know how it looks. And I know you think I'm just the distraught mother who can't accept that her baby has grown up." She managed a rictus of a smile. "That last part's even true." The forced smile faded. "But volunteering to host is the last thing in the world Tommy would do. He *hates* demons. Hates them with a passion."

I wasn't so fond of them myself—hence my career choice—but I had to admit getting to know Lugh, the demon king, had lessened my hate by approximately one hair. "People change their minds."

"Not like this they don't. You see, when my husband and I left for the Bahamas, we'd finally given up hope that we could extricate Tommy—*Tom*—from God's Wrath."

I couldn't suppress a gasp. God's Wrath is the most militant of the anti-demon hate groups. They specialize in roasting people alive to destroy the Spawn of Satan, as they consider demons. They're so radical, they even hate exorcists, because when we kick a demon out of its host, its host gets to live. Of course, about eighty percent of them live the rest of their lives as vegetables, but God's Wrath didn't think that was a severe enough punishment for those sinners who'd invited demons into our world. So I had to admit, the idea of a God's Wrath member volunteering to host a demon was a bit . . . out there.

"We were gone ten days," Claudia continued. "Do you really believe someone could be a card-carrying member of God's Wrath one day, and then ten days later be a willing demon host?"

There was no denying it sounded hinky. Hell, I didn't even see how a former God's Wrath member could get accepted into the Spirit Society in such a short time, much less get accepted, get an appointment with a judge, get all the paperwork approved, and have a summoning ceremony.

"I presume you voiced your concerns to the police?" I asked.

She nodded. "Naturally. Everyone agrees it sounds like an unusual case, but there's no evidence of a crime having been committed." Her voice turned bitter. "Everyone tells me with great sympathy that there's nothing they can do to help me."

"What do *you* think happened?"

Claudia blinked away what might have been the start of tears. "I think he had to have been possessed already when he signed the papers."

I shook my head. "That con hasn't worked for at least thirty or forty years." There was a famous case back in the sixties of a young man who'd turned out to be possessed when he signed the consent forms. Ever since then, the applicant had to be examined by an exorcist first.

"I know the exorcist who was on duty claimed Tommy wasn't possessed, but he could have been paid off."

It sounded plausible, if hard to prove. "Who was the exorcist?"

"His name was Sammy Cho."

I think I managed to avoid making a face. Sammy was a second-rate exorcist—which explained why he was doing shit work like examining host wannabes. However, even the worst exorcist in existence can read auras well enough to spot a demon, and Sammy had such a big stick up his ass I half-expected leaves to sprout from his ears in the spring.

"There's no way Sammy would take a bribe," I said.

"No one is incorruptible."

"Sammy's about as close as you can get. Believe me, I know him well." Only in a professional capacity, mind you, and being an inveterate rule-breaker myself, I tried to spend as little time in his presence as possible. But I'd stake my reputation on the fact that he'd rather die than take a bribe.

Claudia dismissed my assertion with a wave of her hand. "It doesn't really matter in the long run *how* it happened. The fact remains that my son has been possessed against his will." She swallowed hard. "I know it may already be too late, that he may never recover, but I *have* to get that demon out of him."

And I realized now exactly what she wanted me to do. "You want me to perform an illegal exorcism."

She held her chin up defiantly. "We—my husband and I—have money. We're willing to pay whatever it would take."

I wasn't sure whether to be offended that she thought I could be bought, or sympathetic to her terrible situation. What I *did* know was that there was no way I was performing an illegal exorcism.

"You could pay me a king's ransom, and it wouldn't matter to me one bit as I rotted in prison. Illegal exorcism is considered murder." Only because the authorities didn't know that the demons didn't die but were merely sent back to the Demon Realm, but no one was going to believe me if I declared that in my own defense. Besides, I'd been arrested for illegal exorcism once before, and I hadn't enjoyed the experience.

"I understand you'd be taking a great risk," she said, her voice soothing despite the desperation in her eyes. "But once we get Tommy back, he can confirm that he wasn't willing, and—"

"You said yourself it might be too late." If Tommy Brewster really *was* hosting an illegal demon, then there was considerably more than an eighty percent chance of him being a vegetable if he and that demon parted ways. Just a little more of my hard-earned knowledge of the deep, dark secrets the demons keep from the human race—the brain damage is brought on by abuse, and sometimes even legal demons don't treat their hosts all that well.

With a pang, I thought of my own brother, Andrew. He'd hosted Lugh's brother, Raphael, for ten years, and spent weeks in a state of catatonia when Raphael was gone. The good news was that he'd recovered. The really shitty news was that Raphael had recently possessed him once again.

I forcibly dragged my mind back to the problem at hand. What had I been saying? Oh yeah. "If he's a—" I stopped myself, thinking that using the word "vegetable" right now might not be very sensitive. "If he's catatonic when the demon's gone, he can't corroborate a thing. It's not just my own ass I'm protecting, it's yours, too. You and your husband would be accessories. I'm sorry, but I just can't do it. And if you find another exorcist who agrees, you can be ninety-nine percent certain you're about to get scammed. No one's going to risk a murder charge—not when the pool of suspects would be so small."

There are only a couple hundred exorcists in the U.S., and many of them would have alibis. I imagine if someone were stupid enough to take the Brewsters' money, they'd find themselves behind bars in no time.

"So what do you suggest I do?" Claudia asked bitterly. "Just write my son off as dead? Watch that... that *thing* live out my son's life?" She shuddered. "I can't do that. I *won't*." A tear snaked down her cheek, and she swiped it angrily away. She didn't strike me as the kind of woman who cried easily, but it's amazing how much pain family can cause.

She stood up, snatching her purse from the seat beside her. My heart ached with sympathy, the situation with my brother making me feel her pain all the more keenly. Now some might argue that the world was better off without one more God's Wrath wacko tromping around burning people alive, and I might even agree with them. But I'd rather see that wacko in a brick-and-mortar prison than imprisoned helplessly within his own body.

"Look, don't do anything drastic," I advised as Claudia strode to the door.

She stopped and looked over her shoulder at me. "I'll do whatever I have to do to free my son. He's had a hard enough life already. I won't abandon him."

"Yeah, I get that. I've got a, um, friend in the police department." Calling Adam a friend was a world-class stretch, but I didn't have any other way to describe him that wouldn't take five minutes of explanation. "Let me talk to him and see what he suggests."

"The police have already said they can't help me."

"I know, but my friend might be able to pull a few strings. Maybe at least get them to look a little more closely at the case and see if they can find any evidence of coercion."

Actually, Adam was the Director of Special Forces, the branch of the police department responsible for all demon-related crime. He also had a habit of playing fast and loose with the law, which meant he might be able to get things done that a more by-the-books cop couldn't.

Claudia looked skeptical, but managed a nod of

acquiescence. "Thank you. I will, naturally, compensate you for your time."

I could have used the money, but I didn't feel right charging her when Adam was going to do all the work. "No need for that. If I end up performing a legal exorcism for you, you can pay me then. Meanwhile, can I have your assurance that you and your husband won't try anything illegal while I'm looking into this for you?"

She hesitated, then agreed with a nod. "All right. I appreciate your help, and I'm sorry I asked you to risk yourself like that."

No, she wasn't, but I couldn't entirely blame her, so I accepted the apology.

Chapter 2

I put off calling Adam for so long that when I finally talked to him it was nearly six, and he invited me to come discuss the case over dinner. Like Pavlov's dog, I began drooling at the suggestion. Adam's boyfriend, Dominic, is very possibly the world's best cook, and I found it almost impossible to turn down a chance to sample his wares, despite the unpleasantness a visit to Adam's house would likely entail.

Adam just loves making me uncomfortable. Enduring public displays of affection and sexual innuendo was the price I'd have to pay for the free meal, but when I considered the contents of my own kitchen, temptation overwhelmed me.

I arrived at Adam's house at about six-thirty. As soon as he answered the door, I knew it was going to be one of those nights, the kind that made me regret letting my stomach make decisions for me. His eyes were dilated with excitement, and he was slightly short of breath, which told me my arrival had interrupted something I didn't want to know about. Of course, he'd known I was on my way, so my interruption wasn't exactly an accident.

He smiled his typical wolfish smile, and I hoped I wasn't blushing already.

"Come in," he said, stepping aside to let me through the door.

I might have backed out if I hadn't caught the scents from the kitchen at just that moment. My stomach gurgled loudly, and like a zombie I followed that scent, Adam close behind me as if to block my escape.

Dominic is a seriously good-looking guy, tall and olive-skinned, with a sculpted body and meltingly warm eyes. Despite his sexual orientation, he exudes masculinity even when standing over a hot stove. Tonight, he was wearing a chef's apron, which I'd never seen him do before, and he greeted me with a wave of his hand rather than turning to face me.

I suspected immediately he was hiding a boner, and my cheeks flushed. They flushed even deeper when I saw the paddle Adam must have set carelessly on the counter when he went to open the door.

Yeah, "carelessly" my ass. He loved rubbing my face in the more unconventional aspects of his relationship with Dom.

Adam and Saul, Dominic's demon, had been lovers, though from what I could tell they hadn't actually been *in love*. In a moment of candor, Dom had once told me it had always been him, not Saul, who'd loved Adam, though when Dom had been possessed, he'd only been able to love Adam from afar.

When Saul had been declared rogue after his control snapped during a God's Wrath attack, I'd been called in to exorcize him. The fact that I'd exorcized Saul hadn't endeared me to Adam or Dom, but, in my admittedly biased point of view, they were clearly better off without him. It was obvious to anyone with eyes that they were devoted to one another, though I knew that there were aspects of their physical relationship that Adam found less than fully satisfying.

Demons are incorporeal in their own world, and some of them—like Adam and Saul—find *all* physical sensations, even pain, fascinating. Adam's fascination, however, was more in the giving than the receiving. When Dominic had been possessed by Saul, Adam could inflict as much damage as he liked, because Saul could heal his host's body. Saul could also shield Dominic so his host didn't feel any more pain than he found pleasant. Ever since I'd exorcized Saul, Adam had to be content with what Dominic could tolerate as a human being, and I knew sometimes he missed the thrill.

That didn't mean he and Dom didn't have a jolly old time together. And, to my never-ending embarrassment, thoughts of the two of them together really cranked my engine. They were just so incredibly sexy, both of them, and they were so hot for each other I swear they sometimes leaked pheromones.

"I'll have dinner on the table in just a moment," Dom said, his back still turned.

As I moved to the kitchen table, which was set for three, I saw that Dom was dishing out jumbo servings of lasagna. Manners prodded me to offer to help him serve, but I knew from experience he wouldn't let me. The kitchen was his domain, and he wasn't about to let a culinary barbarian such as myself intrude.

I waited in silence—and hunger—as Dominic brought the plates to the table, then retrieved some aromatic garlic bread from the oven, popping it into a napkin-lined basket. I had to wait even longer as Dominic poured wine for himself and Adam; then he finally removed the apron—it seemed the delay had calmed him—and took his seat.

I dove for the basket of bread. Naturally, it was

homemade, and would have been delicious even with-out the butter, garlic, and spices. I practically moaned in ecstasy when I bit into it.

"Have you ever thought of starting your own restaurant?" I asked with my mouth full.

Dominic had been a firefighter when he'd been pos-sessed, but he'd quit once Saul had been exorcized. He still had all the training and experience from his time with Saul, but because of Saul's inhuman healing ability, Dom's experience could very well have led him to take unacceptable risks. I'm pretty sure that it was Dom who'd made the final decision to quit, but I'm also pretty sure his department had encouraged him to get out. I didn't know how long he'd be happy as a full-time housewife, or whatever exactly he was right now. I knew he'd given up his crappy house in South Philly and moved in with Adam, but I had no idea what his long-term plans were.

"The idea has crossed my mind," Dominic admit-ted as he sampled his lasagna and frowned. "Too much oregano," he muttered under his breath.

That prompted both Adam and me to take a bite, and we both assured Dom it was perfect. He blushed with the praise, but it was well deserved. I wondered how come neither he nor Adam weighed three hun-dred pounds if they ate like this every night. I kept eat-ing long after I was full, unable to stop myself because it was so delicious.

Unfortunately, pigging out on the lasagna forced me to turn down the homemade cannoli for dessert. I accepted a cup of strong Italian-roast coffee as a con-solation prize, then finally got around to telling Adam why I'd contacted him.

He and Dom both listened carefully to my sum-mary of Claudia Brewster's story, but they were eerily silent afterward. I looked back and forth between the two of them. Adam was giving me a look that said I was pond scum. Dominic was staring at his coffee cup as if it held the secrets of the universe.

Belatedly, I remembered that Dominic—actually, *Saul*—had been attacked and savagely beaten by God's Wrath. I supposed it was naive of me to expect Adam and Dominic to have any desire to help one of its members.

The silence grew increasingly painful as the seconds ticked away, and I tried to think how to extricate my foot from my mouth.

"Look, I don't have any sympathy for this kid," I said, though strictly speaking that wasn't true. Considering my own aversions, I *did* feel sorry for Tommy Brewster being forced to host a demon in his body, no matter how many ideological problems I had with God's Wrath. "I *do* have sympathy for his parents, though. Claudia Brewster was so desperate, she tried to hire me to commit what the law thinks of as murder. She had to know she'd be arrested herself, but she was willing to do it anyway to free her son. She didn't approve of his involvement with God's Wrath, but sometimes you love your family even if you don't approve of them."

Despite rivers of bad blood between myself and my mother, I was pretty sure we still loved each other, at least a little bit. My general state of happiness increased in direct proportion to the distance between us, but I'd have been miserable if something terrible happened to her. That thought immediately led me to thoughts of the terrible thing that had happened to my father, and I shut that line of reasoning down in a hurry.

"You have one hell of a nerve," Adam snarled at me, shifting his chair closer to Dominic and slinging his arm protectively around his lover's shoulders.

"Don't, Adam," Dom said softly, though he leaned into Adam's embrace. "There's poetic justice in what happened to this guy, but if this really is a case of unwilling possession, how do we know it's the only one? Maybe it's happening more often than we think, and this kid is just the only case weird enough to cause raised eyebrows."

I hadn't thought of that myself, but it was a good point. I decided to keep my mouth shut, though. I figured anything I said would just dig the hole deeper, but Dominic might be able to persuade Adam to look into the Brewster case.

Adam scowled. "It's bullshit anyway. There are too many safeguards in place to believe the guy was unwilling. There's a reason the police have told the mother they can't help."

"And maybe Brewster had some kind of sudden religious conversion and decided it was time to host a demon," Dom agreed, "but it sounds damned unlikely. No matter what the evidence says, I find it hard to believe he could go from being in God's Wrath to being a willing host in ten days."

Adam removed the protective arm from Dom's shoulders and, after giving me another glare, turned his chair to face his lover. "*I* find it hard to believe anyone would bother going through this elaborate scheme to possess some low-level God's Wrath flunky. What would anyone have to gain by it?"

"Well that's a good question, isn't it? What would it hurt to do a little unofficial investigation? Maybe look at his registration video, see if you see something that ordinary human beings wouldn't see. Look into Tommy Brewster's background, see if there's some reason the Spirit Society would consider him a threat. After all, it's beginning to look like most of the Spirit

Society are Dougal's puppets. You never know—this could turn out to be something important."

Adam gave him a sour look. "That's a bit of a stretch." He made a sound between a sigh and a growl. "You really want me to investigate this?"

Dominic thought about that for a minute, then nodded. "Yeah, I do. Maybe it's nothing. Maybe it's none of our business. But I'd feel more comfortable if I knew for sure."

Adam turned his sour look on me, but I knew he wouldn't turn Dominic down, so I met his gaze steadily.

"You'll owe me one for this," he said, and his tone of voice sent a shiver down my spine.

I tried to think of something to say, some clever retort, but nothing came to mind. Dominic ended the staring contest by grabbing another cannoli and plunking it on Adam's plate.

"Here," Dominic said with a little smile. "Eat this and see if it sweetens your mood. I'll walk Morgan to the door." The smile turned impish. "We have unfinished business, remember?"

I forced myself not to glance toward the paddle that still lay on the counter in plain sight. And I tried my best not to visualize what the two of them would do as soon as I was out the door. It didn't help when Adam picked up the cannoli with his fingers and scooped out some of the creamy filling with his tongue. Dominic and I both blushed, and I hastened out of the kitchen without a parting shot.

Chapter 3

I went home after dinner, planning a quiet evening of vegging out in front of the TV. I didn't have many quiet evenings these days, and the prospect held a surprisingly strong appeal.

Because of my uncomfortably eventful life, I never just strolled into my apartment as if it were a safe haven. Before I unlocked the door, I activated and armed my Taser. Once inside, I did a thorough room-to-room check before allowing myself to relax.

For a while, I'd tried the old trick of putting a length of string between the door and the frame when I went out. Supposedly, if that string was still in place when I returned, it meant no one had opened the door. The problem was I didn't always remember to put it there, and any time I returned home and didn't see the string my heart would go into overdrive and I'd conjure the image of hordes of demons invading my apartment. Even when the string was still right where I left it, I found I didn't feel comfortable until I verified with my own two eyes that I was alone. I always felt vaguely silly when I'd finished my search, but that didn't stop me from doing it.

Satisfied that there were no bogeymen waiting to kill me, I plopped down on the sofa, grabbed the remote, and tried to turn on the TV. Nothing happened. I'd forgotten the batteries were dead—I'd meant to stop by the store and buy some on my way home.

I was just mustering the enthusiasm to stand up and turn the TV on by hand when a sudden pain stabbed through my eye.

"Ow! Shit!" I pressed at the space between my eye and my nose, where the pain was most intense, but it was gone before I even got my hand to my face.

Lately, this was the only communication I had with Lugh while I was conscious. For a while, during a period of intense stress, I'd been able to hear his voice in my head, but my subconscious had learned how to block him out. I actually preferred the pain in my eye to hearing his voice in my head, which made me feel like a Looney Tune.

"Do we have to do this *now*?" I complained, and Lugh answered with another stab. I grumbled some more, but figured I might as well get it over with.

Once, when the bad guys had been about to burn me at the stake, I'd voluntarily let Lugh take control of my body to save the day. It had taken a monumental effort, and though he'd ceded control back to me afterward, the experience had left me shaken to the core. Recently, when I'd desperately needed to let him in, I'd found myself unable to do it. Lugh had eventually managed to take control, but by then I very much didn't want him to.

I'd been seriously pissed at him for taking control of my body without my permission, and he'd promised me he'd never do it again—on one condition: that I learn how to let him in voluntarily when the situation warranted.

To that end, I dutifully tried once a night to let

myself cede control to him. So far, I hadn't succeeded, and I had a sinking feeling that wasn't going to change. I'm a control freak by nature, and letting a demon—even one as benevolent as Lugh—take control of my body was my worst nightmare come true.

I took a deep breath and closed my eyes, trying to relax enough to have a hope, however slim, of success. My muscles remained tight, and I was twitchy enough to have trouble keeping my eyes closed, so I got up and turned out all the lights, then reclined on my uncomfortable couch in hopes that that would be more relaxing.

I was still tense, and I noticed I was grinding my teeth. I huffed out a deep breath, then started on the litany of relaxation exercises Lugh had taught me. As usual, my mind kept running on its damn gerbil wheel, analyzing my body's responses instead of letting go and drifting like it was supposed to. I thought I felt a pulse of frustration that wasn't my own, but it was hard to be sure.

I tried my best for a half hour, but I didn't even manage to get myself relaxed, much less let Lugh take control. He gave me another stab of pain when I gave up, but he had to sense how pointless it would have been to keep trying, so he let me be after that.

I didn't go to bed until well after midnight, not because I wasn't tired, but because I knew Lugh was going to have some words for me tonight and I wanted to put it off as long as possible. It was only when I almost nodded off on the couch that I decided it was time to face the music. If I was going to fall asleep and dream of Lugh, I'd rather do it in the comfort of my bed.

Sure enough, the moment I lost consciousness, I

awakened in Lugh's imaginary living room. I found myself reclining into the butter-soft embrace of a leather sofa, my bare feet propped in Lugh's lap as he sat facing me on the matching ottoman.

I opened my mouth to protest the intimacy of the position, but at the same instant, he ran a strong, warm thumb up the center of my right foot. The pressure was just right, and I bit my tongue to suppress a moan as my toes curled in pleasure.

Lugh's hair was unbound tonight, the long, raven's wing tresses partially hiding his face, but I saw one corner of his mouth turn up with satisfied amusement. The bastard always knows exactly what buttons to push.

Before I could get pissy about it, he cupped my foot in both hands, using his thumbs to search out each knot of tension and soothe it away. I decided that protesting something that felt this good was the height of stupidity, so I closed my eyes and let myself enjoy the sensations.

I was warm and mellow when he'd finished with my right foot, and I was practically putty in his hands when he'd finished the left. Then he slid his hands up my calf, kneading the muscles. It felt damn good, but I couldn't help opening my eyes and seeing that the sweatpants I'd been wearing when the dream began had disappeared, and I was dressed in nothing but a T-shirt and panties.

My feet were still in his lap, so I instinctively jammed my heel into his crotch to discourage his now wandering hands. Of course, since his body was just an illusion, he wasn't even slightly discouraged. In fact, he closed his thighs tightly around my foot, holding it in place and pressing his erection against it. I had to suppress a shudder. I've got big feet for a woman, and his hard-on stretched from my heel to my toes.

"Unless you're auditioning for a role as a porn star, you might want to consider a more realistic size," I quipped, though my voice came out breathless.

He laughed, a sound as delicious as the darkest chocolate. "The advantage of dreams is they are not slaves to reality."

I tried to pull my trapped foot away, but I wasn't going anywhere unless he wanted me to. This was one of the reasons I hadn't particularly wanted to see him tonight—his flirting was getting progressively more aggressive. And harder to resist.

"Will you knock it off, already? I'm not in the mood to play games."

He regarded me intensely, cocking his head as he thought. Then he released my foot, and my sweatpants reappeared. "No, I suppose you're not," he conceded. Score one for me!

"Of course, I'm also not in the mood to be lectured, so if that's your plan, you might as well give it up." I sat up straight and put my feet flat on the floor.

The ottoman disappeared, replaced by an armchair that sat uncomfortably close to the sofa, crowding me. Lugh knew perfectly well how much I liked my personal space, but I decided it would take too much energy to protest.

"You need to learn how to let me in," he said simply.

I scowled at him. "Yeah, I know. I'm trying as hard as I can."

"No, you're not."

The nerve of some people! "I don't know what else you expect me to do. I've tried every relaxation technique you've taught me. I just don't know how to turn off my need to be in control."

"You could do it if you truly wanted to, but you're still fighting it."

"I am not!" I sounded like a petulant child, but I couldn't help it. I'd spent at least a half hour tonight trying with everything I had to let him in, and I'd done so every night for the last two weeks. I don't think I'd ever tried that hard to do anything in my entire life.

Lugh crossed his arms over his chest and leaned back in his chair, looking stern. "I'll grant that you're spending time on the project, but your heart isn't in it. You're still afraid that if you let me in, I'll never let you back in control."

I swallowed the protest I'd been about to make, because I recognized the truth when I heard it. Trust had never been one of my strong suits, and what little I'd had had been whittled away by a series of betrayals that still left me reeling.

I stared down at my hands, because it was too hard to look into Lugh's reproachful eyes. "The last time you were in control, you shut me out and killed my father."

Being shut out of my own body had been the single most terrifying experience of my life. And considering my life, that was saying a lot. I'd been completely unaware of what was happening in the real world, my consciousness imprisoned in a deep, dark, claustrophobic oubliette. I'd like to think that him using my body to murder my father—at least, the man who'd raised me as his own for all my life, even though he wasn't my biological father—was the worst part about that memory, but I know it's not true.

"I did what was necessary under the circumstances," he said softly.

"I know that." My father had been possessed by a sociopathic demon who knew far too much to be allowed to return to the Demon Realm. He'd had to die, but despite my less-than-stellar relationship with him, there was no way I could have killed him. So my semi-ex-boyfriend, Brian, had held me down until Lugh fought his way to the surface. I had yet to forgive either one of them.

"Knowing it was necessary doesn't help," I said. Lugh suddenly appeared at my side on the sofa, and I jumped. "Can't you just get up and walk from the chair to the sofa? Do you *have* to poof and startle me?"

Not surprisingly, he ignored my question. "We are inextricably tied to one another for the foreseeable future."

"Yeah, like I needed that reminder."

"If you can't learn to trust me, we'll both die."

A bitter laugh escaped me. "That's just great, Lugh. 'Trust me or die.' Words of wisdom that are guaranteed to put warm, fuzzy feelings in my heart."

He made an incoherent sound of frustration. I expected him to argue some more. Instead, the dream dissolved, and I slept through to morning.

I didn't know why Lugh had let me off so easy last night, but the whole encounter left me unsettled when I awoke. He wasn't one to give up, and I had to wonder what he was planning now.

Of course, whatever he was planning, there wasn't much I could do to stop him, so I told myself to quit thinking about it. To help me follow my own orders, I distracted myself by getting on the Internet and seeing what information I could scrape up on the Brewster family.

I wasn't expecting to find anything particularly interesting, or even particularly relevant. All I really hoped was to keep my mind off Lugh. But I found a lot more than I bargained for.

Claudia Brewster was exactly what she looked

like—an extremely successful career woman. She'd gotten an MBA from Harvard and had eventually brokered that into a position as vice president of a management consultant firm here in the city. Her husband, Devon Brewster III, was old money, and I could see no evidence that he'd ever worked for a living.

But that wasn't what caught my interest. It turned out there was a hell of a lot about Tommy Brewster that Claudia had failed to mention. Starting with the fact that he wasn't her biological son.

It appeared no one knew for sure who Tommy Brewster really was. When he was three years old, he was found at a horrific crime scene in Houston, where a rampaging demon had killed four people. A cop had heard the screams and come running. The demon had grabbed Tommy and was about to smash his head against a wall when the cop reached them. The cop had shot the demon in the head, killing its host and saving Tommy's life.

The story got stranger from there. The police were unable to identify any of the four people who'd been slaughtered, though blood tests proved that two of them were Tommy's parents. Tommy was too traumatized to tell the police anything except his first name. He'd gone into the foster care system and had eventually ended up with the Brewsters, who'd adopted him when he was ten, after he'd lived with them for several years.

The police weren't idiots. They knew the demon who'd killed Tommy's parents wasn't dead—the only way to kill a demon is to burn its host alive—and they knew it was possible it would return to the Mortal Plain to finish the job it had started. When Tommy had gone into foster care, social services had been very careful to cover their tracks and make it impossible for the demon to locate him.

So, how did I learn all this information about him if it was such a secret? Because Tommy had posted the whole sordid story on his MySpace page, along with enough anti-demon invective to get his profile deleted if anyone bothered to complain about it.

It was possible the story was a load of shit. I'd looked up the stories about the slaughter, and there was no denying it had occurred, and that a small child had been found at the scene. That didn't mean Tommy was that child. Still, if it was true, that would explain Tommy's devotion to God's Wrath.

I knew Adam would find out for sure if Tommy Brewster was who he said he was. And if his story turned out to be true, then his case became even more suspicious.

Who was the demon who'd slaughtered those four people and would have slaughtered Tommy if not for a policeman's timely rescue? Why had the demon gone on such a rampage? And could it possibly be a coincidence that shortly after Tommy Brewster turned twenty-one—the age at which he could legally register to host a demon—he turned up possessed?

The demons had shown far too much interest in this kid's life. My gut instinct said it would behoove me to find out why.

Chapter 4

It was a Saturday, and Adam was on duty, so I wasn't surprised not to hear from him. Whatever research he was planning to do on Tommy Brewster would no doubt be off the record, and he probably wouldn't even get started on it until tomorrow. Even understanding this, I chafed at the delay. Of course, some of my impatience was probably due to my desperate desire to find an excuse to cancel my evening's planned activity—dinner with Brian.

I'd barely spoken to him since he'd helped Lugh kill my father. He'd called a number of times, and I'd even picked up once or twice, but my emotions had been far too raw to handle an actual conversation. I couldn't for the life of me figure out how I felt about him right now—though beneath whatever other layers of feelings existed, I had to admit that I still loved him.

Or at least still loved the man I'd thought I'd known. Only I was no longer entirely sure that man existed.

Until that dreadful night, I'd always thought of Brian as the quintessential Boy Scout: virtuous, kind, and law-abiding to a fault. Never would I have imagined him being party to my father's grisly death, and it was the disillusionment, more than the act itself, that put me into such a tailspin of uncertainty.

When Brian had invited me to come to his apartment for dinner so we could talk things through, my first instinct had been to say no. I'm always one to follow my instincts, but Brian is a lawyer, and a good one at that, and whenever I allowed him to draw me into an argument—or "discussion," as he called it—I invariably came out on the losing end. Which was how I'd ended up promising to show up at his apartment at seven o'clock tonight.

I'm not what you'd call a girly-girl, and it was completely unlike me to spend twenty minutes agonizing over what to wear, but I did it anyway—even though my wardrobe was severely limited since everything I'd owned had gone up in smoke. I knew I was procrastinating, but I couldn't seem to stop myself.

I finally settled on a pair of tight, hip-hugging black jeans and a clingy, silk-knit green T-shirt that was a perfect complement to my red hair. It was—for me, at least—an understated kind of sexy. Not something that screamed "fuck me," but not something that screamed "keep your hands off me," either.

I finished the outfit off with a pair of black leather thong sandals with just enough heel to keep the hem of the jeans from dragging on the ground. After a final inspection in the full-length mirror that hung on the back of my bathroom door, I finally decided I was as ready as I'd ever be. I then looked at my watch and saw that I was already fifteen minutes late.

Cursing under my breath, I hurried to the door—but not before I'd double-checked my Taser to make sure its battery was fully charged. Brian's apartment was only six blocks from my own. Maybe I should have driven, seeing as I was already late, but I covered those six blocks at a brisk walk instead.

By the time I got there, the thong on my sandals had rubbed blisters between my toes—they weren't the best walking shoes in the world—and I was sure I'd chewed off all the lipstick on my lower lip. I took a couple of deep breaths to compose myself—like that had a chance of working—before I rang the bell.

I'd expected Brian to be annoyed. After all my dithering, I'd managed to be more than a half hour late, and I'd been too self-absorbed to even think about calling. But his only comment was a raised eyebrow as he opened the door wide enough to let me in. I swallowed hard as I crossed that threshold. I was a mature adult. Mature adults don't run away from conflict like frightened little girls. Okay, so maybe I *wasn't* such a mature adult.

Unlike Dominic, Brian's kitchen skills were mostly limited to simple fare such as hamburgers or spaghetti with jarred sauce. I guess he'd decided that wasn't good enough for tonight. There's a good Italian restaurant approximately every ten yards in Philadelphia, and Brian had ordered takeout from one of them. The fact that the food was still piping hot told me he wasn't surprised by how late I'd shown up.

Tension sizzled and sparked between us. I fidgeted nervously as Brian laid the food on the table. I saw we'd be eating off paper plates, and wondered if he was just trying to be as informal as possible in a vain attempt to make me comfortable, or if he was afraid of what I'd do if he put breakables in front of me.

By the time we sat down to eat, my stomach was tied in such knots I didn't know how I'd be able to force any food down. Brian had said little, but I was very much aware of how closely he was watching me. I cut off a hunk of eggplant parmigiana, but the idea of putting it in my mouth made me want to puke.

I must have been wearing my emotions on my face—not unusual for me—because Brian pushed his own food aside and reached across the table to grab my hand.

"My bad," he said softly. "I should have known we needed to clear the air between us before we ate."

I let out a whoosh of air, wishing my tension would flow out with it, then slumped in my chair. Gently, I extricated my hand from Brian's grip and pushed my own plate aside. I couldn't meet his whisky-brown eyes, afraid of what I'd see in them.

"We can try," I said. "But you know I suck at this."

I could almost feel his frown, even though I still hadn't found the courage to look at him. "What exactly is 'this'?"

I squirmed. "Talking."

"Ah. Yes, I know."

That made me wince, and I finally looked up. "You didn't have to agree that easily," I grumbled.

One corner of his mouth was turned up in wry amusement. "You wouldn't have liked a lie any better."

"Silence is always nice."

"Yeah, that was working really well for us."

Never argue with a lawyer. It's a losing proposition. "What do you expect me to say, Brian? That I'm okay with you helping Lugh kill my father? Well I'm not, and you know it."

Brian leaned forward, propping his elbows on the table and fixing me with an intense look. "You're right, I do. But if I had it all to do over again, I'd do the same thing. If we'd let that demon go back to the

Demon Realm knowing what he knew, you'd be dead by now. I'd rather have you hating my guts than dead."

I rolled my eyes. "I don't hate your guts," I said, though I knew he'd just basically manipulated me into saying it.

He shrugged. "Maybe not, but at the moment, you dislike them intensely."

Even in my muddled state of mind, I couldn't possibly imagine disliking Brian. I might be disillusioned, and I might have made assumptions about him that turned out to be incorrect, but whatever his faults, he was a truly nice guy. At least, I was pretty sure he was. Had I been putting him on a pedestal all this time, seeing only what I wanted to see?

I grabbed the paper napkin I'd laid over my lap and began calmly tearing it into shreds. "The man I thought I knew would never have been party to murder. You wouldn't even lie to the police to give me an alibi when they hauled me in for illegal exorcism."

He let out a long-suffering sigh. "I didn't lie because I could have been caught in it and that would have made you look guilty. Look, I don't like what I did. Just thinking about it makes me sick to my stomach. But I love you. I've always loved you. How could I let you throw your life away like that?"

Of course, he was right. Der Jäger, the demon who'd possessed my father, had *had* to die. Not just for my safety, but for Lugh's. If Lugh died and Dougal took the throne, he'd do his best to make the human race into slaves. There had been far too much at risk to let Der Jäger live. In a way, Brian had even done me a favor, helping Lugh take over so that I didn't have to be directly responsible for my father's death. Logic told me I couldn't hold any of this against Brian. Now, if only emotions were logical . . .

I pinched the bridge of my nose, feeling a non-Lugh-induced headache coming on. The napkin lay on the table in front of me in neat, thin strips. I fought the compulsion to start tearing at those strips. I had to swallow past a painful lump in my throat before I could speak.

"I know all that, okay? I understand why you did it, and I know you were right, but I still can't seem to swallow it." I'm just not as nice as Brian. I hold grudges and nurse my anger like a well-loved baby. Why a man like him loved someone like me was beyond my comprehension.

Brian's chair scraped back from the table, the sound making me wince. Was he about to wise up and wash his hands of me? The thought made my stomach clench with dread.

I must have looked as anguished as I felt. Brian flashed me a comforting half-smile, then came around the table to stand behind my chair. When I tried to get up, his hands came down firmly on my shoulders and held me in place. I felt the warmth of his breath on my neck as he bent to whisper in my ear.

"Maybe we need to do something other than *talk* to break the tension," he said. He nipped my earlobe gently, just in case I was too clueless to get the hint.

I tried to form a coherent protest. Surely we shouldn't even be *thinking* about sex when there were so many issues between us. I even got a husky, grunting sound out of my mouth that was probably the start of a word. Then his hands slid from my shoulders to my breasts, and the protest died in my throat.

"There's always more than one way to attack a problem," Brian said in a smug whisper as my nipples beaded under his hands.

I didn't mean to do it, but my back arched with the

pleasure of his touch. My mind was pretty sure this was a bad idea, but my body didn't give a damn. I tried once more to get up, figuring it was time to take this party to the bedroom, but Brian's hands tightened on my breasts, holding me in place. It was an odd feeling, being held down by my breasts, but trying to get up would hurt if he didn't let go, and it seemed he wasn't planning to.

Against all logic, moisture pooled between my legs. I tried to say something, anything, but my throat was too tight, my breaths too shallow.

When he sensed my capitulation, Brian eased his grip, kneading a breast with one hand as his other hand wandered lower to pull my T-shirt up. I hadn't figured on getting undressed in front of him tonight, so I was wearing a utilitarian tan bra rather than one of my sexy numbers. Brian didn't seem to mind. He nibbled on my earlobe, his tongue occasionally flicking to the shell of my ear as his hands slipped under the bra to cup my breasts.

I moaned and pushed myself into his hands, my skin alive with his touch. The damn bra fastened in the back—another sign that I hadn't been expecting to get any tonight—but instead of bothering to open it, Brian just shoved the cups upward. I'm not exactly flat-chested, so the underwire was painfully tight as he forced it over the fullest part of my chest. I opened my mouth to complain, but then my breasts popped free of the constriction and his hands were back where I wanted them and I forgot what I was going to complain about.

Brian had always been a fantastic lover, and we had so much physical chemistry he could soak my panties with a single smoldering look, but tonight he was . . . different. His fingers played with my nipples, plucking and pinching, creating a sensation just on the cusp between pain and pleasure.

Then suddenly, he wrapped one arm around me right beneath my breasts, hauling me to my feet as he kicked the chair out from between us. I gasped as the chair flew across the dining room floor and hit the wall with a bang. Brian buried his face against the side of my neck, his tongue tracing the vein there as he held me tightly against him and ground his erection into my butt.

The feel of his arousal, even with all those layers of clothing between us, dragged another groan from my throat. I wanted to turn around, lock my lips with his, and wrap my legs around his waist, but he was holding me too tight, and his grip didn't loosen even when I made it obvious I wanted to turn. A shiver trailed down my spine, and I couldn't have said whether it was arousal or unease.

I stopped caring when Brian went to work on the fly of my jeans. My panties were just as utilitarian as the bra, but I doubt he'd have noticed the sexiest underwear on the face of the earth at the moment. His breath was hot and fast against my neck, and he made little hungry sounds in the back of his throat as he burrowed his hand between my legs.

I was almost embarrassingly wet, but no doubt about it, Brian approved. He stroked me, hard, and I tried to reach behind me to get my hand on his cock. To my utter shock, he stopped me by shoving my shoulders down toward the table.

Reflex had me stopping my descent with the flat of my hands. As I was still recovering my balance, Brian dragged my jeans and panties down to my knees and kicked my legs apart as far as they would go—which wasn't very, in those tight jeans.

My breath wheezed in and out of my lungs, and my heart slammed against my breastbone. I heard the distinctive rasp of a zipper being lowered, and the equally distinctive sound of a condom wrapper being torn open. I was breathing so fast I almost hyperventilated.

Brian had never taken me from behind. *Never.* I didn't much care for the position, and Brian was too nice—and too good a lover—to press the issue. But it didn't take a rocket scientist to figure out that's what he was about to do.

Actually, it wasn't just that I didn't care for the position: I hated it. It felt too... submissive. The part of my brain that cared about such things told me that no matter how strange Brian was acting, if I told him to stop, he would. I tried to force myself to say something, to stand up, to close my legs. But just now, my body's demands overrode my brain, and I stayed right where he'd put me.

The sensation of him sliding into me was somewhere between Heaven and Hell. On the one hand, he always felt so *right* inside me, as if his cock had been specifically engineered to fit me. Every sexual nerve in my body sang with that pleasure. On the other hand, I was ignominiously bent over the kitchen table staring at a cooling plate of eggplant parmigiana as my sweet, gentle Brian fucked me brutally from behind.

Emotions rioted within me, bumping into and tangling with each other so wildly that I couldn't have named a single one of them. I tried not to lock my knees and elbows as I braced myself against Brian's thrusts—I was dizzy and unbalanced enough without setting myself up to pass out.

A trickle of sweat ran down the side of my face, but I barely felt it as my concentration narrowed and focused on the place where Brian and I were joined.

Every other sensation became inconsequential as I felt the tension building there, coiling tighter and tighter, until I thought I couldn't stand on the edge of that cliff for another moment. And yet still I stood there, waiting for the fall, desperate for the fall, hardly able to breathe with the intensity of my need.

When the coil finally released, I screamed, the pleasure too much to contain—wave after wave of it weakening my knees until I could barely hold myself up. Dimly, I was aware of Brian reaching his own release, his cry seeming but a shadow of mine.

It wasn't until the last wave of pleasure faded that I became aware of the rest of my body. I was drenched with sweat, shivering in a chill that was only partly physical. My arms and shoulders ached with the strain of bracing myself, and the elastic of my still-closed bra was digging painfully into the flesh at the top of my breasts.

After Brian pulled out, I tried to stand up, but my knees wobbled. If he hadn't steadied me with one hand, I swear I might have fallen down.

I couldn't even begin to absorb what had just happened between us, could hardly believe this was real. I struggled to find words, but before I could form a coherent thought, Brian had scooped me into his arms and carried me to the bedroom. There, he undressed me and tucked me into his bed, climbing in beside me and cradling me in his arms, once more the gentle, sweet lover I knew. And while I still reeled with confusion, Brian—typical male—fell fast asleep.

I lay beside him until his snores told me how deeply gone he was. He must have been exhausted by the intensity of what we'd done. I know I was, but I was far too unnerved to fall asleep. Instead, I slid out from under his arm, cleaned myself up a little, and got dressed.

My body was sore and achy as I slipped out of the bedroom and closed the door quietly behind myself. Our supposed dinner still sat on the dining room table, the mingled scents of sex and Italian food an unusual combination, to say the least. Numbly, I dropped onto Brian's couch and tried to figure out what the hell had just happened.

Brian had never been anything like that before. Oh, every once in a while, we had a good, hard fuck instead of our usual tender lovemaking. The last time we'd made love, he'd left bruises on my wrists. But that time, it had been unintentional, a product of the passion of the moment and of our sexual frustration. What he'd done tonight had felt very much intentional—and premeditated. Was it because he was angry at me for being angry at him?

But no, no matter how dominant and rough he had been, I knew that there had been no anger in it. So what had motivated him to take me like that? And how could he possibly have guessed that a control freak like me would actually let him get away with it?

I gasped as an awful suspicion crept into my head.

Who was the one person who knew and understood me well enough, despite all my layers of camouflage, to guess I might get off on a little show of dominance? But no. He wouldn't *dare* stick his nose into my love life like that! Brian must have figured it out for himself. He was, after all, a fantastic lover.

My hand shaking because I didn't believe my own logic, I moved over on the sofa until I could reach Brian's phone, then began scrolling through his caller ID log. It didn't take me long to find what I was looking for: a call from my number, made at three this morning, when I'd been fast asleep.

"Goddamn you, Lugh," I muttered under my

breath as good, old-fashioned rage flooded my system. Right that moment, if I could have exorcized him and sent him back to the Demon Realm, I think I would have done it, no matter what the consequences to the human race.

Chapter 5

I left Brian's house without waking him up. Maybe I should have confronted him, asked him what the hell Lugh had told him when he hijacked my body during my sleep, but I wasn't sure I wanted to know. Besides, I'd had enough confrontation for one night. Brian would be disappointed to wake up and find me gone, but he knew me far too well to be surprised.

I picked up some Chinese takeout on my way home so that I'd be prepared in the unlikely event my appetite came out of hiding, but it went straight into the fridge and stayed there. I tried to watch TV for a while, tried to keep myself from endlessly replaying the night's events. It didn't work, but my brooding didn't exactly help me make sense of things, either.

I went to bed at ten, exhausted in body and mind. I wasn't sure whether I was hoping to see Lugh, or hoping *not* to see Lugh, but whatever my hopes, he failed to put in an appearance. I slept until eight, and awoke feeling almost refreshed. Still confused, but refreshed.

I was sipping coffee, working my way through the Sunday paper, when the front desk called to let me know I had a visitor. Before I had a chance to work up a healthy head of paranoia, the clerk identified my visitor as Adam White. I can't say the news relaxed me, but surprisingly enough, there were people I was even less eager to see. Go figure.

Naturally, I checked through the peephole when Adam knocked on my door, just to make sure there'd been no mistaken identity. When I confirmed it was just him, I opened the door and let him in. He was carrying a tattered nylon backpack over one shoulder, and after the most perfunctory greeting, he slung the backpack onto one of my dining room chairs and unzipped it, pulling out a manila folder bursting at the seams with papers.

"I thought I'd fill you in on what I found out about the Brewster kid," he said, dropping the folder onto the table.

I was never at my best in the morning, and I was also never at my best when Adam was around. "You couldn't have just called?"

He gave me a dirty look. "I thought you might actually want to *see* what I'd found rather than hear it over the phone," he said with a nod at the folder. "If you'd rather I pack up my toys and go home..."

I huffed out a sigh. "No, please, sit down. Would you like some coffee?" Far be it from me to actually apologize, but I could at least make a peace offering.

"I'm never one to turn down coffee."

I topped off my own mug, then poured one for Adam and brought it to him at the table. "Where's Dom?" I asked, because Adam rarely came to my apartment without Dominic in tow. Which was generally a good thing, since Dominic made such a good referee.

Adam flashed me a wicked grin over the rim of his mug. "I left him at home to sleep it off. He's all tuckered out, poor thing." He winked at me, I guess just in case I didn't get the layers of innuendo.

I willed myself not to blush, but my depraved mind conjured a picture of Dominic bent over a table, gloriously naked while Adam rode him. I then remembered what I'd done with Brian last night and had no hope in hell of quelling the blush.

Adam laughed. "Damn, Morgan. It's so easy to make you blush, it's child's play. At least make me work for it."

My eloquent response was an Italian salute, which of course only amused him more. If I didn't change the subject pronto, this was going to get worse before it got better.

"I presume you found little Tommy Brewster's MySpace profile?" I asked.

Adam visibly took a moment to debate the relative merits of talking business and making me squirm. Thank the Lord, he made the right decision.

"I guess you've been doing some research on your own?"

I shrugged. "Just really basic stuff. So, is it true?"

He took a long slurp of coffee, then nodded. "Every word of it, though it was damn hard to confirm. The court system did its best to keep his identity hidden. If he hadn't gone blabbing on the Internet, I'd never have found out who he was, even with my resources. I guess it's a good thing for us he's such a wack job."

Somehow I doubted Claudia Brewster would see it that way. I cradled my coffee mug between my hands, needing the warmth to fight off the chill as I asked the question that had been bugging me since the moment I saw Tommy's story. "Does it seem to you that demons have been involved in his life far more than they should have been, considering he's not Spirit Society?"

Adam nodded. "Yeah. And the whole story about his origins is a hell of a lot weirder than what got reported in the newspapers." He flipped open the manila folder and pulled out some eight by ten photos, which he laid out on the table in front of me.

It took me a second to figure out what I was looking at, and when I did, I felt like I was hurtling down the steepest roller coaster ever built. I must have turned several interesting, not-very-healthy colors, but Adam didn't notice at first.

"Do you see anything unusual here?" he asked, with the nonchalance of a man who looked at pictures like these every day.

When I didn't answer immediately, he looked up from the photos and saw my face. And he probably also saw how badly my hands were shaking as I gripped my coffee mug. He reached out and plucked the mug out of my hands before I dropped it, then hastily gathered up the pictures and shoved them back into the folder.

"Sorry," he mumbled. "I forget sometimes that other people aren't used to seeing things like that."

I debated the alternatives of sprinting to the bathroom to puke my guts out versus staying at the table hoping I'd be able to keep my coffee down. The bathroom sprint was probably the wisest option, but stubbornness and a fierce desire not to look weak in front of Adam kept me in my chair. I swallowed convulsively a few times.

"So what was unusual?" I asked, my voice raspy and shaky. "Other than the fact that their internal organs weren't internal anymore?" My gorge rose at the memory, but a couple more convulsive swallows forced it back down.

"Several things," Adam answered. "For one, none of the four victims was wearing shoes. The bottoms of their feet were bruised and torn, and it wasn't anything the demon had done to them. For another, they were all dressed identically, in nondescript scrubs."

I was sure this was all fascinating information, and that there was a deep, profound meaning behind it all. But I was too busy fighting nausea to figure it out. "What's your point?"

"This is just a hypothesis, and I could be wildly off base."

"Okay."

"But what if The Healing Circle isn't the only demon-run hospital that's more than meets the eye?"

In the process of investigating my own origins, we'd discovered that Dougal and Raphael had for centuries been involved in a kind of eugenics program, trying to breed the perfect demon host. Their definition of perfection being a superhuman body with the intelligence of a sea cucumber. My biological father had been an escapee from one of those programs, but now that Adam mentioned it, it seemed awfully naive to assume only one such secret laboratory existed. And Houston was the home of Haven Hospital, one of the more well-known demon-run hospitals.

"We have four unidentified victims, with no missing persons reports. Dressed in scrubs, no shoes, and with battered feet."

"As if they'd been running away," I mused.

"Exactly. So this 'rogue' demon was sent to chase them down."

"And how close to Haven Hospital did the attack take place?"

"If you could have looked past the gore of the pictures, you'd have seen the hospital in the background of some of them. They didn't get more than a couple of blocks before they were caught. The demon took out the adults first, probably assuming a three-year-old kid wouldn't get far on its own. According to the papers and to Tommy's MySpace page, the demon was trying to kill him. But I suspect the truth is the demon would have hauled him back to the hospital."

I shuddered. "Unless this was another of those reject strains that the demons decided to destroy." Raphael himself had given the order to kill off my father's strain—and it was my father's escape from that purge that led to my birth.

"I suppose that's possible. Either way, the kid was rescued and got lost in the foster care system, until he decided to post his story on the Internet."

I nodded thoughtfully. "And the fact that he remembers enough to post that story makes the demons behind the project nervous, so they . . . What? How do they get him to agree to host? Did you watch his registration video?"

"Yeah. There's nothing to indicate any coercion. No signs of nervousness or reluctance. No furtive looks, body language completely relaxed."

"So Claudia must be right. He *has* to have been possessed when he signed the papers." I shook my head. "You know Sammy Cho. Can you imagine him lying about something like this? Even if he *tried* to lie, he's bound to suck at it."

Adam nodded. "You're right," he said, but he was frowning.

"What?" I asked.

"If someone in Dougal's camp wanted Tommy Brewster bad enough, they could have arranged for Sammy to be possessed. Then he'd be both willing and able to lie."

I chewed that one over. It would certainly work, but it was awfully risky. There are rarely enough demon-host-wannabes to require more than one exorcist at a time to do aura screenings, but it *did* happen sometimes, and if another exorcist got a look at Sammy's aura—or if Sammy started avoiding multiple screenings to a suspicious extent—the demon could be in serious trouble.

"I'll try to drop by Sammy's office," Adam said. "Given a few minutes with him, I should be able to figure out if he's possessed."

I nodded my agreement. When I had first contacted Adam about my own unwanted hitchhiker, he'd examined my aura, trying to find out if he could "see" Lugh. Unlike a human exorcist, he didn't need a fancy ritual or a trance to see auras—he could do it with the touch of a hand and a few seconds of concentration.

With a very unhappy internal groan, I realized I knew who else we needed to talk to in search of explanations. I met Adam's eyes, and saw that he'd come to the same conclusion.

"If you'd like," he said with uncommon kindness, "I'll talk to Raphael myself."

I really wished I could take him up on the offer. The last thing I wanted to do was to talk to the scumsucking demon who held my brother hostage. Aside from my fury for what he'd done to Andy, I also didn't trust him as far as I could throw him. He claimed to be on Lugh's side, to want to put Lugh back on the throne where he belonged, but I still wasn't entirely sure he hadn't betrayed us to Der Jäger.

"Thanks," I said, and for once I actually meant it. "I appreciate the offer, but he's slightly more likely to tell *me* the truth than you." Only if he was telling the truth about being on our side in the first place, and only if he really respected Lugh as much as he claimed, but we might as well make that assumption if we were planning to question him.

"Let me know what you find out." Adam gulped the last of his coffee. "And I'm really sorry about the crime scene photos. I should have known better than to show them to you."

I gave him a suspicious look. It wasn't like him to be this nice, or this conciliatory. He might not hate me, but he really didn't like me. Perhaps he'd known better than to show them to me, but had shown them anyway, out of spite. "Didn't your host warn you not to show graphic crime scene photos to a civilian?" I asked, and I'm sure he heard the undertone of suspicion in my voice.

The sudden hard glint in Adam's eyes told me he'd heard it, all right. "No. He's as inured to them as I am." He grimaced. "And he asks me to extend his apologies as well."

I had met Adam's host during a brief time when Adam had transferred—most illegally—into Dominic to heal what would have been a fatal gunshot wound. I barely knew the human Adam, but I suspected he and the demon Adam were more alike than not.

"Tell him I accept his apology."

Adam gave me one of those creepy stares of his. I'm sure he hadn't missed the fact that I'd never actually accepted his own apology. But he didn't call me on it. Instead, he shoved the manila folder with its ugly photos into the backpack, then left without saying good-bye.

Chapter 6

The fact that my brother was possessed was not common knowledge. As far as the world at large knew, Raphael had fled my brother's body and gone back to the Demon Realm, never to return. How I wished that were the case!

What this meant as a practical matter was that Andy was unemployed. Like Dominic, he'd been a firefighter when he was a legal host. He'd also begun hosting as soon as he'd turned twenty-one, which meant he hadn't completed his college education and had no particularly useful job skills. The Spirit Society would give him a small pension for a couple of years, but he was young enough that they'd expect him to host again—or get his life together on his own if he chose not to.

The pension wasn't enough to live on, so when I arrived at Andy's apartment, it was to find him poring over the Sunday want ads. It seemed like such a quintessentially human thing to do that I almost forgot this wasn't really Andy. I shook my head to clear the confusion.

"Are you actually going to apply for a job?" I asked.

He gave me a sardonic look. "I do have to support myself, you know. Or did you expect me to ensconce myself in this apartment and spend the rest of my life cackling evilly?"

I wished I could think of a brilliant plan to remove this bloodsucking leech from my brother's body. Unfortunately, since he was a member of the royal family, he was an unusually strong demon. Too strong for me to exorcize. Lugh might be able to overpower him, but I'd have to let him be in control to try it, and we'd already established that I couldn't.

"I really hate you, you know," I said petulantly.

Raphael sighed like I'd hurt his feelings. "I gave you my word I'd take better care of Andrew this time around."

"And you expect me to believe you?"

He shook his head. "I suppose not. But I'll tell you anyway that Andrew is fine. We will never like one another, but we have reached something approximating a truce." He laughed suddenly, though I couldn't imagine why.

"What's so funny?"

"He's testing the limits of our truce. He wants me to tell you that he's all right. He also wants me to tell you, and I quote, 'Get this fucking asshole out of my body.' "

I had no idea whether the message was really from Andy, or whether Raphael somehow thought this would disarm me. "I'm working on it, bro," I said, just in case it really was my brother. Of course, I wasn't working on it all that hard. Not because I didn't want to, but because I had no idea how I was going to manage it.

To my surprise, Raphael reached out and patted

my shoulder. "If you and I can ever reach our own truce, and if you can find someone else to host me, I will leave him. You have my word on that, for whatever you think my word is worth."

I stifled my immediate desire to tell him *exactly* what I thought his word was worth, but no doubt my opinion showed on my face. Raphael looked disappointed in me.

"Why are you here?" he asked. "It's obviously not for the pleasure of my company."

Probably I should be nicer to him when I was here looking for information—particularly information he wasn't overly eager to give me. But I just didn't have it in me to be nice to Raphael, who was the author of so many of my troubles.

Instead of answering, I invited myself to take a seat on his living room couch. Since he was pretending to be my brother, the slob, I had to move aside a pile of junk mail and discarded newspapers to clear a seat for myself. I was glad I was wearing one of my more conservative outfits so that my skin didn't come in contact with the stained upholstery.

"Make yourself at home," Raphael muttered, then took his own seat in the similarly disreputable-looking recliner.

I decided we'd had more than enough preliminaries, so I got right to the point. "Was The Healing Circle the only site where you and Dougal played God?"

Raphael blinked, the question obviously not one he expected. He thought about it a long time before he finally got around to answering. "No."

He didn't say anything else, and I had to quell a surge of impatience. "Care to elaborate?"

"Is there something specific you want to know, or are you just on a fishing expedition?"

"You said you wanted a truce with me, right? So why don't you just talk to me without looking for what's in it for you?"

He closed his eyes and scrubbed at his scalp, once again looking strangely human, even to me, who should know better. "I know it's completely out of character for you, but if you can see your way clear to giving me a break, I'd really appreciate it. Some of this stuff is really hard for me to talk about."

"My heart bleeds for you."

His eyes opened, and there was a flash of something dark and inhuman in them before he managed to control himself. I had to suppress a shiver. I was pretty sure Raphael hated me almost as much as I hated him, and he was not a good enemy to have.

He released his tension on a deep breath, and his voice when he spoke showed none of the anger that still lurked just behind his eyes. "I don't give a damn what you think of me. But no matter how much I wish it were otherwise, I *do* care what Lugh thinks. I don't much relish the thought of talking about things that will make him think even less of me than he already does."

I think it was genuine anguish I saw on his face just then. He and Lugh have one hell of a twisted relationship. I felt a reluctant sense of pity for Raphael, who clearly idolized his brother, but who was doomed to fall short of Lugh's expectations. Of course, that was only because of the choices he made, so I reminded myself not to feel *too* sorry for him.

"I think he'll feel better about you if you tell me the whole story than if you refuse to tell me to cover your ass."

"I'm not—" He shook his head. "Oh, what's the use?" he muttered under his breath. The expression on his face faded until all that was left was a bland impenetrable mask. "We had numerous facilities throughout the country. Even with our considerable understanding of human biology and genetics, what we were trying to do wasn't what you'd call easy. There was a lot of trial and error involved."

I made a sound of disgust. "These are human beings you're talking about, not lab rats."

I expected that to piss him off, but his mask stayed firmly in place. "Some of them were sufficiently altered that I rather doubt they still qualified as strictly human. Certainly your father's strain didn't. The fact that, except in your mother's case, we were unable to crossbreed them with human beings…" He must have realized what thin ice he was treading, for he let his voice trail off. "What is it, exactly, that you want to know?"

"Did you have a facility at Haven Hospital in Houston?"

"Yes, though I personally had little to do with that one." I gave him a skeptical look, and he smiled a bit grimly. "Would you believe I'm scared of flying?"

I thought about that a minute and realized I did. Planes don't crash often, but when they do, there's bound to be a major explosion—and fire. There were plenty of legal demons who worked as firefighters, but their superhuman strength and healing ability could keep them safe in all but the most volatile of situations. Explosions with airplane fuel were about as volatile as you get. It's thought that around twenty-five demons died on September 11, not from the collapse of the towers—which killed any number of demon hosts, sending their demons back to the Demon Realm—but from their heroic attempts to penetrate the fire.

"But even if you weren't there in person, you know

what was going on," I said, shaking off my morbid thoughts.

He shrugged. "Their goal was similar to the goals of The Healing Circle's labs, though they were coming at it from a different angle. The Healing Circle worked on increasing the strength and durability of their subjects. The Houston labs were working on increasing the malleability of human flesh."

"Huh?"

"We wanted stronger, faster-healing hosts."

I started to protest, but he held up his hand for silence, and I complied.

"Yes, we can heal our hosts very quickly by human standards. But our hosts can still die of injuries and send us back to the Demon Realm before we're ready to go. We wanted to create hosts whose flesh could be manipulated well enough to heal even catastrophic injuries quickly. I know I can never expect you to approve of our goals, but this one was actually beneficial to our subjects."

I snorted. "Your subjects who were held prisoner for their entire lives and then killed when they were no longer useful."

He had no answer for that accusation. "Why are you suddenly interested in the Haven project?"

I debated how much to tell him, then decided that if I expected him to talk, I needed to bite the bullet and do some talking of my own. So I told him the details of the Tommy Brewster case, watching his face for any trace of expression along the way.

He was silent for a long time after I'd finished, and I couldn't tell what he was thinking.

"Well?" I finally prompted when I got tired of waiting.

He blinked, as if coming back from a great mental

distance. "From the evidence, it sounds like there's a definite possibility he's a product of the Haven project, but I don't think there's any way to be sure."

"And how do you explain his mysterious change of heart? Why did he leave God's Wrath and register to become a demon host?"

Raphael shrugged, his expression telling me how little this mattered to him. "I'll buy Adam's theory that Sammy was possessed, at least until it's proven wrong. But you know, as fascinating as you might find this puzzle, in the grand scheme of things, it's unimportant."

Yeah, that was Raphael all right—compassion personified. "It's important to the Brewsters."

"I'm sure it is, but that doesn't mean it's important to *you*."

"You don't get to tell me what's important to me," I said through gritted teeth.

He rolled his eyes and looked exasperated. "Fine. Sorry I presumed to tell the demon king's host that she has more important things to do than play girl detective."

I'm usually a master of sarcasm myself, but I don't much appreciate it when it's aimed at me. "How'd you like fifty thousand volts of electricity running through your body?" I asked, though I refrained from actually pulling the Taser. I was sitting too close, and Raphael would be on me before I even got my hand on the damn thing.

Raphael's nostrils flared. "The next time you Taser me, remember you're Tasering Andrew at the same time. I can promise I won't shield him from the sensation."

I growled in frustration. Raphael laughed, but he sounded more bitter than amused.

"What's the good of having a hostage if you're not going to use him, eh?"

My fingers curled into fists, but the emotion that swelled in my chest was more grief than anger. So many people had suffered already because of me.

Raphael sighed, and his voice gentled. "I'm not really threatening to hurt Andrew," he said. "I'm just trying to discourage you from hurting *me*. Surely you can understand that?"

Understand? Maybe. Forgive? No way in hell! "Just don't try giving me orders," I said, but I sounded defeated. "If I want to investigate the Brewster case, it's *my* business, not yours."

"I'm just suggesting you be reasonable. Think it through! Even if you ever figure out exactly what happened, as far as the law is concerned, Brewster is a legal demon host. Your chances of finding enough concrete evidence to prove he's not are slim to none."

There's nothing like being told I can't do something to make me bound and determined to do it. "I'll find a way," I said, and I meant it.

Raphael dismissed my assertion with a wave of his hand. "No, you won't. But we've argued enough for one day, don't you think?"

"Fine." I stood up and managed about three steps toward the door before Raphael stopped me in my tracks.

"There's something else I need to talk to you about."

My instincts were to get the hell out of there now that I'd gotten as much as I could out of him, but I fought those instincts. I still wasn't convinced whose side Raphael was on, but I couldn't deny he was an important player in this deadly war of succession. And if he was actually willing to divulge information for once, it would behoove me to listen.

I forced myself to return to my seat. "I'm all ears," I said, my voice brittle as broken glass.

"I wish you would let Lugh surface so I could talk to my brother directly," Raphael said, and I snorted out a laugh.

"Not gonna happen." Lugh was peeved enough at me to send a spike of pain through my eye, but that didn't exactly endear him to me.

"So I gathered." Raphael's expression changed, the forced blankness disappearing as a mischievous grin took over his face. "I suppose there are some advantages in being able to talk to him without him being able to talk back."

I felt my lips starting to curve into an answering grin, but stopped myself cold. I was *not* going to allow Raphael to disarm me. "So what is it you're so desperate to talk to him about?"

Raphael sat back in the couch, the humor fading from his face. "I'm wondering if he's formed anything that even vaguely resembles a plan."

"If he has, I don't think he'd tell *you* about it."

Raphael ignored my comment. "Dougal will keep sending his forces after you. He might not know that you're still hosting Lugh, but as far as he knows, you know the identity of Lugh's current host."

"Thanks to you," I pointed out. Of course, I had to admit to myself that when Raphael had been playing inside man in Dougal's conspiracy, he'd had no choice but to tell Dougal the name of the host into which he'd summoned Lugh. But just because I had to admit it to myself didn't mean I had to admit it to Raphael.

His only acknowledgment of my jab was a brief dirty look. "Maybe even without having me on the inside, we'll be able to protect Lugh. Adam is a powerful ally, and I'll help as much as you'll let me. But hiding out on the Mortal Plain is only a temporary solution. Eventually, you're going to die."

I must have made some kind of outraged face, because Raphael patted the air soothingly.

"I mean of old age, not necessarily by violence. Lugh can help you lead a longer-than-normal life with greater health than someone who's not hosting a demon, but eventually the human body wears out. One of the many traits Dougal and I were trying to improve upon in our program."

"Don't even—"

"Forget I said that last part," he interrupted. "What I'm trying to tell you is that demons are essentially immortal beings. The span of a single human life—even one that has been artificially extended by a demon—is a relatively short time to us. If Dougal decides he's losing too many people and wasting too much energy trying to destroy Lugh right now, all he has to do is wait until you die and Lugh is forced to return to the Demon Realm.

"You . . . That is, *Lugh*, must come up with some kind of long-term plan. If that plan doesn't involve me, I'll understand."

Maybe he'd expected me to rush in with reassurances, because when I didn't say anything, his lips pressed tightly together, and a muscle ticked in his jaw.

"Is that it?" I asked. "Can I go now?"

He stared down at his hands and nodded briskly. "Yeah, that's it," he said in his flattest voice.

I supposed I'd hurt his feelings, and a small part of me felt kind of bad about that, because I couldn't help but see the occasional echo of myself in him. But I had little trouble hardening my heart. "If you want any sympathy from me, you need to stop holding my brother hostage."

He raised his eyes to mine, and the expression in them chilled me. "Has it ever occurred to you that I trust you as little as you trust me?"

"What's that supposed to mean?"

Raphael's capable of one of the most malevolent stares I've ever seen, and he was giving it to me right now. "It means you're a vindictive, reactionary bitch, and if I weren't inhabiting Andrew, you might do any number of unpleasant things to me—like send me back to the Demon Realm to face the brother I betrayed. That is not a reunion I anticipate with any great joy."

I almost laughed. "So what you're trying to tell me is that it's *my* fault you're holding Andy hostage? What a crock of shit!" His face turned a shade of red that should have warned me to silence. Naturally, I ignored the warning. "I'm not powerful enough to exorcize you, and I'm not about to murder your host just to get revenge on you. *You're* the vindictive one. You're holding Andy just to hurt me. And maybe hurt him, too."

The fire flared in his eyes once more. I got the impression he briefly tried to control himself, but that effort didn't last long. "Here's what I'd do if I wanted to hurt you," he snarled.

He moved so fast I didn't have a chance in hell of protecting myself. He leapt out of his seat and crossed the distance between us in a heartbeat, taking my arm in a bruising grip to hold me still while his fist connected with my chin. My head snapped back with the force of the blow, my jaws clicking together so hard I think I cracked a tooth.

I'd have fallen down if he weren't holding me up by one arm. I didn't quite black out, but the room spun dizzily around me, and nausea roiled in my gut. I saw his fist coming at me again, but there was no escaping it. It occurred to me that it sure would be nice if I could voluntarily let Lugh surface just about now.

The second punch never connected, and through my blurry vision, I saw Raphael standing with bowed head, his fist clenched as his ribs heaved. I sure had a way of bringing out the worst in people.

He was still holding me up by my arm, though the floor was looking mighty inviting. I was pretty sure he hadn't broken my jaw, but the nausea and blurry vision suggested I had a concussion. Still, enraged as he might have been, he'd pulled that punch, or I'd have been dead.

We stood like that for what felt like forever, my head throbbing in time to the beat of my heart as Raphael gathered the shreds of his temper together. By the time he managed that, I'd recovered enough that my legs could hold me, though I had a severe case of double vision.

Raphael's voice when he spoke was soft and contrite. "It would hurt less in the long run if I went ahead and knocked you out so Lugh can fix you."

The side effects of the concussion couldn't stop the bark of laughter that escaped me. "Thanks for the kind offer," I lisped, and realized for the first time that I'd bitten the side of my cheek and my mouth was full of blood. I spat the blood on Raphael's carpet, but my vision was too blurry to make out the expression on his face to see how much that pissed him off. "I think I'll pass."

"Can you get home all right?" he asked. I wondered if he thought I'd missed the fact that, contrite though he might sound, he hadn't bothered to apologize. "You can lie down on my couch if you want. I'll go into another room and stay there until you're well enough to leave."

The idea of lying down held a great deal of appeal. But then, so did the idea of getting the hell out of there. I chose the latter.

"It's been a pleasure," I said as I made my way carefully to the door. Raphael didn't answer, and that was just as well.

Chapter 7

I managed to get home without passing out on the sidewalk, but it was a close call. No doubt about it, I had a concussion. The doorman asked if I was all right as he opened the door for me. I lied and said yes.

The elevator ride almost made me toss my cookies, but I made it into my apartment and onto my bed without embarrassing myself. The bed felt like a combination bucking bronco and tilt-a-whirl, but I closed my eyes anyway and tried to let myself relax down into sleep. Eventually, it worked.

I half-expected Lugh to patch me up without bothering to talk to me. After all, I was pissed off at him for whatever he might have said to Brian, and he had a history of avoiding me when I was pissed at him. He's nothing if not smart. This time, however, avoidance wasn't his strategy.

When I opened my eyes, I found myself in a room I'd never seen before—a long, cavernous hall, its ceiling supported by massive stone pillars, its windows and doorways topped with Gothic arches. At the head of the room sat a dais, and on that dais loomed what could only be called a throne. In keeping with the scale of the hall, the throne was huge, its legs and back carved from some kind of dark wood, maybe mahogany. The seat, which didn't exactly look comfy, was a thinly padded red and gold tapestry, and a swath of red velvet—a rug, apparently—surrounded the throne like a halo.

The only light in the room came from a series of candle-bearing iron chandeliers, which left most of the arches and corners in impenetrable darkness. The hair on the back of my neck prickled, and I shivered.

"Lugh?" I called out, my voice echoing against the stone as I turned in a circle, looking for him. When I came around full circle, the throne was no longer empty.

I had never seen him looking remotely like this before. He was dressed all in wine-dark red with accents of gleaming gold—a matching set of coat, waistcoat, and breeches adorned with buttons even where buttons weren't needed. White lace frothed from the cuffs of his coat and foamed beneath his chin. White stockings clung to shapely calves and disappeared into red velvet shoes with gold buckles. His hair was unbound, held back from his face only by a simple gold band that I gathered was a crown.

The face beneath the crown was the same familiar face—Lugh, my demon and, maybe, my friend. But for the first time ever, I truly felt as though I was facing the demon king. My mouth went dry, my throat tightened, and I couldn't think of a thing to say. How could I stand in a king's hall and scold said king for speaking out of turn?

Lugh crossed those elegant legs of his at the knee and leaned back into the throne as if it were a cushy recliner rather than hard, carved wood. I wouldn't call the expression on his face a smile, but there was definitely a hint of amusement in his eyes.

"Have I finally found a way to overawe you, then?" he asked.

I tried a snort, but the sound was feeble and unconvincing. "If I'd known this was a costume party, I'd have dressed up," I said, determined not to let him make me feel uncomfortable.

He didn't say anything, merely raised his eyebrows. With a sigh of resignation, I looked down at myself and found that I was dressed in a voluminous green brocade gown. My breasts were pushed up and in by what I could only assume was a corset, and were covered—barely—by a triangular, lace-covered panel that appeared to be pinned to the gown's bodice. If I breathed too deeply, my nipples would probably make a surprise appearance. I was pretty sure I hadn't been wearing this getup when the dream had started, but since I hadn't thought to look at myself, I couldn't be sure.

"It's so me," I muttered dryly as another shiver chilled my spine.

"It would be a sensual delight to strip you out of it," Lugh said. "A tease in the truest sense of the word. All those little pins holding the stomacher in place, then all the undergarments with their tapes and laces..."

"You sound like you've stripped women out of outfits like this before."

Again, he didn't answer, but his silence was answer enough. He was a long-lived, possibly immortal, being, and I knew he'd walked the Mortal Plain before. Perhaps what I was wearing had been the height of women's fashion when he'd last been here.

Since he'd brought up the subject of sex himself—

albeit indirectly—I went on the offensive rather than questioning him about this sudden change in milieu.

"What did you say to Brian when you called him in the middle of the night?"

He sighed and gave me a disappointed look. "Is that what you consider the most important thing for us to talk about?"

Not really. It was just my attempt to wrest control of this dream from Lugh, and *that* was important to me. "What did you say to him?"

Lugh shook his regal head, making me feel childish even as he answered my question. "I told him you would respond well to a little dominance." He held up a hand to stave off my protest. "From *him*. Another lover might not have survived the attempt."

I was pretty sure he was laughing at me, even though he wasn't smiling. I wished like hell I could deny what he was saying, but since neither one of us would believe it, I refrained.

"Why?" I asked, my voice little more than a scratchy whisper. Bad enough to have Lugh invading my mind and learning each and every one of my most hidden thoughts and desires. But to have him share them with someone else, even Brian . . .

Lugh cocked his head and regarded me closely. I knew he was trying to figure out what he could get away with telling me, and though I would have liked to demand he tell me *everything*, I wasn't sure I dared.

"We both know you have trust issues," he finally said.

"No kidding?" He gave me a quelling look, and I shut up.

"But you desperately long for the ability to trust someone even as you keep sabotaging your own attempts at it."

"Now wait just a minute—"

Not surprisingly, he talked right over me. "The part of you that isn't *thinking* all the time trusts Brian. That's what makes your bond with him so special. I advised him to communicate with that part of you."

"Huh?"

"You would never have put up with, much less enjoyed, what he did if you didn't trust him implicitly. For someone like you, trusting another person enough to give up control is something of a Holy Grail. I wanted to show you that it was within your grasp, if only you're willing to reach for it."

I shook my head violently, and I could swear I felt marbles rattling around in there. I didn't know what the hell he was talking about, but I was pretty damn sure it had something to do with his machinations to get me to cede control to him on occasion.

"Whatever. Don't screw with my love life again! It's none of your business."

Lugh laughed, though I didn't know what was so damn funny.

"Besides," I continued loudly, "I thought you wanted me for yourself. I bet you didn't mention *that* to Brian."

The laughter faded, replaced by a gentle condescension I liked even less. "Brian and I are not in competition. You will never have to choose between us, because I can only come to you when you sleep, and he can only come to you when you wake."

Somehow I didn't think Brian would see it that way if he knew the whole picture. I was also damn sure Lugh hadn't mentioned his own seduction attempts when he was having his little chat with Brian.

I guess I was getting used to being possessed, because until that moment, I hadn't thought through all the ramifications of my liaison with Brian—ramifications that had loomed large in my mind when Lugh had first possessed me. My jaw set into what I felt certain was an unattractive line as I glared at the demon king.

"So, did *you* enjoy it when Brian bent me over the kitchen table to fuck me?" I might not be able to be with Lugh and Brian at the same time, but Lugh was *always* in residence.

Lugh flashed me a completely unrepentant smile. "I have never inhabited a female host before. I must admit the differences in sensation are fascinating, and quite pleasant. And as you have no doubt gathered, demons don't have the same hang-ups as humans about sexual orientation."

I suppressed a groan. Not only did I have to worry about Lugh seducing *me,* I now had to worry that he was using me to seduce *Brian.* Argh!

I suspected Lugh could read the direction of my thoughts and decided he needed to head me off before I could work my way into a world-class fury.

"Enough talk about your personal issues," he said, his tone raising my hackles even more. "I believe Hell may have frozen over, because for once I am in agreement with my brother." The momentary flash of humor in his eyes took a bit of the edge off my anger, though I was still poised to go for his jugular if he made one wrong move.

"Raphael said we were in need of a long-term plan," Lugh continued. "Somehow, that plan will eventually need to include a way to contain Dougal and all his minions who know my True Name, but my first goal must be to gain myself—and, of course, you—some measure of security."

Angry as I was, I couldn't argue with that logic. "And how do you plan to do that?" I asked.

Lugh sat up straight in his throne, his back held stiffly upright, his chin held high, his eyes blazing amber. "I may have been ousted from my throne in the Demon Realm," he said, "but unless Dougal succeeds in his attempts to kill me, I am still the king. It is time for me to set up my court, and in the face of necessity I shall do so on the Mortal Plain."

Chapter 8

Lugh's words rang in the empty hall, full of weight and portent. The thing was, I hadn't the faintest idea what they actually *meant*. Set up his court? I was trying to frame a question that wouldn't make me feel like an idiot, but Lugh answered before I succeeded. Sometimes, I don't know why I bother actually *talking* to him, seeing as he knows perfectly well what I'm thinking at all times.

"I need to gather a core of faithful supporters. In the Demon Realm, I have a council of advisors, although I don't know how many of them are truly loyal to me. I inherited them from my father, and some of them are no doubt as enamored of the old ways as Dougal and would be happy to be rid of me. I need to build a new council, one that will serve me on the Mortal Plain."

"Okay," I said slowly. "How do you plan to do that?"

"I will start with those I already know are loyal to me."

I frowned. "In other words . . . Adam. Not much of a council."

He watched me warily. "I am including Raphael. I know you aren't convinced of his loyalty, but I think he genuinely wants to put me back on the throne."

"But—"

"He told you far more about what happened in the Houston facility than he had to."

I laughed, the sound swallowed by the cavernous hall. "Were you listening to the shit he was telling me? He's not one of the good guys, Lugh."

He shrugged. "Consider him a necessary evil, then."

I didn't like it, but the fact was Raphael was too deeply entangled in my life and Lugh's to exclude. "Fine. Your council consists of Adam and Raphael."

"And you and Dominic."

"Practically an army."

I wasn't sure, but it looked like Lugh was counting backward from one hundred. I had that effect on him, and it wasn't exactly by accident.

"At this point," he said when he overcame his apparent desire to strangle me, "I can think of only one other demon I would trust enough to draw into my inner circle."

I don't know if it was an out-and-out premonition or whether I just made an assumption based on the look on Lugh's face, but the stupid corset suddenly seemed to be squeezing the air out of my lungs.

"Please don't say what I think you're going to say," I begged, and the regret in his eyes told me I'd guessed right.

"Saul was particularly targeted because of his loyalty to me, and he and Dominic proved to be compatible. There will be . . . complications if he joins us on the Mortal Plain once more, but I need more allies."

I shook my head as I struggled to breathe. Never

mind that this was just a dream, and I didn't actually need to breathe. "No!"

I had never met Saul. I don't consider the short time we spent together while I was exorcizing him as a real meeting. But despite my sometimes bad attitude toward Dominic, I had to admit I considered him a friend. I didn't want to lose him, as I'd lost everyone else who'd ever mattered to me.

Okay, that was melodramatic. I hadn't actually lost Brian, though it wasn't for lack of trying. But I'd lost my best friend, my father, my brother . . . It was enough.

After my moment of self-pity, I allowed myself to think of others. "You can't do that to Adam!" I protested. I might not like Adam, but even the most clueless idiot could see that he loved Dom. He'd been in a relationship with Saul before, but from everything I'd observed, I knew that relationship hadn't had the same emotional intensity.

"I know Adam will be unhappy," Lugh said, "but he will understand it's for the greater good."

I thought I'd been angry before. Now I knew what angry really was. "You cold-blooded, cold-hearted bastard! What about Dominic, huh? You'll just volunteer to sacrifice him for the common good?" I dragged up the hem of my skirts and petticoats or whatever the hell it was I was wearing and stomped up the steps to the dais until I could glare down at Lugh. "How *dare* you?" I suppose I'd gotten over being awed by his kingly mien. I dropped my handful of skirts and seriously considered throwing a punch, fat lot of good it would do. But it might give me a little outlet for the rage and hurt and, yes, fear that boiled in my gut. Every time I started to think of Lugh as a pretty decent guy, I'd get some kind of a reminder that he was a *demon,* and that demons don't think like humans.

"Calm down," Lugh said, looking up at me and showing no outward reaction to my outburst.

I doubt there was anything he could have said that would have calmed me less. I decided to throw that punch after all. He made no attempt to avoid it, but then it wasn't like I could hurt him. His head jerked back with the impact, and his crown slid sideways, but his facial expression didn't change.

"When you're through having your temper tantrum, let me know and I'll finish saying my piece." He crossed his arms over his chest and affected a pose of exaggerated patience.

I was sorely tempted to continue my "temper tantrum," as he called it, but I fought that temptation. Maybe I'd misunderstood what he was trying to say. Maybe he wasn't planning to offer up Dominic like a sacrificial lamb.

Nah. That was exactly what he'd meant, and I knew it. But as satisfying as yelling, screaming, and otherwise making a fool of myself might be, I knew it wouldn't do me—or Dom—a bit of good.

I sucked in as much air as I could manage, my head feeling light and fizzy from lack of oxygen. "Get me out of this damn corset," I snarled at Lugh.

Once the words left my mouth, I wished I could suck them back in. Whenever I complained about the way he'd dressed me, I always seemed to end up in something worse. I braced myself for something embarrassingly flimsy, but for once he declined to torment me.

My breathing came easier, and when I glanced cautiously down at myself, I saw that I was now dressed in loose, comfy gray sweats. The outfit didn't exactly blend in with the grand hall or Lugh's kingly red and gold, but it was definitely more me than the Marie Antoinette getup. I clamped my jaws together to stop myself from saying anything else as I glared at Lugh, who remained calmly seated on his throne.

When he was satisfied that I wasn't going to light into him anymore, he spoke again.

"Adam is one of my subjects. If I command him to step aside while Saul takes his lover, he will do it."

If I ground my teeth any harder, they would break. However, I managed to keep my temper in check, waiting for him to finish.

"However, Dominic is *not* one of my subjects, and I have no authority to give him orders. I will request that he agree to host Saul once more, but in the end, it will be his decision."

Dominic, like most legal demon hosts, had a hero complex. He might agree to take Saul back even if he knew it would mean losing what he now had with Adam. And even if losing *him* would break Adam's heart. But *I* wasn't one of Lugh's subjects. Perhaps I could conveniently "forget" to mention his request.

Lugh shook his head at me. "Would you rather I take over the next time you're asleep and give Adam a call myself?"

My heart sank at the thought. "You're probably doing that right this moment, aren't you?" It would hardly be the first time.

Slowly, Lugh unfolded from his throne, forcing me to take a couple of steps back to maintain my personal space. I'm a tall woman, but Lugh is at least six foot five, and he towered over me. He reached for me, and I'd have backed up farther if I didn't think I might fall off the edge of the dais. His hands landed on my shoulders, and he gave them a firm squeeze.

"I'll do you the courtesy of giving you the chance to do it yourself, first. But the request will be made, one way or another."

I swallowed past a lump that had formed in my

throat. "I hate you." I couldn't stand to look up at him anymore, so instead I stared at one of the ornamental gold buttons on his waistcoat.

"I'm sorry."

"Why does it have to be Dominic? Can't someone else host him?" I was still staring at the button, but it didn't seem to bother Lugh.

"Do you have someone else in mind?"

I scowled, because, of course, I didn't. We no longer had anyone on the inside with the Spirit Society, so it wasn't like we could get Saul into a legal host. So just who would I "volunteer" for the role?

"Keep in mind also what you know of Saul's ... inclinations, shall we call them?" Lugh said, forcibly reminding me of the kind of relationship he'd had with Adam. I didn't know—and sure as hell didn't *want* to know—what kind of S&M "play" they'd engaged in, but I knew it was brutal enough to be too much for Dominic—and to require a demon's healing ability.

"Many, if not *most* hosts would have trouble coping with his particular tastes," Lugh continued, hammering away at me. "I know his union with his last host before Dominic was not a happy one." He frowned. "I'm afraid Saul can be most abrasive when he doesn't like someone."

"You mean more abrasive than Adam?" I asked incredulously, and I forgot to stare at the button and looked up into his amber eyes.

"There's a reason he and Adam are friends."

"You mean because they're each the only creature in existence who can tolerate the other?"

Lugh smiled crookedly. "A bit of an exaggeration, but fairly accurate." The smile faded, and his grip on my shoulders tightened. "We already know Dominic and Saul get along well. Any other host might ... suffer."

I wasn't keen on the idea of shoving a demon, especially an abrasive one, into *any* human host. If Saul ended up in another host, I'd feel guilty as hell at the idea that the host was suffering and being ill-treated. But better some stranger than Dominic. I suppose that was selfish of me, but I didn't care.

"Don't do this," I begged. "Don't ask this of me, or of Dom."

His hands slid up the sides of my neck until he was cupping my face in his palms. His eyes were wells of regret, but there was no hint of yielding in them. His thumbs caressed my cheeks in a way that was either supposed to be soothing or sexy, I wasn't sure which. And for the first time ever, my body failed to respond to him in any way.

"Take your hands off me," I said, and I'd never heard my own voice so cold.

Lugh's jaw tightened with what might have been anger, but he let go. "I'll give you twenty-four hours to approach Dominic and Adam with the proposal. If you haven't done it by then, I'll do it myself."

There were times I'd been angry, even furious, with Lugh before. None of them compared to how I felt now. I glared at him, for once glad that he knew *exactly* how I felt. His face didn't change expression.

Knowing things were only going to get uglier if I stuck around, I mustered my mental forces and slammed the doors of my mind shut.

I woke up back in my own room, the rage still burning high. I wanted to break something, but I settled for hurling my pillow across the room instead. It wasn't anywhere near as satisfying.

It was only a little after four in the morning when I woke up, but I knew I wasn't getting back to sleep.

Cursing Lugh some more, I gave up the effort and hauled my sleep-deprived carcass into the kitchen to brew some extra-strength coffee. After I'd gotten the first cup down, a few of my still-sleeping brain cells woke up, and I realized I'd forgotten to ask Lugh an important question.

Lugh was talking about summoning Saul to the Mortal Plain, but as far as I knew, the only way to summon a specific demon was by its True Name. As Lugh had explained it, only demons who were extraordinary in some way earned the dubious honor of being granted a True Name. Lugh and his brothers had them because they were part of the royal family. The only other demon I'd known who had a True Name was Der Jäger, and he'd earned it through being a sociopath with the unique ability to hunt demons on the Mortal Plain.

I could only assume if Lugh meant to summon him that Saul had earned a True Name, but I had no idea how. Maybe that wasn't important, but if he had any special abilities, I'd rather know about them. Of course, since I was planning never to speak to Lugh again—yes, I knew I'd have no choice, but it made a nice fantasy—I wouldn't be able to question him. I could ask Adam, but since Adam wouldn't tell me squat without Lugh's permission, I knew it wouldn't do me any good.

When the sun came up, I made myself a cold breakfast of Cheerios with slices of a banana that was past its prime. I had until four o'clock tomorrow morning, give or take, to tell Adam and Dominic what His Majesty had requested. Until then, I would keep my lips tightly zipped, and I would do my best to ignore the problem.

Instead, I focused on the problem of Tommy Brewster. Even if Adam dropped by Sammy Cho's office and discovered he was possessed, there would be no proof that he'd been possessed when he'd examined Tommy. Demons might not have the same rights as humans in our legal system, but I still had to have *some* concrete evidence that Tommy's demon had done something wrong in order to legally exorcize him.

However, if Raphael believed that reality would cause me to drop the case, he didn't know me as well as he thought. I'd just have to figure out a way to *get* proof.

Easier said than done, naturally. I wasn't what you'd call a private investigator. But it occurred to me that perhaps the best way to prove that Tommy's demon had possessed him illegally was to get the demon to admit it.

I supposed that meant it was time for me to have a face-to-face chat with Tommy, the superhost, and the scum-sucking bottom-feeder who currently inhabited his body.

Chapter 9

I wasn't sure exactly how I was going to engineer this meeting with Tommy Brewster. After all, exorcists had very little excuse to hang out with legal demons, and I didn't imagine I could just call him up and ask him to meet me for a friendly chat. Well, I *could*, but I sort of doubted he'd agree.

In the end, I decided the easiest way to go about it was just to drop by his apartment and use my charm and persuasion to convince him to talk to me. Okay, so charm and persuasion aren't my strong suits, but I didn't see a whole lot of other options, so it would have to do.

Tommy lived near U. of P. in an ancient brownstone that had no doubt once been a single-family home, but had been converted into tiny apartments catering to students. It turned out Tommy was auditing some classes while he waited to start med school in the fall. I couldn't imagine how he'd gotten into an Ivy League university with his God's Wrath affiliation; unless, of course, they didn't know about it. I also wasn't sure why he was still going there now that he was possessed. It wasn't that unusual for legal demons to go through med school and become doctors, but it seemed like an odd thing for a demon in Dougal's camp to do. Unless he was in training to become another of Dougal's mad scientists. And wasn't *that* a cheerful thought?

Tommy wasn't home when I stopped by, and his roommate informed me that this was the status quo. Being a helpful sort—and being at just the right height to stand eye-level with my breasts, a convenience of which he took full advantage—the roommate informed me that my best shot at running into the new demonic Tommy was at his favorite nightclub, The Seven Deadlies.

My friendly, if false, smile died on my face when the roommate—whose name I'd already forgotten—mentioned that proverbial den of iniquity. He was too enamored of my chest to notice, and I decided the little creep was icking me out. I forced myself to thank him relatively politely before I hastened away, wondering if I really had the nerve to show my face at the club where Raphael had held and tortured Brian.

The easy way to handle it would have been to call Adam and ask him to meet up with Tommy there. Adam was a card-carrying member, and far from being repulsed by the club's sickening purpose, he actually *liked* the place. At least, he'd liked it before he and Dom had had a run-in with Shae, the club's owner. I doubted Adam would set foot in there again for any reason other than official business. Besides, I didn't want to talk to Adam, not with Lugh's request/order looming. Yes, I'd rather present it to Adam and Dom myself, but I'm a big fan of procrastination.

I wasn't what you'd call happy with my decision, but I suppose you could say I was resolved to it. I spent the afternoon and much of the evening loading myself up with caffeine to get me through a long night and trying not to think about what I was about to do. At around ten, I put on my favorite pair of black leather pants along with an emerald green halter top that left my belly button bare and revealed the tattoo on my back. It wasn't the kind of top I could wear a bra with, but it had a flimsy built-in shelf bra that slightly reduced the jiggle factor. I finished the outfit off with some platform sandals that added another couple of inches to my already greater-than-average height, then looked myself over in the mirror.

I looked far more demure and conservative than I'd looked the last time I'd set foot in that club, but I was dressed sexy enough to fit right in. I was also dressed sexy enough that I could probably persuade some hormone-crazed demon groupie to take me in as his guest, seeing as I wasn't a member myself. I'd then have to find a way to ditch said hormone-crazed groupie, but if there's one thing I'm good at, it's the cold shoulder.

The Seven Deadlies is located on South Street, home to some of Philadelphia's most outlandish citizens. Bars, clubs, tattoo parlors, fetish shops, New Age bookstores. You name it—if it's off the beaten path, you can be sure you'll find it somewhere along South Street.

I looked downright conservative next to some of the South Street regulars I passed as I made my way from the garage where I'd parked to the club. Mohawks, funky dye-jobs, ostentatious body piercings...Maybe I'd need to get another tattoo or ten. Nah. I didn't plan to come here ever again.

On the outside, The Seven Deadlies looks relatively ordinary, just a normal South Street alternative club. Even on a Monday night, there was a steady stream of customers going in. Still, I decided I'd try to get in on my own merits before going for the charming-a-helpless-male technique.

I was glad to see the Guardian of the Gates was a young, handsome guy. That upped my chances of conning my way in. When I approached the window, I put on my friendliest smile and pressed my shoulders back a bit to make sure the halter top clung to my breasts just right. Handsome Guy gave me a thorough once-over with his eyes before greeting me with a bland "Can I help you?"

I might have been insulted that he didn't seem to be reacting to my appearance if I hadn't caught the quickly suppressed gleam in his eyes when he'd looked me over.

"I've heard great things about this club," I gushed, trying to look young and brainless. "I was wondering who I could talk to about maybe buying a membership."

He gave me another of those up-and-down looks, then smiled at me with what looked like regret. "Sorry, but our membership roster is full. The waiting list is about three months."

Yeesh! There were that many people who wanted to hang out at a demon sex club? I made a pouty face—maybe I was laying it on a little thick, but I've never been a big fan of subtlety.

"Is it possible to buy a guest pass? I'd love to look around, get a feel for whether the place is worth waiting for." A line was forming behind me, and I could feel the impatience at my back. Handsome Guy seemed to feel it, too, since his expression hardened into full authority-figure mode.

"I'm sorry, ma'am, but the club is only for members and their guests."

"We can make an exception for this one, Deke," said a voice from over my left shoulder.

I turned slowly, my fists automatically clenching at

my sides, my teeth grinding as I struggled to control my primal impulses.

Standing behind me, where she must have emerged from a nearby door marked Employees Only, was Shae, last name unknown to me, the owner of The Seven Deadlies. Approximately my height, with deep ebony skin and hair cut so short she was practically bald, Shae reminded me of a black panther, a creature of deadly grace and beauty. She was also a predator, a mercenary, and an illegal demon, whom Adam refused to arrest because she served as his snitch—when it was convenient to her.

She was dressed all in red and black, an outfit that only heightened the aura of danger that clung to her. A black leather bustier, only half a shade darker than her skin, made the most of her minimal cleavage, the bloodred bow at the center drawing the eye. Her black leather pants were even tighter than my own, and her shoes—red patent leather pumps with spiky, four-inch heels—were a hell of a lot showier. She topped the outfit off with a dramatic floor-length black and red brocade duster.

I'd taken an instant dislike to Shae when I'd first met her, and nothing since then had persuaded me to change my opinion. I had sort of hoped she either wouldn't be here, or at least wouldn't recognize me, but I should have known my luck wasn't that good.

She smiled her shark's smile and put a hand on my arm, drawing me away from the window so the next schmuck in line could pay his way in. I let her touch me for about ten seconds, then jerked my arm from her grip. It was probably a good time to cut my losses and get the hell out of here, but as you may have noticed, I'm a bit stubborn. I had a plan, and I wasn't going to let Evil Bitch from Hell ruin it.

"I had no idea you enjoyed yourself so much the last time you were in my club," Shae said, still smiling.

I tried desperately not to think about the things that had happened the last time I'd set foot in here, but of course it didn't work.

"What can I say, I'm a glutton for punishment," I responded, then instantly regretted it as Shae's eyes gleamed.

"You've come to the right place, sugar. Perhaps you'd like to venture down into Hell tonight as a participant, rather than an observer?"

I managed to suppress my shudder, but I'm sure the revulsion showed in my eyes. Shae laughed, and I wondered what would happen if I gave in to my temptation to introduce her face to my fist. I didn't wonder very long, though. She was a demon, and my own demon was helpless against her unless I let him take over. I had no particular desire to get my ass kicked tonight, so I reluctantly kept my temper in check.

"Are you going to let me in or not?" I asked, not in the mood for a game of cat and mouse.

"I already said I would, didn't I?" She reached into what must have been an inner pocket in the duster, then handed me a voucher. "I'll even throw in a free drink."

I took the voucher from her even as I wondered what the hell her game was. I don't suppose she had any particular reason to dislike me—after all, she'd earned lots of money on me when one faction of demons paid her to help capture me and Adam paid her to help me escape. But I didn't imagine she was welcoming me into her club with open arms because of any great affection she bore me, either.

"What's your angle?" I asked her suspiciously.

"I have no angle," she said, though her claim was patently false. "I regret some of the . . . difficulties you experienced the last time you were here. Since you were kind enough to stop by again, I figured it was the least I could do to show you the true face of The Seven Deadlies."

I knew full well I'd seen the true face already, and it was uglier than even I could have imagined. Common sense told me that if Shae wanted me to come into her club, then the intelligent thing to do was to run the other way as fast as I could. But I wanted to talk to Tommy Brewster, and here of all places he would be most likely to be willing to talk to me. After all, who would ever suspect a patron of a demon sex club of being an exorcist?

"Your generosity is overwhelming," I told Shae, and her eyes crinkled with amusement.

"Suspicious little thing, aren't you?" she asked, then continued before I could slip in a cutting retort. "As a sign of good faith, I won't even make you check your Taser at the door."

That had been the part of this adventure I'd been dreading most. I'd been sure my Taser would be confiscated before I would be allowed into the heart of the club. The idea of walking unarmed into a club full of demons hadn't exactly thrilled me, but I hadn't thought there was an alternative.

I was caught between two aphorisms that seemed particularly relevant to the situation: "Don't look a gift horse in the mouth," and "If it sounds too good to be true, it is." Shouting down my more sensible side, I told myself that as long as I had my Taser, I couldn't get into too much trouble.

Shae nodded approvingly as she saw the decision on my face, then led me past the line at the entrance and into the club itself.

The music was so loud it almost knocked me over,

and I couldn't hear whatever Shae said to me in parting. Probably just as well. She smiled at me, her eyes glinting, then melted away into the crowd.

I stood in the entrance for a while, trying to adjust to the sensory assault. The last time I'd been in here, the music had been a heavy, tuneless techno with a beat that made my teeth rattle. This time it was ear-splitting hip-hop, but it still made my teeth rattle. I figured it was just as well I couldn't understand the lyrics.

The dance floor was packed with gyrating bodies, some dancing in couples, some in groups, and some just doing their own thing. Here and there, I spotted people wearing angel halos or devil horns, picked up from the table just beside the entrance. They were cheesy as hell, but somehow seemed sinister now that I knew what they meant. People wearing the halos were in the market for some "vanilla sex," and if they found a compatible partner, they would go up the stairs under the sign that said Heaven and rent a room for a little old-fashioned roll in the hay. Those wearing horns wanted to go down into the basement aptly named Hell, where the sex was anything but vanilla.

It was in Hell that the demons had held Brian, hiding him in plain sight in a place where screams weren't necessarily sounds of distress. If Tommy was down there, you could bet your ass I wasn't going in after him.

Of course, considering how packed the club was, I wasn't sure my chances of finding him were all that great no matter where he was. Not knowing what else to do, I weaved and elbowed my way through the crowd until I reached the bar. I used the voucher Shae had given me to buy my favorite drink, a piña colada, then snagged a stool at the far end of the bar, where I had a decent view of most of the club.

It was a nightclub of course, so it was mostly dark as a pit. I stared out into that darkness, examining faces in whatever scraps of light I could find, hoping to spot Tommy. No luck, but then the night was young. I sipped my drink and wondered what the hell I was doing here. It wasn't like Tommy was going to spill his guts the moment I started talking to him, or like I could do anything about it even if he admitted to being an illegal.

I sat there for maybe an hour, alternately scanning the crowd for a glimpse of a familiar face, and trying to talk myself into giving up. I'd already been hit on three times, twice by guys who were probably demons, once by a guy who definitely was not. The Spirit Society has strict standards as to what makes an acceptable host for their damned Higher Powers, and a five-foot-four man with a beer belly and no neck definitely did not qualify. The fact that he was wearing the devil horns did not improve the impression he made.

When he came back for another try, I decided I'd had enough. Without even speaking to the little twerp, I started making my way toward the door.

By what had become habit, I continued to scan the crowd. I stumbled to a halt when I finally caught sight of a familiar face. Only it wasn't the familiar face I'd been expecting.

There across the room from me, looking loose-limbed and relaxed as he closed the door to Hell behind him, was Adam. And the man exiting Hell at his side was most definitely not Dominic.

Chapter **10**

I stood rooted to the floor, staring across the room, hardly believing what I was seeing. For all of Adam's faults, I never for a moment would have suspected him of cheating on Dom. I felt a stab of pain in my heart for Dom's sake.

I don't know what made Adam look up and meet my eyes, whether it was just chance or some kind of gut instinct. But when he saw me, his eyes widened in shock and he froze in his tracks. His shoulders slumped, and then his gaze flickered upward and landed somewhere above my left shoulder.

I couldn't not look, even though I knew he might be trying to fake me out so he could escape the club without having to face me.

He wasn't faking me out. Standing on the balcony above the dance floor, smiling smugly, was Shae. And now I understood exactly why she'd let me in.

Shae cooperated with Adam because if she didn't, she'd either be exorcized or executed, but she'd made it abundantly clear how much she resented it. She would happily take advantage of any chance to hurt him, even if it meant hurting Dominic in the process.

Maybe even *especially* if it meant hurting Dom—she had certainly seemed to enjoy it before.

I dragged my eyes away from Shae and found that, far from fleeing, Adam was making his way through the crowd toward me. I was torn between wanting to avoid him and wanting to rip him a new one. I hadn't reached a decision yet when he came to a stop directly in front of me.

I'd never seen him looking anything like this before—embarrassed, uncertain, maybe even vulnerable. But considering he was as good as tearing Dom's heart out, I didn't feel the least bit sorry for him.

"At the risk of sounding like a cliché," he shouted into my ear, the music almost drowning out his words, "it's not what you think."

My hand itched to draw the Taser and give him a good zap in a vulnerable spot. I managed to refrain, though my opinion of him must have shown clearly on my face.

His eyes darted away from mine. "At least hear me out before you jump to conclusions," he begged.

I'd have loved to tell him to go shove it up his ass, but no matter what I thought of him, he was going to be part of Lugh's inner circle, which meant I would have to find a way to tolerate him no matter how much I loathed him. I couldn't force a civil word out of my mouth, but I indicated my willingness to listen with a brief, jerky nod.

"Let's go somewhere quieter," he shouted. I didn't answer, but when he started heading toward the door, I followed. I had to wait until he could retrieve his sidearm from the coat-check girl, or whatever she was, but soon we were out the door into the relatively fresh air.

Exiting the club—the noise, the crowd, the demons,

the unpleasant vibes—was a relief, even though South Street was far from deserted at this time of night. Adam started down the street, and I fell into resentful step beside him, watching him out of the corner of my eye.

Unlike many of the regulars at The Seven Deadlies, Adam didn't dress like an S&M cover model when he visited. Instead, he wore conservative khaki pants, a white oxford shirt, and a light linen jacket to conceal his shoulder holster. He had both his hands shoved into his pants pockets right now, and his eyes were fixed on the sidewalk ahead of him.

My lip curled up in a sneer. "If it wasn't what I thought, why do you look so goddamn guilty?"

A muscle in his jaw ticked, and I saw him swallow hard. "I didn't have sex with that guy," he said, still staring at the pavement.

I barked out a laugh. "In the same way Bill Clinton didn't have sex with that woman?"

He looked at me now, anger flashing in his eyes. But he must have been feeling really crummy, because he didn't lash out at me. "Let me rephrase that more emphatically—nothing of a sexual nature happened. I don't go to Hell for the sex."

I thought about that a moment and realized I understood what he was saying even though he wasn't willing to put the whole ugly truth into words. "You go there so you can get your rocks off torturing demons in a way Dominic could never handle now that Saul is gone."

"It's not about sex!" Adam insisted, loudly enough that a couple of passersby turned to look. Adam caught the eye of the most blatant of them and snarled. The Goth chick lowered her pierced eyebrow and looked quickly away.

Once upon a time, I'd allowed Adam to "play"

with me, to satisfy his lust for pain in return for his aid in rescuing Brian. I remembered all too well the feel of his body pressing against my back as he bound my hands above my head.

"I've had up-close-and-personal experience," I snapped in a furious undertone. "I know—"

"You know *nothing*!" he interrupted.

I stopped, unable to keep walking casually down the sidewalk while simultaneously fighting Adam and my insidious memories. Adam stopped, too, crowding into my personal space and glaring down at me. I matched him glare for glare.

"I *felt* how you reacted, you asshole," I said, poking him in the chest for emphasis.

He grabbed my wrist and wrenched it painfully downward. I suppressed a cry of protest, afraid he'd enjoy it too much. "I told you, it was a conditioned response, not true sexual desire. I have no interest in fucking anyone but Dom."

My eyes started to water from the pain as his hand closed ever more tightly on my wrist, but I didn't back down. "And would Dom see it that way if he knew what you were up to?"

I knew I'd read the guilt in his eyes correctly when he suddenly shoved me away from him, hard. My back slammed into a metal grille that protected a plate-glass window advertising Tarot readings and "spiritual advice." The air whooshed out of my lungs, and my knees buckled beneath me. Apparently, this was my week for being beat up by my supposed allies.

My ass landed on the pavement with a teeth-clacking thump, and for half a second I thought I was going to pass out. Then I managed to drag some air into my lungs, and I realized I would stay wide awake so I could feel the bruises as they began to spring up all over my back. I wondered if they'd make a diamond-shaped design to match the grille that created them.

Adam did another of his intimidating glares at the passersby, and when one didn't take the hint, he pulled his badge. That caused the crowd to disperse in a hurry, so Adam was able to focus his attention on me once more. He came to squat in front of me, and there was no apology in his eyes.

"You'd better not say a goddamn thing to Dom about this," he growled. "He *might* understand. My host thinks he would. But I'm not willing to risk hurting him."

I swallowed my impulse to ask him what exactly he would do to me if I told Dom. As I knew from personal experience, he could do any number of awful things to me without killing me, and since Lugh could fix me right up, he'd probably even get away with it. Instead, I met his eyes and asked him a question he had every reason to think was purely hypothetical.

"So if you could get Saul back into Dom's body, would you do it?"

"No!" he answered with gratifying speed. "I *like* Saul. He's my friend, and has been for centuries. We enjoyed ourselves immensely walking the Mortal Plain together, and I'll see him again when my time on the Mortal Plain is up." He swallowed hard. "But I *love* Dominic, and *he* won't be waiting for me in the Demon Realm. I don't want to risk hurting him. It has nothing to do with covering my own ass."

This was as candid as I'd ever seen Adam, and there was no longer any doubt in my mind that what I saw in his eyes was indeed vulnerability. The only strong emotion I'd ever seen from him before was fury. This was a whole different side to him, one I wasn't sure I wanted to see. Not with the message Lugh had tasked me with delivering.

I let out a long sigh, and my voice when I spoke was devoid of the judgmental overtones that had filled it before. "Can we go somewhere more comfortable? We need to talk."

Adam blinked as though surprised by what must have sounded almost like capitulation. Then he nodded briskly and rose to his feet, offering me a hand up. Internally wincing in case he should squeeze as hard as he had before, I took his hand and let him drag me to my feet. A quick glance at the grille showed me a Morgan-sized indentation in the middle. It looked like I was lucky not to have any broken bones.

Adam stuffed his hands back into his pockets and continued down the street. I supposed I had no choice but to follow.

"Are you going to tell Dom?" he asked.

I let out my breath with a whoosh. "No." I didn't want to hurt Dom any more than Adam did.

He slanted a look at me. "Are you sure?"

It was tempting to snap out a yes, but I knew exactly what he was asking, and it was a fair question. No, I didn't *plan* to tell Dominic anything. But sometimes my mouth had a tendency to run away with me, especially when my temper was roused. Might I let something slip in a moment of anger? I had the uneasy suspicion the answer was yes.

"You should tell him yourself," I said instead of answering the question. "There are ways he can find out other than me blabbing, and they'd all make you look far worse than you would if you just fessed up."

Adam shook his head. "I can't do that."

I shrugged. "Then maybe you should stop going to the goddamn club. That idea ever occurred to you?"

Adam stopped in front of a café that billed itself as a teahouse, then pushed the door open and gestured me in. It seemed as good a place as any to talk, so I stepped inside.

It was pleasantly quiet, with the scream of the cappuccino machine the only exception. New Age music played softly on the speaker system, and though the place was hardly empty, it wasn't exactly hopping, either. Most of the people inside looked like tourists, here to take in the sights of South Street but needing a break from the craziness every once in a while.

There were tables set up in the middle of the café, with a long bar lined with stools against one wall, and cozy arrangements of easy chairs in each corner. One of those corners was empty, and Adam and I made a beeline.

"What can I get you?" he asked, indicating the line at the counter.

"Just sit down."

He pointed at a sign that informed us the seating areas were for customers only, then repeated the question. He could probably pull his badge and the staff would be happy to let us sit there without buying anything, but maybe we both needed a couple minutes to cool down.

"Just plain coffee," I finally said. When I leaned into the soft chair, my back informed me that the bruises were well on their way to setting in.

Adam came back before I was ready to face him again, but then that would probably have been true if he were gone for an hour. He laid my coffee, along with one cream and two sugars, on the end table between our chairs. From the scent that wafted over to me from his cup, I gathered he was drinking mint tea himself. It seemed a strange choice for a tough guy, but then people thought the froufrou drinks I ordered at bars were strange for a tough broad with a tattoo and multiple ear piercings, so who was I to judge?

Adam took a sip of his tea as I began doctoring my coffee. When I was finished, I leaned back into the chair—more carefully this time—and waited for him to say something. It didn't take long.

"I don't want to hurt Dom," he said, staring into his tea.

"Yeah, you said that already."

But he shook his head. "That's not what I mean." He looked up and met my eyes. "Since Saul's been gone, I've come to realize that what we did together served more than one purpose. Yeah, it was a sensual pleasure, for both of us. But it turns out it was a good way for me to blow off a little steam, too." His eyes slid away from mine once more. "I have to be so careful with Dom," he said softly, his breath stirring the steam that rose from his cup. "If I don't...let loose every once in a while, I'm afraid of what might happen."

"Shit," I muttered as I finally understood what he was getting at. "You really think you'd hurt Dominic if you didn't play your little games at the club?"

"I don't know. I don't want to find out."

I let out a long sigh. Obviously, Adam wasn't my favorite person in the world, but in this one instance I suspected he wasn't doing himself justice. "Far be it from me to suggest you have any redeeming features," I said, "but if there's one thing I know about you, it's that you'd never do that to Dom."

He looked up at me, obviously startled. "You really believe that?"

"Yeah, I really believe that. I also really believe you need to talk to Dom about this. If you can convince *me* to cut you some slack about it, then I'm guessing you can convince him, too."

Adam laughed, and I could almost see the weight

lifting off his shoulders. I laughed a bit, too, but for different reasons. How ridiculous was it for someone like me to be giving relationship advice to *anyone*, much less to a sadistic demon?

"Maybe you're right," Adam conceded when he stopped laughing. "I'll think about it, I promise. Now tell me, what on earth were you doing in The Seven Deadlies?"

"Good question," I muttered under my breath, then proceeded to tell him all about my lame-ass plan to meet with Tommy. I'd drunk half my cup of coffee by the time I was through, but the jolt of caffeine didn't make my plan sound any better.

Out of the corner of my eye, I saw Adam shaking his head. "And what were you going to do if by some miracle he blurted out a confession?"

I shifted uncomfortably. That had always been the weakest part of my plan.

"That's what I thought," Adam said, then leaned forward in his seat, drawing my gaze. "You're not a cop. You're not a private investigator. You're an exorcist. Leave this to the professionals, love."

Yes, he was totally right, but that didn't stop me from bristling. "It was *me* Claudia Brewster hired, not you." Well, maybe technically she didn't *hire* me. I hadn't accepted any money from her.

Adam seemed less than impressed. "You brought the case to me for a reason, and it wasn't because you wanted to hang out with me. Let me do my job, okay?"

I'd have loved to argue with him if he weren't making so much sense. Of course, being me, I wasn't about to agree with him, either, so I just gulped more coffee instead of speaking.

"You said we needed to talk about something," he

said when it became obvious I wasn't planning to say anything more. "Obviously it wasn't about this, so what's up?"

He'd already said he didn't want Saul back in Dominic, but when I'd asked him, he hadn't known that's what Lugh wanted. I believed Lugh was right, and Adam was a good little soldier. What his king commanded, he would do, no matter how much it hurt him, or anyone else.

I knew eventually I'd have no choice but to tell him what Lugh wanted me to. But that didn't mean it had to be now. Lugh shot me a little headache to let me know he disapproved of my decision, but it was only a brief stab of pain. If he really wanted to show his displeasure, he could hit me with a pain so bad it could bring me to my knees.

"Never mind," I told Adam. "It's not important."

I'm sure he saw through my lie, but he didn't challenge it. I glanced at my watch and was startled to discover it was already two in the morning. I hadn't realized how long I'd sat in that damn club! The twenty-four hours Lugh had given me were almost up, which meant that if I didn't tell Adam now, Lugh would hijack my body the next time I fell asleep.

I took one more look at Adam, then decided it was time to get a refill on my coffee.

Adam gave me a bit of a funny look when I returned to the table with my fresh cup of coffee. Despite a concerted effort, I still haven't learned how to keep everything I'm feeling from showing on my face, and he probably knew something was wrong. Something other than his cheating on Dominic, that is. And though I fully understood why he was doing it, as long as Dom didn't know, it seemed like cheating to me.

"I gather you haven't had a chance to visit with Sammy yet?" I asked, hoping that would stave off any questions he was tempted to ask.

Adam raised an eyebrow. He knew a diversionary tactic when he saw one. Luckily, just this once, he decided to let me off the hook.

"I dropped by his office today and found out he's on vacation. I'll talk to him as soon as he gets back. But meanwhile, I'll focus on Tommy. I suspect I'll have no trouble getting some, uh, private time with him." He stared at his cup of tea, though I suspected it had been empty for at least fifteen minutes.

It wasn't hard to guess what he meant, and I had to fight my surge of disgust. "You mean he likes the hardcore shit," I said, my voice rising, "and you're going to cheat on Dom with him."

I was loud enough that a few people turned to look at me. I swallowed hard and lowered my voice. "I'd rather you let me question him myself."

Adam put his cup down and leaned toward me, anger glinting in his eyes. "I am *not* cheating on Dom," he snarled. "And with your *charming* personality, you'll have him clammed up and suspicious within the first five minutes. If I take him down into Hell, I can get him into a frame of mind where he's not thinking straight. And since I'm a police officer, I can act on it if he tells me something he shouldn't. You've done your part by bringing the case to me. Now stay out of it like a good little exorcist and let me handle it."

I was getting pretty damn tired of being told to stay out of it, but for once my common sense spoke up in time, and I kept that thought to myself. I doubt Adam expected me to heed his warning, but I didn't think arguing about it was going to help my case.

"Fine," I muttered, slurping down more coffee. "You go on back to Hell. It's where you belong anyway."

I stood up, meaning to make a dramatic exit, but Lugh sent a stab of pain through my eye, and I stumbled. I almost pitched face-first into Adam's lap, but with demon-quick reflexes, he caught me. For a moment that felt like forever, I looked into those dark brown eyes, my nose inches away from his. I caught the scent of the spicy aftershave he favored, and beneath that, a salty undertone that reminded me of an ocean breeze. Despite my dislike of him, despite his sexual habits, despite him being a demon, I had to admit to myself that he was one hell of a sexy specimen of manhood. Against my every wish, images flashed through my mind. Images of Adam, naked and aroused, images of him with Dom, images of—

With a jerk, I shoved myself away from him, shutting down that line of thought with all the ferocity I could. I did *not* want to think of Adam that way. I was already in love with Brian and in lust with Lugh. I didn't need any more . . . complications.

One corner of Adam's mouth rose in a half-smile, but it wasn't a nice expression. There was no question in my mind that no matter how much I wanted to deny it to myself, Adam knew I found him attractive. I had a distinct feeling he would use his knowledge against me if he had half a chance.

Knowing that anything I said would just make things worse, I settled for shaking my head before I turned on my heel and strode to the door. Lugh did the eye-stab thing again, but it was merely a brief annoyance. It wasn't like this was a battle I could win. No matter how much caffeine I ingested, eventually I would fall asleep and he would take over. But *eventually* was better than *now*.

Wondering how I was going to keep myself occupied during the wee hours of the morning, I made my way back to the garage to retrieve my car.

Chapter 11

It was past four when I finally let myself into my apartment, so I didn't have as many wee hours to kill as I'd expected. The day was getting a head start toward being really shitty. On my way home, I'd gotten pulled over for speeding. Naturally, the cop who pulled me over was female and not a good candidate for the eyelash batting that had gotten me out of tickets with the testosterone brigade. I wasn't really going that fast, but I guess she was bored and I made an easy target. Always happy to help our women in blue pass the time.

I shoved the speeding ticket into a drawer with my growing pile of unpaid bills and then made myself a pot of coffee. My body ached for me to throw myself onto the bed and sleep for a week, but this was a case of mind over matter, and I wasn't going to give in.

I had to find a way to keep myself busy, otherwise the lure of sleep would be too much to resist, but I couldn't think of anything useful to do on the Brewster case. I could drop by Tommy's apartment again, but I didn't think it would do me much good.

Besides, I had semi-promised Adam I'd let him handle things. Not that I felt particularly bound by that promise, but I figured it would be decent of me to at least let him make first contact. Besides, for all I knew, he'd gone back to the club last night and convinced Tommy to confess everything.

I settled for going in to the office again. This would be two times within the space of one week. I was being positively productive! Of course, I hadn't gotten much work done the last time, Claudia Brewster's visit having thoroughly interrupted my efforts.

Doing paperwork wasn't the best way to keep myself awake, I realized a couple of hours later as my eyes crossed and my mind wandered. I took an extended break to get a grande cappuccino with an extra shot of espresso from the nearest Starbucks, and felt marginally more alive after my first few sips. I had almost psyched myself up for the singularly unpleasant task of chatting up my insurance company when I stepped off the elevator into the hallway leading to my office. I was spaced out enough that I took two more long strides toward my door before I noticed the figure standing before it.

In the pictures Claudia had shown me, Tommy looked like a typical sulky, rebellious teenager. Unkempt hair. Ill-fitting pants. Face fixed in a long-suffering expression that said his life was fucked up beyond recognition, but somehow he'd manage to muddle through.

Apparently, demonic possession agreed with him. He still wasn't exactly what you'd call a snappy dresser. His jeans were baggy, the fraying cuffs dragging on the floor, and his T-shirt had probably once been black but had been washed so many times it was an uneven and particularly unattractive shade of gray.

But he carried himself entirely differently. His shoulders were straighter, his posture more confident, his expression much...older.

He was leaning casually against the wall, arms crossed over his chest as he watched me approach. I had no idea what he wanted, but I made an educated guess and decided it wasn't anything good. I shifted my coffee into my left hand, then reached into my purse and fished out my Taser, arming it while keeping a close eye on him. I didn't really think he was going to attack me in a public place, not when he'd gone through so much trouble to make himself seem like a legal demon, but I wasn't one to take chances.

Tommy was a little bit shorter than your average demon host. Most of them topped six feet, but I'd have put him at about five-ten. Give me a good pair of heels, and I'd be able to look down on him. He had the requisite good looks, though. His face was a little rounded, giving him an almost cherubic expression with his small, curvy mouth and apple cheeks. But all you had to do was look him in the eye to kill that illusion. They were a deep shade of blue I'd have called beautiful if it weren't for the malevolent presence I sensed behind them.

Maybe it was all in my mind. Maybe the fact that I knew he was possessed by an illegal demon made that glint in his eye look evil. Maybe if I had no idea who he was and had just run into him on the street, I wouldn't have given him a second glance. But I *did* know what he was, and I hated him before he even opened his mouth.

Tommy pushed away from the wall and gave me an assessing look, one that made me bristle. He watched me pull the Taser from my bag but didn't seem particularly concerned about it.

"Morgan Kingsley, I presume?" he asked in a cultured tone that I suspected sounded nothing like Tommy Brewster.

"What are you doing here?" I asked. I suppose I won't win any prizes for politeness, but I couldn't think of any pressing reason to treat him as a decent human being.

"I'd heard you were looking for me," he said.

I narrowed my eyes at him. "Where did you hear that?"

"My roommate informed me that I had a visitor yesterday. He also said he suggested you look for me at The Seven Deadlies." He grinned at me, a creepy expression that made my skin crawl—no doubt just the effect he was going for. "I *am* sorry I missed you last night."

I was trying to think of a good retort while simultaneously trying to keep my face from showing how much he was creeping me out, when the elevator dinged, signaling it was about to open.

There was only one other tenant on my floor, a mid-sized and terribly respectable accounting firm. I doubt they were thrilled to be sharing space with me in the first place, and they would be even less so if a customer stepped off the elevator to see me holding a cherub-faced youngster at Taser point.

With great reluctance, I turned the Taser off and stuck it back in my bag just in time. Tommy and I waited in silence for the professional young couple to step off the elevator and push open the accounting firm's door.

"Wouldn't you prefer we take this conversation somewhere more private?" Tommy asked, jerking his thumb toward my own closed door.

I wasn't sure I wanted to be trapped in a closed

room with him, but it wouldn't do to risk having innocent bystanders caught in the crossfire if things turned ugly. My hand hovered near my bag, though if Tommy wanted to attack me, I was dead meat. I wouldn't have time to reach into my bag, pull out the Taser, arm it, and fire before he was on me. Even knowing that, I felt better having it within reach.

"Give me some space," I demanded. Tommy hesitated, a smirk on his face as he waited for me to acknowledge that if he did as I ordered, he was merely humoring me. I gave him my fiercest scowl, which seemed to satisfy him, and he backed away.

I was twitchy as hell as I approached my door, uncomfortable with the idea that between the coffee and the keys, both my hands were occupied. I needed a third hand for the Taser. But despite my worries, Tommy made no move to attack me, and his lips remained stretched in that infuriating smirk.

As soon as I got my door open, I hurried into the office and put my desk between myself and Tommy. He humored my skittishness, keeping his distance while making it obvious how much he was enjoying himself. I threw my keys onto the desk and drew and armed my Taser once again. *Now* I felt safe.

I leaned back into my chair and propped my ankles up on my desk, the Taser never wavering. I took a nice long gulp of my rapidly cooling coffee before addressing my surprise guest once again.

"What do you want?" I asked, though I was pretty sure I already knew.

Tommy's smirk hadn't faltered at my newfound confidence. Moving slowly, and keeping a close eye on the Taser, he pulled out a chair and took a seat in front of my desk. "As I said, I'd heard you were looking for me. Perhaps I should be asking *you* that."

"Cut the crap and get to the point."

One corner of his mouth tugged downward in a hint of a frown. Maybe I was getting to him more than I thought. I surreptitiously glanced at my Taser, reassuring myself that it was fully charged.

"Fine," Tommy said with a pout he must have learned from his host. "The point is I know my parents want you to exorcize me."

"They aren't *your* parents," I snapped. "They're Tommy's."

He rolled his eyes. "All right. I'll rephrase: I know my host's parents want you to exorcize me. They are under the delusional impression that Tommy was coerced into hosting me. Let me assure you, that's just their wishful thinking. Tommy is a legal, registered demon host, and if you exorcize me, you'll be guilty of murder."

"Yeah, that's a real news flash. Thanks for letting me know."

His frown was more pronounced now. Apparently that hadn't been the reaction he was hoping for. "I have warned my . . . associates that I have been threatened. If I were to leave Tommy's body, you would be up on murder charges before you knew what hit you."

"Again, not a news flash. I told your parents no. I'm not a moron."

He raised his eyebrows as if surprised. "No? Then what were you doing looking for me at The Seven Deadlies last night?"

"How did you know I was at the club?" I countered.

He gave me a droll look. "Because Shae told me."

Warning bells clanged in my head. Shae wasn't exactly my bosom buddy, and she hadn't even bothered to question what I was doing at her club last night. How could she possibly have known I was looking for Tommy? My question must have showed on my face, because Tommy answered it before I had a chance to ask.

"An exorcist who I know has been hired to exorcize me shows up at a demon nightclub and stakes the place out like an amateur detective. It wasn't hard to put the pieces together, especially since I asked Shae to tell me if you showed up."

I supposed that made a kind of sense, though it suggested a closer relationship between Tommy and Shae than I would have guessed. Of course, since they were both illegals, they had things in common that perhaps would lead them to be close friends. Nah, I didn't think Shae was into the whole "friends" thing. She was a mercenary through and through. If she and Tommy had teamed up, it was because she was being well paid. The question remained, what for?

"Now that I've satisfied your curiosity," Tommy continued, "why don't you satisfy mine and tell me what you want?"

I'd had enough of my pseudo-relaxed pose, so I put my feet back down on the floor and sat up straight. "I sympathize with your host's mother. If I were in her shoes, I'm sure I'd be doing the same thing she is. But I'm not stupid enough to perform an illegal exorcism. If you'd like to confess to me that you're an illegal, I'd be delighted to hear it and I'd set up that exorcism so fast it'd make your head spin. But somehow, I don't see you being that obliging."

He chuckled. "No, not likely. But none of this explains why you were looking for me."

At this point, I wanted nothing more than to get rid of him. I knew Adam was right, and that I should leave the investigating to the professionals. But it wasn't like I was going to admit that to Tommy.

I shrugged. "If I ignore your mother's request without looking into it at all, I'll never be able to live with myself. It's hard for me to imagine a God's Wrath fanatic agreeing to host you. I just wanted to hear your explanation firsthand for why he's doing it."

His smile looked genuinely amused. "And if you don't like my explanation?"

I shrugged again. "I haven't figured that part out yet."

He laughed softly. "You're almost as entertaining as Shae said you were." He pushed his chair back and stood. "It's been lovely talking to you."

"If you're here legally, then there's no reason you shouldn't explain to me why Tommy decided to host you."

"There's also no reason why I *should*." He smiled at me pleasantly. "And here's a friendly word of advice for you: wasting your time trying to find evidence that Tommy didn't summon me of his own free will is not your wisest career move."

Naturally, I bristled. "That sounded suspiciously like a threat." Making a threat—even one more blatantly phrased than that—isn't considered a "violent crime," so I couldn't earn the right to exorcize him that way. But in a manner of speaking, it could be considered a step in the right direction.

There was a predatory gleam in Tommy's eyes, though his smile remained firmly in place and he made no response to my accusation. He mimed tipping his hat, then turned to the door.

For a moment, I considered shooting him just on general principle. But of course, the authorities frowned on that sort of thing.

I'm not sure just what he'd hoped to accomplish by

confronting me like this. If he thought I'd be intimidated and back off, then clearly he and his cronies didn't know me at all.

Reciting a list of curses under my breath, I let him go.

Chapter **12**

I was still in my office at four o'clock that afternoon when Brian called. I hadn't exactly gotten much done, and the ring tone I'd assigned to Brian jerked me out of a reverie that had been on the verge of becoming a doze. I cursed myself roundly, knowing that it would only take a few short minutes for Lugh to use my body to make the phone call I didn't want him to make.

On some level, I knew I was being needlessly stubborn about this. After all, I couldn't go without sleep indefinitely. But so little of my life was under my control these days, I'd take any excuse I could find to hold on to the reins, even if just for a little while.

I should have expected Brian's call. He'd given me the requisite two days to think about what had happened between us, and now he was going to start pushing. It was an MO with which I was intimately familiar. I'd have liked to ignore the ringing phone and let him stew awhile, but I figured wrangling with him was sure to keep me awake. With a sigh of resignation, I dug my phone out of my purse and answered.

"Hey," I said, a neutral greeting.

"You sound tired."

On cue, I yawned. "You could tell that from one word?"

"I can read you like a book, remember?"

I shook my head, refusing the second yawn that tried to bubble up. "Especially when Lugh's given you the CliffsNotes?"

There was a moment of silence. "Was it that obvious?"

I scrubbed at my gritty eyes. "Yeah." I didn't elaborate.

Another silence, longer this time. "Aren't you going to tell me what you think of me?" he finally asked.

"No. I already reamed Lugh out about it. I'll let you off with a warning: don't do that again."

"Do what?" I made a snarling noise, and Brian hastened to clarify. "Talk to Lugh, or—"

"Either!" I snapped. Of course, my treacherous mind called up the intoxicating sensations he'd awakened in my body when I'd surrendered to him, and my pulse kicked up. Damn it, it had felt so good! And here I was telling him never to do it again. Not that my words were likely to have much of an effect.

"Maybe this is something we should discuss in person," Brian suggested, and I could almost see the suggestive waggle of his brows.

As usual, my first instinct was to push back. It was on the tip of my tongue to tell him no, but then I considered my alternatives. I could sit here in the office for another hour or two, getting little to nothing done and struggling against sleep. Or I could go home by myself and face the same struggle. Or I could meet up with Brian. At least if I was with Brian, I'd be facing a struggle that would keep me awake.

"You're right, it is," I said, smiling as I imagined the look of shock that his face must have been wearing at the moment. "If you want to talk, meet me at my apartment at six-thirty. And bring food." I hung up before he could answer, but there was no doubt in my mind that he would come.

I hoped he'd had fun with his little dominance game. Because tonight, I was going to make him pay for it.

Feeling decidedly more awake than I had all day, I shut down my computer and stuffed my unfinished paperwork into my desk.

My mood sank a bit when I got home and listened to my messages. Adam had called and asked me to call back. I didn't much want to talk to him, but if he'd managed to get anything out of Tommy last night, I had to know. I started a pot of coffee, then dialed his number.

"Tell me you have some good news for me," I demanded when Adam answered, though I knew if he'd had *really* good news, Tommy wouldn't have stopped by this afternoon.

"Afraid I can't do that, love," he confirmed. "However, I did find out something *interesting*."

I raised an eyebrow, even though he couldn't see me. "Oh?"

"I went back to the club after we talked last night. Tommy'd just gotten there and I assumed he was trolling the place. I approached him, hoping I could get him to spend a little time in Hell with me . . . and he turned me down."

I swallowed a laugh. "Wow, that's just *amazing*! To think that there's a person on this earth who might turn down the incredible Adam White." I put a hand to my chest and groaned dramatically. "What *is* this world coming to?"

"You're just a laugh a minute," Adam said, but though he was striving for an air of nonchalance, I heard the simmering anger beneath it. The bruises on my back flared to life, reminding me what Adam could be like when he was pissed off. Not that he could do anything to me over the phone, but still . . .

"Sorry," I said, but I don't think I sounded too sincere. "I couldn't resist."

"It isn't the fact that he turned me down that's interesting. It's the why."

"Okay, I'll bite—why did he turn you down?"

"I hung around the club for a couple hours afterward, and I saw a very definite pattern. Apparently, he's only interested in women."

I blinked a couple of times. "And this is interesting because . . . ?"

"Because it's highly unusual for a demon to have a strong sexual preference when on the Mortal Plain. Sex for us here has nothing to do with reproduction and everything to do with physical sensation."

I'd always suspected that Adam swung both ways, but up until now I hadn't been completely sure. I'd never felt *safe* with Adam, but a part of me had taken comfort in the idea that he was gay and therefore not a sexual threat. I'd have preferred to keep that illusion.

"What do you think it means?" I asked, hoping my voice sounded absolutely normal.

He gave a frustrated sigh. "I don't know. But my instincts say it's important. I'm going to go to the club again tonight and keep an eye on him, see if I can figure out what he's up to."

"Have you told Dom yet?" I blurted, and the guilty silence on the other end of the line was answer enough. "You know that the more time you spend at the club, the more likely it is Dom will find out."

Adam didn't answer, but I knew he heard the truth in my words.

"I know you're about as eager to take advice from me as I am to take it from you," I continued, "but I'll say this anyway. Don't go to the club tonight. You probably wouldn't learn anything anyway." I then told him about Tommy's visit to my office this afternoon. "Obviously," I concluded, "he's on high alert right now. If you start staking out the club, he's going to figure out something is up."

"Do you have a better idea?"

I frowned. "I'm working on it. I know you think I should let the professionals handle this, but I'm just not convinced there's anything you can do right now."

"You're probably right. But if anyone's going to risk their neck going after Tommy, it had better not be you. Much though I hate to admit it, you're too important to risk."

That made me wince, though I was immediately pissed at myself. There was no reason in hell for me to care if Adam liked me or not. Especially considering how little I liked him. But every time he hinted at what he thought of me, it brought a little stab of pain. Pathetic! You'd think I'd have gotten over the fruitless quest for approval by now.

"I've got other concerns anyway," I said, hoping my voice didn't betray the hurt. Then, because I knew if I said anything more I wouldn't be able to hide how I felt, I hung up.

I'd downed half my pot of coffee by the time Brian arrived, and my nerves were stretched taut by caffeine while my eyelids still tried to droop. There's nothing like that special feeling of being sleepy and jittery at the same time to put a girl in a warm fuzzy mood.

Brian arrived right on time, bringing a large pizza that quickly filled my small apartment with the scent of garlic. He took one look at me and tossed the pizza onto my minuscule dining room table.

"What's wrong?" he asked, putting both hands on my shoulders and peering into my eyes with his trade-mark gentle concern.

I tried to muster my usual snappish response, but sleep deprivation had eroded my carefully constructed defenses, and for a moment I feared I would burst into girly tears for no particular reason. When Brian pulled me into his arms for a hug, I had to bite down hard on my lip to keep myself under control.

"Nothing's wrong," I murmured unconvincingly into his chest. "I'm just tired."

His lips whispered over the top of my head. "I know you far too well to believe that," he said. "But I also know if I push, you'll just get pissed at me, so I'll try my hardest to be on my best behavior."

He set me away from him, and I looked into his eyes. Once upon a time, he wouldn't have been able to resist pushing. My inability to share my feelings with him had caused more arguments between us than I can count. If he was finally learning to back off...

But no. Those whisky-brown eyes of his held sym-pathy, but also a hint of calculation. This was a tacti-cal retreat, not a change of heart. I stifled a sigh, then turned to the table and opened the pizza box.

Extra cheese, and plenty of pepperoni, swimming in greasy goodness. My stomach grumbled, and I tried to remember if I'd eaten any lunch today. Brian re-trieved plates and paper towels from the kitchen; then we dug into our pizza without speaking. Brian used the paper towels to dab some of the grease off the top of his pizza, but I figured with the amount of caffeine in my system, I must be burning up calories at an impressive rate, so screw the grease.

For a while, we ate in companionable silence. I reveled in Brian's presence, in his calm strength and kindness, and, yes, in his love. It sounds pathetic, but before Brian, no one had ever really loved me for who I was. My parents had always wanted to change me, as had my brother—at least once the Spirit Society had gotten its claws into him. My boyfriends before Brian had all been under the illusion that they could somehow tame me. They had never lasted very long.

What kind of fool was I to work so hard to hold Brian at arm's length when he really, truly loved me? And when I loved him in return? Once upon a time, I'd told him—and myself—that it was for his own protection, but that was bullshit.

"You look like you're thinking very hard," Brian said, and I'd been so spaced out I practically jumped out of my chair.

I shoved away my plate, which was littered with pizza crusts, and tried to drag my mind back into the real world. Introspection was not my thing, but the lack of sleep was making me loopy.

"Sorry," I said. "I'm just really, really tired."

He raised an eyebrow. "Oh?"

It was a very gentle invitation for me to tell all, and usually I would have declined that invitation without a second thought. But today I overrode my own instincts.

"Lugh and I are having a bit of a disagreement," I admitted. "If I go to sleep, he's going to take matters into his own hands. I know I can't stay awake forever, but..." I shrugged.

True, it wasn't much of an explanation. But it was more than I would usually give him, and I could see by the look on Brian's face that he knew it. He leaned over the table and wrapped his hand around mine, giving me a comforting squeeze despite my greasy fingers.

"I can stay with you tonight," he said softly. "And if Lugh tries to take control, I can wake you up."

My throat tightened. "You would do that? Even when you don't know what the disagreement's about?"

His hand squeezed mine more tightly. "I'm on your side, Morgan. No matter what. So yeah, I'd do that."

The intensity of his gaze unnerved me, and I tried to pull my hand away. He didn't let me.

Fine, let him have my hand! But I escaped his gaze by staring at the table. "You and Lugh teamed up against me once before," I said. "Why should I believe you won't do it again?"

Brian reached across the table and tried to lift my chin to force me to look at him. A little of my usual fire returned, and I jerked away.

"Don't treat me like a child!" I snapped, then cursed myself because I couldn't help looking him in the eye when I was pissed off. The faint smile he tried to suppress told me he'd done it on purpose.

"What if I promise you that no matter what, I'll wake you if Lugh tries to take control?" he asked. "Will you accept that promise?"

He finally released my hand, and I drew it back gratefully.

Could I trust Brian's promise? "What if Lugh tried to convince you it's the right thing to do? You *have* sided with him before."

"I sided with him because I wanted to protect you. I won't do it again." He held up his hand in the Boy Scout salute. "Scout's honor."

It was a chancy proposition at best. I wasn't entirely certain Brian would be able to wake me up if Lugh took control. Come to think of it, I wasn't sure he'd be able to tell whether Lugh was in control or not. Demons are damn good at mimicking their hosts when they want to. But I couldn't stay awake forever, and this sure seemed like my best chance to get some sleep while still avoiding being Lugh's instrument.

"You know that Lugh can overpower you," I said, wondering just how determined Lugh would be to make this phone call. Might he hurt Brian?

Not unless he wanted me as a permanent enemy. He *had* to know that.

Brian shrugged. "Yeah, I know. But if he has to overpower me, then the struggle should give you time to wake up."

"True," I agreed, stifling yet another yawn. I made one last attempt to look the gift horse in the mouth. "You have to go to work in the morning, don't you?"

"I'll be all right," he assured me. "I'll just pretend I'm a college kid pulling an all-nighter."

I laughed weakly. Obviously, I had no defenses strong enough to defeat Brian. God, I loved him. Why didn't that make everything easy between us?

"Thank you," I said, though the words were inadequate to express what I felt.

Figuring I'd turn into a gibbering idiot if I stayed awake any longer, I gave Brian a quick, appreciative kiss, then led him to my bedroom.

Chapter **13**

You know that feeling you get when you're too tired to sleep? Well add the jitters of a couple gallons of coffee on top of that, and you'll know exactly how I felt as I lay there in my bed trying to force myself to knock off.

Brian sat on the easy chair in the corner, reading by the light of a bulb so dim that it would give him eyestrain. I had my back turned to him—and to the light—but though I tried to pretend he wasn't there, my every nerve seemed aware of him. I wanted him beside me in the bed, not across the room from me. I wanted his warmth and strength pressed up against me, his arms wrapped around me. I was too tired to want sex, but oh how I longed for that simple companionship.

If Brian was feeling any of the same feelings, he wasn't showing it. I could tell by the steady turning of the pages that he actually was reading that book, not just staring at it blankly. I sucked in a deep, quiet breath and let it out slowly, trying to let my body relax.

Easier said than done. Even if I felt sure that Brian

wouldn't side with Lugh, even if I felt sure he'd recognize Lugh if he took over, I still figured I was in for some unpleasantness when I finally gave in to sleep. Lugh would no doubt tell me his opinion of my stubbornness, and he would try to lay a guilt trip on me. I was confident in my ability to resist his persuasion, but I wasn't looking forward to the battle.

The bed dipped beside me, and I jumped. I hadn't been even close to sleep, but I had been spaced out enough that I hadn't heard Brian get up. His hand landed on my shoulder and gave a firm squeeze.

"Having trouble sleeping?" he asked.

Damn. I thought I'd been faking sleep better than that. I rolled onto my back and squinted up at him. He was silhouetted by the single light in the room, and I couldn't see the expression on his face.

"I've had a lot of caffeine today," I murmured in response. "The exhaustion will take over eventually."

"Hmm," he said, but it didn't sound like an agreement. Without another word, he stood up and crossed the room, turning off the light and leaving the room cloaked in darkness.

I propped myself up on my elbows. "How are you going to stay awake in the dark all night?" I think there was a tinge of hysteria in my voice, but Brian just chuckled.

"I'll turn it back on once you're sound asleep," he said.

Once again, the bed dipped under his weight. I was going to say something else pithy—though I don't know what—but my words died in my throat when Brian pulled the covers slowly down my body.

When I'm by myself, I generally wear super-comfy PJs to bed, but when Brian's around it's either a slinky nightgown or nothing. Tonight, I'd gone with nothing.

I'd been sure Brian wouldn't make sexual overtures when I was so desperately in need of sleep. Shows how much I know.

"Brian . . ."

He chuckled again. "I know. Not tonight, you have a headache."

I couldn't help a little bark of laughter in response. "Something like that."

His fingers came to rest at the base of my throat, then traced softly, slowly down my middle. I tried to protest, but my body had a will of its own, arching into the caress even though he didn't touch any of my erogenous zones.

With a resigned sigh, I reached for him, but he gently nudged my hands away.

"No, no," he said. "Tonight, I'm taking care of you. You don't have to do a thing."

I snorted. "You've got to be kidding me."

Those maddening fingers of his brushed over my nipple, and my breath hitched. "Nope," he said, sounding cheerful. "I'm just going to give you a little stress relief to help you sleep."

I squirmed under his touch. Although my body couldn't help reacting to him, I really, truly wasn't in the mood. Let me tell you, I have to be *very* off my game not to be in the mood when Brian is around. But before I could muster another protest, he had leaned over me and planted his lips on mine.

I resisted the pleasure of his kiss for, oh, ten seconds or so. But the brush of his tongue was so incendiary that it felt like every nerve in my body spontaneously combusted. To hell with being too tired for sex! I wrapped my arms around his neck and clung, a greedy, whimpering sound rising from my throat.

Once again, Brian pushed my hands out of the way, this time circling my wrists with his fingers and pinning them to the bed beside my head. He raised his head just enough to give him room to speak, even as I strained toward him. My eyes had adjusted to the dark, and I could see the mingled heat and determination in his eyes.

"I mean it, Morgan," he said, then punctuated the statement with a delicate lick across the seam of my lips. "Tonight, it's going to be all about you. So keep your hands to yourself and let me take care of you."

My heart beat irregularly in my chest. I am *not* a passive lover, and the idea of lying here like some frigid Victorian lady while Brian had his way with me did not sit well. What the hell had gotten into him?

But, of course, I knew all too well.

"This is one of those goddamn dominance things, isn't it?" I asked, trying to sound as irritated as I thought I ought to feel.

He nipped at my lower lip, then soothed the sting with his tongue. "It has nothing to do with that," he assured me. "All I want is to give you some pleasure. I want to *give*, not take. No ulterior motives, no hidden agendas."

I'd have argued with him, but he plunged his tongue into my mouth, and the only sound I could make was a moan.

The part of me that never stops thinking knew that whatever he might say, there was more to this than the simple giving of pleasure. If he hadn't had his little chat with Lugh, it never would have occurred to him to do this. But my body told me in no uncertain terms that thinking was highly overrated. With my defenses weakened by sleep deprivation, I gave in to my body's demands and stopped struggling to free my wrists.

As soon as I surrendered, Brian let go of my wrists, using one hand to draw maddening circles on the slope of my breast while his tongue tangled with mine. Instinct urged me to wrap my arms around him again, to hold him close to me and feel the warmth of his skin under my hands. I fought those instincts, kissing him back with every drop of my passion while I lay still beneath him.

There was an unaccustomed glitter in his eyes when he raised his head, along with a hunger I knew he planned not to sate, at least not tonight. I shivered, again not sure if it was because of anticipation or unease.

His head lowered once more, and he trailed kisses down my throat. I had to curl my hands into fists to keep from running my fingers through his hair. As he worked his way down, those circles he'd been drawing on my breast finally shrank until a single finger brushed my nipple, over and over. My back arched into that touch, but his hand moved away far before I was ready. The good news was his mouth was moving steadily south.

I didn't completely understand the game he was playing until his mouth started circling my nipple, mimicking the pattern his fingers had made before, and his hand slid down past my navel. When I realized that his mouth was going to continue following the trail blazed by his fingers, I practically came right then and there. Maybe if I hadn't been so tired, I would have.

He moved so slowly it was all I could do to keep myself from screaming my impatience. Mouth and fingers working in perfect synchronization, circling, circling, circling, but never quite getting to their final destinations. When I arched my back to try to get my nipple into his mouth, he carefully compensated for the movement, just as his fingers did when I lifted my hips.

"You bastard," I gasped, and his laughter buzzed against my skin, yet another erotic stimulus. Note to self: don't amuse him again, it only makes the torment worse.

I groaned when his fingers circled close enough to my clit that, with just the tiniest hint more speed or pressure, I'd have gone off like a rocket. But he knew me too well, knew how to read every nuance of my responses so that he could keep me on that razor's edge without pushing me over. I swallowed a number of curses and considered using a quick burst of power to roll us over so I was on top and could impale myself on him.

My few rational brain cells reminded me he was still fully clothed, but perhaps he'd sensed that thought, for his mouth left my breast and began once more following the trail of his fingers. I grabbed a double handful of the covers to remind myself to keep still. Because no matter what other emotions and desires were jumbling together within me, I knew with perfect clarity that I wanted his mouth to complete that journey.

He didn't move any faster, despite my increasing desperation. I bit down on my lip to keep myself from begging. My breath came so short it was a good thing I didn't hyperventilate, and my skin quivered and twitched under the artful caresses of his tongue.

I took a certain savage satisfaction in the fact that once Brian had made his way down to the juncture of my thighs, some of that inhuman control seemed to snap. Instead of teasing me mercilessly as he had with his fingers, his tongue took only a brief sample before he settled in to work in earnest. And then pleasure overrode every other thought and sensation until I swear I almost forgot how to breathe.

When the last spasm fluttered into oblivion, I felt like every muscle in my body had been transformed to jelly. My heart continued to gallop, my breaths continued to come out in short gasps, but there was no question that I was much more relaxed. Even with the lingering buzz of caffeine in my nerves, I found my eyelids heavy, my mind free.

Brian didn't say anything, and he seemed content to let me drift in the afterglow while he himself went hungry. My eyes slid closed, and the last thing I remembered was Brian tucking the covers up under my chin and planting a chaste kiss on my forehead.

I awoke the next morning to the enticing scent of coffee. For a moment after I awoke, I just lay there, smelling the coffee while debating whether to let myself drop back into sleep. Then my brain cells started waking up, and I knew there would be no more sleep for me.

Rubbing bleary eyes, I sat up just as Brian pushed through my bedroom door carrying a mug that smelled heavenly.

"Good morning," he said, smiling at me as he held out the mug.

I grunted something incoherent and tried not to spill anything as I snatched the mug from his hand and took a big gulp. I burned my tongue in the process, but I didn't care. Even in my morning stupor, it occurred to me that the last thing I remembered was Brian tucking me in, which meant Lugh hadn't bothered to ream me out last night. I should have been grateful. Instead, I merely felt uneasy.

"What time is it?" I asked, since he was standing between me and my bedside clock.

"Quarter after eleven," he said, and I almost choked on my coffee.

Shaking my head in a futile attempt to clear the cobwebs, I leaned past him to double-check the clock, just in case he was yanking my chain, but he wasn't.

"Shouldn't you be at work?" I asked, stifling a yawn.

"I took a personal day."

For some reason, that admission made my eyes sting. Maybe just because Brian is usually so uptight, and I knew what a concession it was for him to stay home from work.

"Lugh and I had a bit of a chat last night," he continued, and I froze.

"Shit," I mumbled.

Brian laughed. "Relax. We didn't discuss your sex life."

"Glad to hear it," I said unconvincingly. "What *did* you discuss?" I wrapped both hands around my mug, my skin soaking in the warmth as inside I shivered in a phantom chill. I really didn't like the idea of Lugh and Brian talking.

"He told me about Tommy Brewster."

"Tattletale," I muttered under my breath.

"Were you ever going to tell me about this?" He didn't sound particularly angry, which made me feel guilty. If he'd started scolding me for holding back, I could have torn into him for not letting me have my space. I'd probably have liked that better.

I shrugged, hoping I didn't look as guilty as I felt. "Do you tell me about the cases you're working on every day?"

"My cases aren't likely to get me killed."

I dismissed that with a wave of my hand. "This

case isn't dangerous. And I'm not doing anything official on it anyway. I've handed it off to Adam, so if anyone's in danger, it's him."

"Hmm," Brian said, and he didn't sound particularly convinced. He did, however, drop the subject. Too bad I didn't like the next subject any better. "Lugh also told me what you two are arguing about."

I winced and mumbled another curse. Lugh and I were going to have another talk about respecting my privacy. "So he's convinced *you* to argue his case, which is why he didn't bother me last night."

Brian grinned at me. "Actually, no. He *tried* to convince me to argue his case. I even told him I would. But frankly, I'd much rather stay out of the middle."

I drank a little more coffee as I pondered his position. I supposed it made sense. Unless Lugh had convinced him that my safety was at stake, there was no reason to suspect Brian of siding against me. Of course, suspicion is second nature to me.

"He's right about one thing," Brian continued, and my suspicious nature leapt to the forefront.

"Aha!" I practically shouted. "Now comes the part where you argue his side while trying to sound like you're not."

Brian gave me a look of long-suffering patience. "If you'll let me finish..." I bit my tongue and nodded. "As I was saying, he's right that this is a battle you're eventually going to lose. I can't stay here to keep you awake every night, and you can't stay awake indefinitely."

Pissed off at him even though I didn't really have any reason to be, I shoved the covers off and made a beeline for my closet to grab my robe. At least, that's what I intended to do, but Brian took hold of my arm to stop me.

"Why are you angry with me?" he asked quite reasonably. "I'm not telling you anything you don't already know."

I glared at his hand until he let go of me. I felt at a distinct disadvantage arguing with him while I was stark naked, so I put on my robe, giving myself a couple moments to calm down. I knew I was overreacting. I knew it wasn't really Brian I was angry with. But somehow, that didn't seem to help me fight off the anger.

"Instead of getting pissed about it," Brian said, "why don't you just sit down and talk to me and we'll see if we can come up with a way out of the problem."

I let out a huff of frustration. "There *is* no way out, as you just pointed out."

Brian crossed the room and turned me to face him, his hands warm and solid on my shoulders. "We'll find one, okay? Can you just assume I'm not the enemy and talk to me?"

The hint of hurt in his eyes made my heart ache, and before I knew what I was going to do, I had put my arms around him and squeezed tight.

"I know you're not the enemy," I murmured against his collarbone as he returned my embrace. "And I'm sorry I'm such a bitch. I just . . . I want my life back, and I know I'm not going to get it, at least not anytime soon."

"I understand," he assured me. "And I love you even when you're being bitchy."

I couldn't help laughing. "Good thing, that."

His lips brushed the top of my head. "Yup."

I laughed again, slapping his chest and taking a step back. "Jerk! You didn't have to agree with me."

He just grinned. I let the humor bleed out of me and retreated back to the bed, grabbing my coffee once more. Brian joined me, sitting close enough that I could feel the heat of his body beside me as I quietly sipped my coffee. He didn't say anything, choosing instead to sit beside me in supportive, companionable silence. It felt surprisingly good. Domestic, even. And then Brian had to go and ruin it.

"You know," he said softly. "If we were living together, we could have quiet mornings like this every day."

My hand clenched on my mug, and I ground my teeth. It had been quite a while since he'd trotted that one out. I'd turned him down enough times in the past that I would have thought he'd have learned his lesson. I shook my head and refused to look at him.

"I'm really grateful to you for staying with me last night," I said, "but we still have . . . issues. You know that."

"You mean *you* have issues," he countered, but he didn't sound particularly upset.

I should have bristled, but somehow I couldn't find the energy. "If one of us has an issue, then we both have an issue." I put the coffee mug down and turned to face him. He was wearing his lawyer face, the one he wore when he didn't want me to know what he was feeling. I hated that face, but I couldn't blame him at the moment.

"Even if I totally forget about how you and Lugh have teamed up against me, I can't forget that there are a lot of people out there who want to kill me, and they're not the sort to worry if an innocent bystander gets hurt in the process."

"We've been through all that before. I'll be in the line of fire no matter what." He smiled, but it was a half-hearted expression. "But don't worry. I didn't expect you to fall into my arms and give me everything I want. I just wanted to remind you that I still want it."

What can I say? The man is just too good for me, but I can't seem to convince him of the fact.

"So now that we have that out of the way," he said, "let's talk about what you should do with the Adam and Dominic situation."

Neither one of us actually believed that it was "out of the way," but I decided I could pretend as well as Brian. "If you have any brilliant ideas, I'd love to hear them."

He shrugged. "I don't know if this counts as a 'brilliant idea,' but I do have a suggestion. You think that if Lugh gets to introduce the idea to Adam, Adam's going to agree, right?"

I nodded. "He won't like it, but when Lugh says to jump, Adam's one of those idiots who asks 'how high?'"

"And you think Dominic will agree because he wants to be a hero."

"Yeah, that about sums it up."

"So maybe you should try to convince Dominic to be a different kind of hero."

I raised an eyebrow. "Go ahead, I'm listening."

"Adam will agree because he thinks he has no choice but to obey his king, but it's going to tear him up inside. So make sure Dominic understands what putting Saul back in his body will do to Adam. Maybe then he won't be willing to host Saul."

I bit my lip, thinking about it. It made a certain amount of sense. But timing could be very important. If Adam mentioned his extracurricular activities and Dom didn't take it well, then he might not be in the right frame of mind. I suddenly wished I hadn't badgered Adam into agreeing to tell the truth.

"That sounds like as good a plan as any," I told

Brian, "but I'm still going to wait before I say anything. I'd rather have something more foolproof."

Brian gave me a grave look. "I don't think foolproof is going to be an option."

He was probably right. But as they say, hope springs eternal.

Chapter **14**

Brian left shortly after lunch—actually, breakfast for me, if you want to be technical about it. He said he need to catch a few Zs, and I figured he was more than entitled.

I was still feeling pretty groggy after my long night's sleep. I wasn't sure what to do with myself today. I could try to harass Tommy in hopes that he'd let something slip, but aside from the fact that I didn't think it would work, I was also pretty sure it wouldn't be good for my health. Probably Tommy wouldn't stoop to any kind of violence against me, not when he would be the immediate prime suspect and a conviction could get him killed. But this was one of those instances where I'd really hate to be proven wrong.

With my brain feeling so fuzzy, I decided to set myself to the patently uncerebral task of doing laundry. I spent most of my afternoon sitting in my building's creepy basement laundry room watching my clothes spin in the dryer. I'd have gotten through it much faster, but apparently Wednesday was Little Old Lady Laundry Day, because there was a steady procession of them hogging the machines. I had to hang around like a vulture waiting for its prey to die.

I was in a decidedly grumpy mood and still had one more load to do when I gave up for the day. That damn laundry room was super-heated from all the hot air of the dryers, I was soaked with sweat, and my throat was parched from the dry heat. I couldn't take any more, so I dragged my current clean load upstairs and told myself I'd finish up later.

My cell phone rang while I was putting the laundry away, and I debated whether I wanted to answer or not. When the caller ID told me it was Claudia, I decided I should take it.

Turned out it wasn't Claudia, it was her secretary. Claudia was stuck in important meetings all afternoon, but she wanted to meet with me. Her secretary asked me if seven o'clock at Bookbinder's would fit into my schedule.

I was momentarily speechless. I wasn't officially working for Claudia, so could this actually be considered a business meeting? It seemed not, and yet surely she wouldn't have tasked her secretary to make her social arrangements. And surely she wouldn't have assumed I could afford to eat at places like Bookbinder's at the drop of a hat. I really wanted to ask the secretary who'd be paying for this meal, but I figured that would be kind of tacky.

In the end, I agreed to the meeting. If I ended up having to pay, at least I'd be getting a first-class meal out of it. And if I didn't have to pay, it would be a *free* first-class meal. Yeah, yeah, typical me, thinking with my stomach.

I gathered from Claudia's secretary that she would be coming straight to dinner from work. I figured I should try to dress a little businesslike to put her at her ease, but I didn't own anything appropriate for a boardroom. I decided on a pair of white pinstriped pants that might have looked like business wear if they hadn't ridden so low on my hips, paired with a metallic silver tank top that dipped low enough to show some pretty serious cleavage. I looked more like I was going clubbing than going out to eat at a fancy restaurant for business, but it was the best I could do. I hadn't even come close to replacing the extensive wardrobe I'd lost in the fire.

The Old Original Bookbinder's is located near the Delaware River and is either a first-class seafood restaurant, or a tourist trap, depending on whom you ask. When I was a kid, every time we had someone come visit from out of town, there'd be a requisite trip to Bookbinder's for a lobster dinner. It used to be there was another restaurant called Bookbinder's on Fifteenth Street. They both billed themselves as being the "original" Bookbinder's, and my dad would regale visitors with stories—possibly more urban legend than history—about the bitter battles between the two for the right to use the name. The one on Fifteenth Street—which was "original" because it was owned and operated by the original Bookbinder's family—is gone now, but the one by the riverfront—which is "original" because it's the location of the original Bookbinder's restaurant—is alive and well.

I arrived before Claudia and tried to keep myself from staring at the huge lobster tank. When I was a kid, I'd always been fascinated by the lobster tanks, where customers could handpick which lobster was going to die to feed them that night. At the time, I didn't really make the connection that those bright red crustaceans that appeared on our plates were the same dark, drab creatures that crawled around in those tanks. Now that I knew better, I felt sorry for the poor,

doomed things. Yeah, I'm a tough broad all right—
with a bleeding heart.

Claudia arrived at quarter after seven, full of pro-
fuse apologies. She had indeed come straight from
work, where one of her meetings had run late. I silently praised my own wisdom in choosing a job that
would let me set my own hours. I didn't make the kind
of money Claudia Brewster did, but at least I had as
much free time as I wanted. Or I used to, before I
became the demon king's human host.

"So, what's the occasion?" I asked Claudia once we
were seated and our drink orders were placed. I didn't
know her well enough to be sure, but she seemed a bit
nervous. That didn't do my own nerves much good.

She smiled at me a bit sadly. "I really appreciate
you looking into Tommy's case for me. I wish you'd let
me pay you, but since you won't, I thought I'd at least
buy you a nice dinner. You can order anything you
want."

Well, that answered the question of who was paying. But I didn't think it answered the question of why
she'd called this meeting.

I could have pressed her for more information
ASAP. That would be my usual MO. But despite her
spiffy gray power suit and her confident corporate
facade, I sensed she was brittle underneath. Tact and
diplomacy aren't usually my strong suits, but my instincts were telling me to back off, and I usually listen
to my instincts.

Claudia ordered a lobster, probably as an addi-
tional signal that it was okay for me to do so as well.
She declined the opportunity to go to the tanks and
pick her victim. Even if the tanks hadn't bothered me,
I'd never dream of ordering lobster at Bookbinder's.
All around me, well-dressed businesspeople, dating
couples, and families wore the embarrassing bibs they

put on you when you ordered lobster. None of them seemed the least bit uncomfortable about how silly they looked, but I'd have been self-conscious the whole night. Of course, you didn't *have* to wear the bib, but somehow it felt a little like cheating to refuse it.

I managed not to laugh when they put the bib on Claudia. I think the struggle showed on my face, because her eyes twinkled a bit and her lips lifted in a hint of a smile.

"I haven't been here in years," I said, feeling the need to make small talk even though I sucked at it. "I think we came here for every special occasion I could name when I was growing up, so I kind of burned out on the place." I realized that could be taken as a complaint and felt my cheeks redden with embarrassment. I should really keep my mouth shut.

Luckily, Claudia didn't take offense. She grinned, and it was almost an impish expression—or maybe it just looked impish because the stupid bib was hiding the power suit. "Were you a chocolate cake kid or a strawberry shortcake kid?" she asked me, and I laughed.

Bookbinder's has the most ginormous desserts I've ever seen, and ordering that slice of chocolate cake the size of my head had always been the highlight of eating here when I was a kid. "Chocolate all the way," I answered. "I was crushed when they stopped serving it."

"Me, too. Tommy always liked the shortcake, though. And he always managed to eat the whole thing without even being sick afterward." Her smile wilted a bit at the memory.

I'd never thought of myself as socially awkward. Abrasive, and maybe even bitchy, but not *awkward*. Claudia was making me reassess myself. It occurred to me that even before my life had gone to hell, I'd spent very little time with female friends. There'd been Valerie, who turned out not to be a friend at all, but most of the other women I'd known when I was younger now had husbands and young children. I'd never exactly fit in with the mainstream crowd, but I'd never felt quite so far on the outside as I did now.

I really had to settle this thing with Adam and Dom. Messing up my sleep schedule was having a negative impact on my mood. In an effort to snap myself out of it, I fished out an oyster cracker from the jar on the table, then scooped out a tiny bit of horseradish from the condiment tray and dabbed it on the cracker. I popped it into my mouth, and the stinging bite of the horseradish cleared my head better than smelling salts.

"If you don't mind my asking," I said when I could talk again, "why did you and your husband adopt Tommy? Given his past, he must have been quite a handful."

Claudia took a dainty sip of the fancy French wine she'd ordered before answering. "I was in a very bad accident when I was twenty-two," she said. "The damage was extensive enough that I'll never be able to have children of my own." She swirled the wine around her glass, looking kind of lost. I wished I hadn't asked, but before I could think of a graceful way to change the topic, she continued.

"When my husband and I decided to adopt, we both agreed that we'd take in a child who'd be hard to place instead of going on a waiting list for the perfect baby. We fostered several children before Tommy came into our lives, but when he did . . . we knew he was meant to be ours. It sounds corny, I know, but there you have it." Again the sad smile.

I couldn't imagine how a child like Tommy, as troubled as he was, had managed to win the

Brewsters' hearts, but despite my big mouth, I knew better than to voice that particular opinion. As usual, though, I apparently wore my opinion on my face.

"He was a very sweet child," Claudia hastened to assure me. "He didn't seem to remember anything about . . . what happened to him. He was a great student and was popular with the other kids at school. It wasn't until adolescence that things started to change."

"Yeah, puberty sucks," I said, thinking of the changes that had overtaken my brother when he'd gone through puberty. That was when he'd turned into a Spirit Society drone, and I felt like I'd lost my big brother.

Our food arrived, and I thought I was in for a reprieve from the unwise conversation I had started. But after the waiter left, Claudia ignored her steaming lobster and met my eyes over the table.

"The sweet child I once knew is still in there," she said. "Under all the baggage he carries and all the anger, there's a decent human being."

"I believe you," I lied, then turned my attention to my grilled salmon in hopes she wouldn't read the lie on my face.

"I don't suppose I ever mentioned it," Claudia said, and I hoped that her easy tone meant she hadn't caught the lie, "but Devon and I also adopted two little girls." Still ignoring her food, she dug through her purse for her wallet, then showed me a photograph of two children.

I'd guess the older girl was about five, with thin brown hair, and a face I would have called plain if it weren't for the infectious smile. The smaller girl was probably around three, and would have been adorable in her little froufrou pink dress even if she hadn't been caught in the middle of a delighted laugh. The older girl stood behind her sister and had bent down to put her arms around her sister's waist so that their smiling faces were on the same level.

"They're lovely," I said, because what else were you supposed to say to someone who shows you pictures of their kids?

"Yes, I think so, too." There was something strangely sad in her voice as she tucked the wallet back into her purse. I wondered if I should ask about the girls' backgrounds. They were probably hard-luck kids like Tommy. But Claudia was finally turning her attention to her lobster, and I decided I'd rather eat than talk.

After the awkward and uncomfortable beginning, Claudia did us both a favor and took over the small talk reins for the remainder of the meal. The conversation wasn't what I'd call stimulating, but it got us both through the meal without too many of those uncomfortable silences. My dinner was delicious, and Claudia and I shared a piece of strawberry shortcake afterward. In my opinion, it wasn't as good as the chocolate cake they'd mysteriously dropped from the menu, but it was still a decadent treat. We managed to eat about half of it, which considering the size of the piece was an impressive accomplishment.

I'd have been just as happy to hit the road after dessert, but Claudia ordered coffee, so I followed suit. And that was when she broached the *real* reason why she'd asked me to dinner.

I could tell it was coming from the way her fingers tightened on her coffee cup. I'd known from the moment I'd laid eyes on her that there was something bothering her, and now I was going to find out what.

"My husband and I are very thankful for everything you've done for us," she said, not looking me in the eye.

It didn't take a rocket scientist to figure out I was about to be fired—though since I technically wasn't working for her, it wasn't really possible for her to fire me.

"But you've decided you don't need my services anymore," I finished for her. I'd have been pissed as hell if I thought she was dropping me of her own free will. But there was no way the desperate woman who had first shown up at my office would give up on her son, unless she was under duress somehow.

Strain showed in the stiffness of her posture and the tightness of her lips. She raised her chin and met my gaze. "I know it's pointless," she said, but there was no conviction in her words.

We stared at each other a long while. Usually, I'd have bet on myself in any staring contest, but there was so much pain and unhappiness in her expression that I was the one who looked away first.

"Who threatened you?" I asked, though I supposed it had to be Tommy and/or his cronies.

"No one threatened me," she said, but I didn't believe her for a moment. "My husband and I have decided it's time we accept reality and move on with our lives. We have to care for the children we still have."

Claudia didn't strike me as the type who'd give in easily to threats. Either her husband was a wuss and convinced her to be a wuss with him, or the bad guys had come up with one hell of a scary threat. What would be enough to convince a mother to stop fighting for the life of her son? I remembered the picture of those two smiling little girls and figured I had my answer right there.

Now, a wise person might have taken this as some kind of cue from the universe that it was time to back off of Tommy Brewster. I wasn't exactly making a whole lot of progress, and I didn't suppose my chances of finding an excuse to exorcize him were too good. If the bad guys were threatening the little girls, then any efforts I made could endanger innocent lives. Not to mention that as the demon king's host, I had enough problems on my own without letting myself get obsessed with others'.

But no one has ever accused me of being wise, and there was no way I was letting the demons get away with this.

"You can accept whatever reality you want," I said, "but I believe you're right and that Tommy's been possessed against his will. As an exorcist, I can't just let that go."

Claudia stared into the depths of her empty coffee cup. "Did you know that that exorcist, Sammy Cho, committed suicide?"

My heart made a very unpleasant thud in my chest, and I shook my head in disbelief. Adam had said Sammy was on vacation. I guess it turned out to be a *permanent* one.

"I hadn't heard," I said, feeling a wave of sadness even though I hadn't liked Sammy.

"Maybe he felt guilty over what he did to Tommy."

It wasn't hard to follow her train of thought. "Or maybe someone wanted to make sure he wouldn't blab."

I hadn't mentioned to Claudia the possibility that Sammy had been possessed, and I saw no reason to bring it up now, even though his "suicide" practically confirmed it. Whatever demon had taken him wanted to make absolutely sure no one could get proof that Sammy had lied, and it was no skin off the demon's metaphorical teeth to have his host commit suicide. I could also see why Sammy's death had left Claudia shaken.

"If you or your family are being threatened, we have grounds to bring in the police."

"We're not being threatened," she reiterated, though I still didn't believe her. "Your heart is in the right place. I really meant it when I said I appreciated all you've done. But it's time for you to step aside."

I knew there had to be a good reason she was being like this. I knew she hadn't just capriciously changed her mind, just like I knew her suddenly cool tone wasn't personal. That didn't stop my blood pressure from soaring.

I pushed back my chair, threw my napkin on the table, and stood up. "Thanks for the lovely dinner."

I started to walk past her toward the door, but she caught hold of my arm and looked up at me beseechingly. "Please, Ms. Kingsley. Leave it alone." Her eyes pleaded with me, and I felt almost like she was trying to convey some kind of secret message.

Whatever the message was, I wasn't getting it. I dropped my voice so it could barely be heard in the noisy restaurant. "Tell me who threatened you, and tell me what bad thing will happen if I keep investigating, and I'll consider your request."

Her hand squeezed painfully tight on my arm, and her eyes flashed with mingled anger and alarm. "I can't do that," she answered just as quietly.

"Fine." I jerked my arm out of her grip, and this time when I headed for the door, she let me go.

Chapter 15

Because the LOLs had held me up so much this afternoon, I still had one load of laundry to get done when I got home from my wonderful dinner. Not feeling in the mood to do anything else, I schlepped my load down to the laundry room.

I was in luck. All the machines were empty. I shoved my clothes into the washer and dug out some quarters. The small, claustrophobic room echoed with the sound of the water gushing in, covering the sound of footsteps so that I never heard anyone approach. When I picked up my laundry basket and stood, there were suddenly two super-sized men standing in the laundry room doorway.

I live in a big building, so it's not as if I would know all the tenants by sight, but these guys would have set my mental alarms ringing even if they hadn't been wearing dark, wraparound sunglasses in a basement. Goon #1 smiled at me in sadistic anticipation, while Goon #2 made a meaty fist and held it up for display.

They were too squat and ugly to be hosting demons—legal ones, at least—but they probably didn't need supernatural strength to make my life miserable. I'm a pretty good fighter—when you're family's Spirit Society, you learn to stick up for yourself at an early age, unless you enjoy getting beaten to a pulp on a regular basis—but I didn't like my chances against two men who had the look of professionals.

In tandem, they advanced on me. My Taser was in my purse. I was paranoid enough to carry it around with me at all times, but now that I actually needed it I realized I wasn't paranoid enough. I had to have it out and armed already, not tucked neatly in my purse.

I didn't have any brilliant ideas, but one thing I knew for sure was the laundry basket wouldn't help my defense much. I screamed as loud as I could, the sound echoing nicely through the unfortunately deserted basement, and threw the laundry basket at my would-be assailants.

As I'd hoped, they were momentarily startled, which gave me time to put the folding table between me and them while I shoved my hand in my purse. Very much contrary to my hopes, they recovered before I could even *find* the Taser, much less draw it.

Goon #1 wasn't about to let a little thing like a folding table get between him and his quarry. He leapt over it, coming straight at me while his partner continued to block the doorway. I didn't have time to get my hand out of my purse before he was on me, but I managed an off-balance kick that hurt him just enough to annoy him. He charged me again, and I jabbed at his eyes with my fingers while I tried for his groin with my knee. He ducked out of the way of my jab, and turned his hips to take my knee on his thigh. Damn. Apparently he wasn't expecting me to fight like a girl, and my self-defense moves weren't surprising him.

He grabbed both my arms to keep me from trying to hit him again. I would have gone for another kick, except Goon #2 had waded in while I was distracted. His punch connected with my cheek, and if I hadn't known better, I'd have sworn he'd just hit me with an anvil.

I didn't fall down, but only because Goon #1 still had hold of my arms. My head spun, and while I was trying to remember which way was up, a punch to the gut drove all the air out of my lungs. The goon hit me again, this time in the eye, and pain stabbed all the way through my head. But it wasn't the pain of his fist that caused it. Lugh was trying to surface, coming to my rescue like a knight in shining armor. Considering these guys could probably beat me to death if they wanted to, I supposed I should let him.

But then Goon #2 let go of my arms and allowed me to collapse to the floor in a puddle of misery.

"This is just a friendly warning," he said in a low, gravelly voice. "Stay out of Tom Brewster's business."

I realized that meant the beating was over, and I no longer needed Lugh's services. I'm sure he realized that, too, but he didn't let up. He was going to exploit my semi-dazed state and steal the reins to my body. I concentrated on holding him off, but a poke in the gut with a toe reminded me I had more than one problem.

"You hear me?" the goon prompted.

Forming words while fighting for air, fighting nausea, fighting dizziness, and fighting Lugh wasn't exactly easy. However, I figured if I didn't answer, I was in for more pain, and Lugh was even more likely to win our battle. "Loud . . . and . . . clear," I managed to gasp, and the goons, satisfied with a job well done, disappeared as silently as they had come.

Lugh continued his barrage against my mental barriers, the pain spiking through my head so hard it drew a whimper from my throat. If that were the only pain I had to battle, I probably would have prevailed.

Knowing I would eventually have to sleep and leave myself open to him, he would have bided his time rather than submitting me to what amounted to torture. But combined with the pain of the beating, it was too much. Hard though I tried to hold on, my mind slid closer and closer to oblivion. Tears of frustration welled in my tightly shut eyes.

And then my entire body eased, the pain disappearing as if it had never existed. I took a moment to sigh in relief before I let the panic set in.

Driving my body, Lugh pushed me up into a sitting position. I felt the touch of my own hand as he made me wipe away the traces of tears. He was blocking the pain so thoroughly that in any other circumstance, I'd probably have been grateful to him. Well, maybe not.

My body was no longer my own, but if a mind could shudder, then that's what mine did. The last time Lugh had taken control, he'd shut my conscious mind out completely, trapping me in a dark, claustrophobic, terrifying oubliette. I had panicked then like I've never panicked before in my life, and had I actually been there in body, I would have done myself considerable physical harm in my frantic attempts to escape. If he did that to me again...

"I won't," he said, using my own mouth to speak to me. I really hate it when he does that. "Those were extenuating circumstances," he explained as he rose to his feet. "I would not do that to you on a whim."

I couldn't speak, couldn't control a single muscle in my body, but I imagined any number of colorful suggestions for what he could do with himself, and since he knew all my thoughts, I knew he could "hear" them.

He sighed. "We've been through this before," he said patiently. "I have a responsibility to my people—

and to yours—that has to take precedence over your desires. I'm not in any way *trying* to hurt you."

He picked up my laundry basket and carried it out into the darkened hallway, where he summoned an elevator. If I couldn't wrest back control before he made it to my apartment and my phone, he was going to make the damning call to Adam, and there would be nothing I could do to stop him.

Fool that I was, I'd forgotten about the cell phone in my purse. Lugh hadn't. While he waited for the elevator, he fished the phone out. I struggled against his control, but he had a firm hold. It would take time to wrest control back, time I knew I didn't have.

It showed something about the mess my life had become that I had Adam on speed-dial.

Something hard and cold solidified in my center—metaphysically speaking, I suppose, since without a body, I didn't really have a center. This was not a battle I was willing to lose, not a battle I could *afford* to lose, not if I wanted any say at all in the rest of my life.

I focused all my thoughts into getting one clear, cold message across to Lugh. *Do this, and from now on, we will be enemies.*

He gasped, and from that I knew he'd heard my message. Adam's phone began to ring just as the elevator doors opened. Lugh stepped inside.

"You can't mean that!" he objected.

You know I do. And, because there was no corner of my mind he couldn't see into, he did. *I'll find a way to get back in control eventually, even if you decide to toss me in that oubliette again. Do you want to be at war with me as well as with Dougal?*

He shook his head. "Why?" he asked. "Why do this over a request you don't even know if Adam and Dominic will honor?"

Why ask questions when you already know the

answers? But in case you need me to verbalize it—it's because I have to take a stand somewhere, sometime. This is where I'm drawing the line in the sand.

"Hello?" Adam said, and Lugh didn't immediately respond.

"Perhaps I should have put you directly in the oubliette after all," Lugh muttered very softly.

"What?" Adam said. "Morgan? Are you all right?"

Lugh made a soft growling sound that my throat shouldn't have been able to make. "Actually, it's not Morgan, it's Lugh."

Even without a body, I felt as if I were holding my breath, nervously waiting to see which path Lugh would choose. I didn't want to be at war with him, but that decision now rested firmly in his hands.

"Morgan was just attacked in the basement of her apartment building," Lugh said, and I mentally breathed a sigh of relief. "She wasn't hurt too badly, and I don't dare heal her injuries since her attackers got away. However, she should make a police report, and you should be the one to take her statement."

"Of course. I'll be right over."

"And, Adam?"

"Yes?"

"Morgan has a request from me that I've tasked her with making. I'll allow her to phrase it however she wants, but don't leave her apartment until she conveys the request. Understood?"

"Er . . . yeah, I guess."

"Very well. We shall see you soon."

Lugh hung up just as the elevator doors opened on my floor. He stepped out into the hallway. "I hope you will consider that a fair compromise," he muttered.

I wasn't sure what I thought about this "compromise" yet, so I didn't answer.

Lugh let himself into my apartment, dropped the

laundry basket by the door, and drove my body to the couch. He sat down, and then suddenly my entire body ached and throbbed, and nausea roiled in my stomach.

With a groan, I lay down on the couch and clutched a throw pillow over my face, blocking out the light in hopes that it would ease the pounding in my head.

Chapter 16

Eventually, I hauled myself off the sofa and headed for the kitchen to make up an ice pack for my aching head. My left eye was on its way to swelling shut, and any motion of my jaw sent fingers of pain stabbing throughout the side of my face. Holding a baggie full of ice to my eye, I made my way to the bathroom and downed three ibuprofen. I didn't think it would help a whole lot, but it couldn't hurt.

I'd taken a lot of physical abuse since I'd begun hosting Lugh, but most of the time he'd been able to heal the damage so that the suffering didn't last terribly long. But this beating he hadn't healed, and I understood why. No one was supposed to know I was possessed, so I couldn't miraculously turn up uninjured after I'd taken a thumping like that. I cussed him out for it anyway. Hey, pain makes me grumpy.

I'd gone back to lying on the couch, moving the ice pack back and forth between my eye and my cheek, when the front desk called to let me know Adam had arrived. The walk from the couch to the door seemed to take forever, and my face throbbed to the beat of my heart. I detoured to the kitchen to dump the ice, which was mostly melted by now anyway, before opening the door to let Adam in.

"Wow," he commented as soon as he saw me. "You look like shit."

I scowled and tried not to slam the door behind him. "Thanks. Your compassion knows no bounds."

He laughed, and I seriously considered decking him just to vent a little of my frustration and fury. But no, I was bruised and battered enough already. The last thing I needed was to start a fistfight with Adam.

"Tell me what happened," he said as we sat on opposite ends of the couch.

I did. I wasn't able to give much of a description of my attackers. Short, squat, powerfully built, with blah-brown hair and no identifying marks. At least, none that I'd been able to see while I was being pummeled. It wasn't a whole lot to go on.

"I'll check with building security," Adam promised. "See if I can figure out how they got in. One assumes they aren't residents." I gave him a sour look, but didn't comment. "Do you have a theory on who they were?" he asked.

I shrugged. "I assume they're in league with Brewster."

Adam looked thoughtful. "Maybe. But let's keep an open mind. Who else has reason to want you to leave Brewster alone?"

My stomach did a backflip as an unpleasant possibility came to mind. "I had dinner with Claudia Brewster tonight. She was suddenly very anxious for me to butt out. She wouldn't confirm or deny it, but I'm sure someone must have threatened her."

Adam didn't look any happier with that idea than I was. "I'm not sure she has the connections to hire a rent-a-thug on such short notice, but she certainly has the money. Anyone else been bugging you about the case?"

"Well, there's *you*."

He grinned. "Love, if I wanted you roughed up, I'd do it myself."

I was too miserable to work up a good retort, so I settled for a dirty look. "There's also Raphael," I said. "Maybe he wasn't as forthcoming with me as he claimed. Maybe there's more to the Houston project than he was willing to admit, and he wants me to stay out of it." I bit my lip, remembering my last conversation with him. "He *did* tell me to back off. He claimed it was because it was a hopeless cause, but maybe he had other motives."

Adam looked grim. "I suppose that is a possibility. Damn, that guy is a pain in the ass."

I had other, less charitable ways to describe him, but I'd voiced my opinion on the subject plenty of times already. "Is there any point in questioning him?"

"Doubtful. I don't think he's going to come clean if he's the guilty party, and if he's not, he could be offended."

I snorted. "Like I care about offending him!"

"Your brother might care."

I winced at the reminder. I might not be able to convince myself whose side Raphael was on, but one thing I did know—he wouldn't hesitate to hurt Andy to punish me if I pissed him off too much.

Adam folded up the little notebook he'd been jotting notes in and tucked it into an inner pocket in his jacket. It would have been nice if he'd forgotten all about Lugh's little "suggestion," but of course, he hadn't. "So," he said, his voice conspicuously neutral, "what's the request Lugh wants you to make?"

I swallowed a groan, hopefully before any sound left my throat. I did *not* want to do this. And I wasn't sure if this could technically be considered a compromise, seeing as Lugh and I hadn't agreed on the terms before he'd taken matters into his own hands. Unfortunately, my options were limited in the extreme. Despite the threat I'd made earlier, I really, really didn't want to be at war with the demon who possessed me. My life was tough enough *now*.

I nearly jumped out of my seat when Adam's hand came to rest on my shoulder. I'd been staring at my hands, which were clenched in my lap, but now I looked up to meet his eyes. And I saw something in his expression that I'd never seen before, at least not directed at me—concern.

"What is it, Morgan?" he asked, and damn if I didn't feel the prickle of tears in my eyes.

I swallowed hard, taking in a deep breath and banishing that hint of tears. "Have you told Dom about your extracurricular activities yet?" I asked.

Adam's hand slid off my shoulder, and his posture stiffened. "What does that have to do with anything?"

"Did you?"

The concerned expression disappeared as if it had never existed. Perhaps it hadn't. Perhaps I'd just *wanted* him to look concerned. Now he was wearing his hard, cold face, the one that probably scared the shit out of any criminals who found themselves in his custody.

"No." His voice was curt and clipped, and I had the feeling a full-fledged explosion of anger was on its way.

"Good."

That took him by surprise. His eyes widened, and his mouth dropped open. "What did you say?"

I knew he'd heard me, so I didn't bother to repeat it. At least Dominic wouldn't already be in a vulnerable state of mind when Adam asked him to host Saul again. I swallowed the lump in my throat and mentally reminded Lugh what I thought of him at the moment before I continued.

"Lugh's decided to set up his court here on the Mortal Plain," I said.

Adam nodded cautiously. "That seems like a reasonable thing to do."

"You'll be part of his inner circle, of course, and he's counting on Raphael to be there, too, though he and I disagree on that." I stalled out.

"Okay. Now tell me about whatever bombshell you're going to drop."

I clenched my hands in my lap so tight I heard my knuckles crack. But there was no turning back now. "He wants Saul to be in that inner circle, too."

Silence descended like a heavy winter fog, dense and thick. Adam's face closed off entirely, not a hint of expression showing through his impassive mask. But I knew thoughts and worries were pinging back and forth behind that mask. At least, I hoped they were. They sure were having a field day in *my* head, and my own mask was far from secure. A tear trickled down my cheek.

Damn. I thought I'd managed to suppress them entirely. I wiped the single tear away and willed myself to stay calm as I waited for Adam's inevitable answer.

This shouldn't matter to me so much, I told myself. Yeah, I liked Dom and considered him a friend, but it wasn't like we were super close. He wasn't someone I'd turn to in times of trouble. But then, who was? I noticed I was grinding my teeth and forced myself to stop.

"The suspense is killing me," I said, trying to sound dry and sarcastic. It didn't work. I noticed Adam's hands had clenched, the knuckles turning white. His mask wasn't perfect after all. But he didn't say anything.

Minutes ticked by—at least it felt like it—and the tension grew worse and worse. I suppose I must not have been as sure of Adam's answer as I'd thought, or else why would I have been such a wreck?

When I finally couldn't stand it anymore, I stood up and headed for the kitchen. A cup of coffee wouldn't cure all that ailed me, but at least it would be hot and soothing and delicious. Adam remained unmoving on the couch while I went through the ritual of making a pot of coffee. Not until I'd poured a mug and started to doctor it did he leave the couch and come to join me in the kitchen.

"May I have a cup?" he asked. Whatever he was thinking or feeling, he was still keeping it off his face.

"I wish I knew how to do that," I said, and I finally saw a hint of expression: bafflement.

"Huh? Do *what*?"

"Keep my face from showing how I feel. I've never seen anyone as good at it as you. I mean, Brian does good lawyer face, but he can't do it under extreme duress—"

"May I have a cup of coffee, or not?"

Okay, so I'd been babbling. It wasn't the first time. "Depends on whether you're going to give Dominic up to Saul or not."

He blinked. "It matters to you that much?"

I was seriously tempted to throw my scalding hot coffee in his face. I managed to refrain, but it wasn't easy. "He's my friend," I said. "I don't want to lose him to some demon I don't know. Hell, I don't want to lose him at all! He's a truly good, decent human being, and he doesn't deserve to be tossed aside!"

"I don't want to lose him, either," Adam said, his voice quiet, his eyes haunted.

"But you'll give him up to your good buddy Saul anyway," I said bitterly. I almost said something scathing about how he'd be able to practice his more sickening habits in the privacy of his own home once more, but for once I managed to think about my words before blurting them out. I might never understand how demons think, I might never be able to forgive Adam for giving up Dom, but only an idiot wouldn't see how much the idea hurt him, and there was no point in making it worse.

Adam shook his head, and for the first time since I'd conveyed Lugh's request, he met my eyes. "Not without a fight, I won't."

My jaw fell open, and I put the cup of coffee down before I dropped it. "You mean to tell me you're *not* going to do what Lugh wants?"

He leaned against one wall of the kitchen, folding his arms over his chest in what might have been a defensive gesture. "I told you before. I *like* Saul. I *love* Dom."

"Yeah, but you also told me once before that if you were put in a position where killing Dom would be the 'right' thing to do, you'd do it and not feel guilty." And in telling me that, he'd made me see just how foreign demons could be, even though their psyches so resemble those of humans.

"Turns out that's easier said than done."

My opinion of him improved exponentially. I even poured him a cup of coffee, which he accepted gratefully. I guess *he* needed warmth and comfort, too.

"Just so we're clear," I said, picking up my own coffee once more, "you're *not* going to tell Dom about Lugh's request?"

Adam's mouth tightened into a grim line. "I'll tell him." He held up his hand to stop the sharp retort that I'd been about to make. "He's a grown man. It's not my right to make this decision for him. If he wants to take Saul back, then I won't stand in his way." He closed his eyes and took a deep breath.

I was still indignant over what seemed to be a change of mind on Adam's part, and I was moments away from telling him exactly what I thought of him, when once again I managed to restrain a knee-jerk reaction. This was twice in one day, and I was beginning to think I might be gaining some maturity. What a concept!

Adam wasn't hiding his expressions now, and I found I could read him easily. He'd give Dom the chance to take Saul back, because if he didn't, he'd never know whether Dom would have chosen Saul over him. Was there, perhaps, a hint of insecurity under that usually arrogant facade?

"As long as you make it clear that it's Dominic you want, not Saul, he'll make the right decision," I said, and I really believed it. Yeah, Dom was the hero type, but there was no question in my mind that he'd choose love over heroism, as long as Adam didn't make it sound like he'd rather have Saul.

"Ah," Adam said, "that's why you asked whether I'd told him about my visits to Hell."

I nodded. Better for Dom not to know about that, not to doubt that Adam was completely satisfied with him.

Adam scrubbed a hand through his hair and put his coffee down, having not taken a single swallow. "I'm going to go downstairs and question the security people." One corner of his mouth lifted in his trademark sardonic grin. The expression was a bit off, but it was a valiant effort. "That'll give me some time to pull myself together before I talk to Dom."

"Good idea," I agreed, though I wasn't sure he was in the best frame of mind to do any investigative work right now. "Will you call me later? Let me know what happens?"

He nodded, but didn't say anything. His poker face had definitely deserted him, and he looked worried and unhappy as he headed toward my door. It wouldn't be at all unusual for him to leave without another word, and it wouldn't be at all unusual for me to let him. But today I just couldn't let him walk out like that.

"Adam?" I said before he'd gotten halfway to the door. He turned back to face me. He didn't speak, just raised an eyebrow in inquiry.

An instinct I didn't understand made me approach him and, to our mutual surprise, give him a hug. "It'll be all right," I said.

I felt ridiculous speaking words of comfort to Adam. I felt even *more* ridiculous hugging him. I don't want to know what shade of red my face turned, and I released him so fast I'm sure it would have looked comical to the outside observer. I didn't have the nerve to look at him, and I told myself that if he laughed, I was going to deck him and damn the consequences. But he didn't laugh.

"Thank you," he said softly, but I still didn't have the courage to face him. He patted me awkwardly on the shoulder, his own unpracticed gesture of support.

My face was still burning, my eyes still fixed on the floor, when I heard the door close behind him.

Chapter **17**

Apparently, even in the midst of his inner turmoil, Adam was an effective investigator. He learned that the two goons had gotten in by convincing Mrs. Schwartz, one of my building's ubiquitous LOLs, that they were insurance agents. She'd met them at the coffee shop around the corner, and they'd followed her into the building like little ducklings. Mrs. Schwartz had then spent a half hour discussing her insurance needs with the two "charming" young men. They'd left her apartment at around five in the afternoon, which meant they'd been loitering around the building for hours before their quarry—me—had finally shown up. The security personnel were much more interested in who was coming *in* the building, rather than who was going out, so no one noticed that the goons had remained far longer than insurance agents would have.

They hadn't been wearing the dark glasses when Mrs. Schwartz had brought them into the building, but once she vouched for them, neither the doorman nor the front desk clerk paid any attention to them.

They barely even remembered seeing them, and certainly couldn't give a reliable description. Mrs. Schwartz couldn't either, on account of her cataracts. There was footage from the security camera in the elevator, but the goons must have been aware of it, for they were careful not to show their faces.

Adam had informed me of these meager details by phone on his way home to Dom. He'd then made a point of telling me he'd call me tomorrow, which meant I'd be spending the rest of the night sweating the results of their conversation.

I thought I'd have a lot of trouble falling asleep that night. I was wrong. I suppose sometimes pain and stress can make you toss and turn all night, and sometimes it can just exhaust you until you can't keep your eyes open.

I doubt I got more than a couple of minutes of blissful, uninterrupted sleep before I "awoke" to find myself in Lugh's throne room. I was seated on a short, hard chair at the base of the dais, looking up at Lugh on his throne. I guessed that meant I was supposed to be some kind of supplicant, but I doubt he was surprised that I rejected the role.

I stood up and mounted the stairs to the dais. It was easier this time than last, since he hadn't bothered to dress me in period costume.

He was dressed once more in crimson velvet with gold accents, though I don't think it was exactly the same outfit, just a similar one. Naturally, he looked good enough to eat, even if the throne and crown were just a tad off-putting. He sat ramrod straight, his gorgeous, chiseled face set in an expression I couldn't read. I didn't think he was happy. But then, neither was I.

"You rang?" I asked when the silence seemed to stretch.

"You're angry with me."

I shrugged. Of *course* I was angry with him. He'd forced me into this lame-ass "compromise" of his. I don't take well to being forced into anything. But he knew all that, so I didn't bother to say it.

"And you're angry with me," I said instead. "I suppose that makes us even." I frowned. "Well, as even as we'll ever be."

He shook his head. No doubt he was wishing Raphael had chosen anyone else on the planet to host him.

"I won't explain myself to you again," he said, and there was a distinctly sharp edge to his voice.

"Ditto."

He reached up, I think meaning to run his hand through his hair in frustration. At the last moment, he remembered the crown and stopped himself.

"As I'm sure you know," I continued, "I'm really, really tired. Is there some vital reason we absolutely have to talk tonight? Because if not, I'd rather get some sleep."

He seemed to think about that one for a while before he answered. "Actually, it's not you I need to talk to. It's Raphael."

I let out a sound that I'm afraid was something like a squeak of alarm as I realized what he meant. I then put as much concentration as I could into trying to close my mental doors.

"Relax, Morgan," Lugh said in what was probably supposed to be a soothing croon, but I think both our tempers were too brittle for soothing or being soothed. "I'd like us to work together to make this happen. You see, I've had an idea as to how we can ease your way into letting me take control when necessary."

I probably shouldn't have let him disarm me so

easily. Maybe my exhaustion was affecting my mental processes in my sleep as well as during my waking hours. But whatever the reason, I stopped trying to struggle free of him. I didn't, however, drop my guard.

"All right. I'm listening. Let's hear this idea of yours."

He rose slowly from his throne, towering over me. He *always* towered over me, but those red velvet shoes of his had a considerable heel on them, and I felt like I was straining my neck to meet his gaze. Instinct urged me to take a step back from this dangerous creature, but I fought it. Sure, he already knew he was intimidating me, but that didn't mean I had to show it.

"I'd like to try staying in control while you wake up," he said. "Through sleep, you've already dropped your guard enough to let me take over. Getting you to drop that guard is the key, so perhaps if you try not to fight me, we'll be able to make that transition to wakefulness together."

I realized with a bit of a shock that when Lugh had first started communicating with me, my subconscious had consistently managed to kick him out without any effort on my part. Now, unless I made a concerted effort to fight my way free, he could remain in control of my sleep for however long he wanted. I couldn't help thinking that wasn't a good thing, that I was slowly giving him more and more power over me. And I decided I didn't want to wake up and find myself the passenger in my own body.

I started trying once more to close my mental doors.

"Don't!" Lugh ordered sharply, and the look on his face now was pure steel. "We *need* to do this, and what you want doesn't really matter. If you keep fighting me, you'll find yourself in the oubliette."

I gasped in shock, the sick sense of horror and betrayal in my gut momentarily derailing my efforts to wrest control from him.

"You promised you would never do that again!" I said, though the sound came out more like a wail.

Lugh's face remained grim. "And you promised you'd learn to let me take control when the situation warrants it. Keep your promise, and I'll keep mine. It's as simple as that."

At that moment, I think I actually hated him. Not so long ago, I'd *liked* him, started thinking of him almost as a friend. A very sexy friend, whom I had the reluctant hots for. What had happened to *that* Lugh, who'd been kind and gentle, and who'd seemed to care about me?

I didn't say any of that out loud, but Lugh answered me anyway.

"Nothing has changed, Morgan," he said in a much softer voice. "And I do care about you. More than you know. It's just..." He blew out a sigh, and the throne room dissolved around us.

I felt a moment of intense disorientation. When it passed, we were no longer in the intimidating throne room. Instead, we were back in the cozy living room where we'd often talked before. And Lugh was back to what I thought of as his usual self. Gone were the crown and the red and gold velvet, and back were the tight black leather pants tucked into knee-high black boots and the plain black T-shirt that clung so appealingly to the muscles of his chest.

"Whether I'm here, or whether I'm in the throne room," he said, "I'm still a king. As a king, I have to do things that, as a man, I'd prefer not to do." He sat beside me on the butter-soft leather sofa. He took one of my hands in both of his, and it didn't immediately occur to me to object.

"Please, Morgan," he asked, and his eyes echoed that plea. "Please honor your agreement with me. We will disagree at times, and we will argue. That is inevitable given who we are. But we should choose our battles carefully. And this isn't something we should battle over."

I had the distinct impression I was being shamelessly manipulated, but there was no doubt he was wearing me down. Perhaps I was just too tired to care anymore.

"All right," I said grudgingly. "I'll do my best to let you stay in control as I wake up." I frowned. "Though to tell you the truth, I'm not sure how to wake myself up without fighting you. The two have always gone hand in hand before."

"No, not always," he said cryptically.

"Morgan?" said a voice, one that didn't belong to Lugh, one that seemed strangely distant.

My eyes locked with Lugh's. That sounded suspiciously like...

"Time to wake up," the voice said again, a little less distant.

And this time, there was no doubting whose voice that was. It took every ounce of my willpower not to immediately start struggling against Lugh's control as I realized what he must have done.

"Please don't," he said simply. "I had to talk to him, and I needed someone to wake you."

I had a few colorful suggestions for him, but I didn't fight his control. The living room dissolved, just as the throne room had. Only this time, when I opened my eyes, it was to look up into Andrew's face as he gently shook my shoulder.

No, not Andrew. Raphael. And unfortunately, this time it wasn't an illusion or a dream.

Chapter 18

I wanted to reach up and rub the sleep from my eyes, but Lugh didn't seem to feel the same need. He pushed himself into a sitting position, then swung his legs out from under the covers. Raphael backed up to give him room.

"Am I speaking to Morgan, or Lugh?" Raphael asked.

"Lugh. At least for the moment."

There was a chair in the far corner of my bedroom. It was too heavy to move easily, but that didn't stop Raphael from dragging it over to face the bed and then sitting in it. Sometimes, it must be nice to have demon strength. Of course, I currently had it myself, and I'd just as soon have done without. I wasn't used to letting Lugh control me like this, and all my primal survival instincts shouted at me to fight, to run, to do something to win my way free.

I felt Lugh's muscles tense, then relax when I resisted the urge to struggle.

Was this what it was like for Andy? Could he feel everything Raphael did with his body, feel the coarse fabric on the chair's upholstery under his hands while being powerless to move those hands? If so, how could he stand it? Could I really believe my brother was alive and well inside his body?

"How is your host faring?" Lugh asked, shocking me and, judging by the look on his face, Raphael as well.

"The first time we've been able to talk to each other outside of an immediate crisis for perhaps a century, and *that's* what you want to ask me?"

Mentally, I started. I knew, of course, that demons were long-lived, if not immortal. And I knew how badly Lugh and Raphael had gotten along. But it had never occurred to me that they hadn't spoken to one another for so long.

"Remember, brother," Lugh said, "unlike yourself, I'm in partnership with my host. Which means her concerns are important to me. So tell me how Andrew fares."

Raphael shook his head. "Why should I bother? Neither you nor Morgan will believe me if I tell you he's fine." I'd never seen my brother's face look petulant before. It wasn't a flattering expression.

I felt my teeth grinding and knew that Lugh was struggling to control himself.

Don't throw a conniption fit on my behalf, I thought at him. *You know I've already had this conversation with him, and his assurances haven't made me feel any better.*

"Do you blame us for not fully trusting you?" Lugh asked. "Would *you* trust *me* if our positions were reversed?"

Raphael crossed his arms over his chest and slumped in his chair. I swear he looked just like a sulking teenager. "Nothing I ever do is enough for you. No matter how many risks I've taken for you, no matter—"

Lugh growled. "Stop whining! If the only reason you're helping me—if you are indeed helping me—is so you can use your cooperation as emotional blackmail, then don't bother."

The demon Raphael flared in Andrew's eyes, and for a moment I thought he was going to launch himself at us. Lugh tensed, apparently sharing my suspicion, but Raphael managed to keep his ass in the chair. He gripped the arms of his chair with both hands, and the knuckles turned white.

Uh, Lugh, I don't think goading him and telling him what a shit he is is terribly productive, I said. Funny how much more rational I could be when it was Lugh arguing with Raphael rather than myself.

"And who was it who goaded him into hitting her the last time she spoke with him?" Lugh asked aloud.

If my body had been my own, I'm sure I would have flushed beet red at the reminder. I definitely wasn't in a position to throw stones.

To my surprise, Raphael chuckled and seemed to relax. "I have mentioned before that you and Morgan make a surprisingly compatible team." The humor faded from his face, but at least the sullenness didn't return. "Andrew is fine. We are neither of us happy with our forced alliance, but we are making the best of the situation."

Lugh snorted. "No one's forcing the alliance except *you.*"

Raphael leaned forward in his chair. "You're forgetting something, brother. Andrew and I have despised one another almost since the first moment we met. I have the power to destroy him, but because of you and Morgan, I'm not doing it. So yes, I am being forced into an alliance I'd very much prefer to give up."

Then give it up, you asshole, I wanted to say, but of

course my voice wasn't under my own control at the moment.

I felt my lips curl into a smile that was more like a snarl. "I'd be happy to help you give it up, little brother," Lugh said, and it seemed like every muscle in my body tensed.

Raphael tensed, too. "You think you can exorcize me?" His lips curled into a snarl very like his brother's. "Are you certain which one of us would win if we fought?"

Lugh had told me once that he wasn't sure, that he and Raphael were evenly matched. But he seemed to have forgotten that doubt now.

"Let's find out," Lugh said, and before the words had left his mouth, he had propelled himself off the bed and slammed into Raphael's body.

What are you doing? I screamed in my mind. If they fought and Lugh lost, then it was all over. Dougal would gain the throne, and everything I'd gone through—that *we'd* gone through—would be worth diddly squat.

Lugh didn't answer me. The chair crashed to the floor, and Raphael ended up trapped on his back, with Lugh holding him down. Andrew was a lot bigger than me, but Lugh was strong enough to compensate, especially when he was already on top. Their eyes locked, and although the effort to exorcize a demon is not a physical one, I was still aware of Lugh mustering his energy, of his aura pressing down on Raphael's.

I desperately wanted to take back the reins of my body, but it was too late now. If I started fighting against Lugh, I could destroy his concentration, and it would all be over.

Never in my wildest dreams had I imagined that Lugh would let his temper get the better of him. Yes, I'd seen flashes of that temper before. And yes, I knew how deep-seated was the animosity between him and his brother. Still, I'd thought the same sense of responsibility that I spent most of my time cursing would keep him from doing something so rash. I mentally held my breath, hoping and praying that Lugh turned out to be stronger.

Raphael's eyes widened as his gaze locked with Lugh's.

"Please don't send me back," Raphael said in a choked whisper. "You know what Dougal will do to me. Please!"

What the hell . . . ?

Lugh's aura continued to push against Raphael's, but there was no resistance. Just a little bit more pressure, and Raphael would be shoved back into the Demon Realm. And my brother would be free.

Raphael lay still under Lugh's body . . . under *my* body. There was still no resistance against the pressure of Lugh's aura, and it finally occurred to me that there was no resistance because Raphael wasn't fighting back.

"You're going to make it this easy?" Lugh inquired, his voice calm despite the ugly temper that had prompted the attack.

Raphael swallowed hard. "If one of us is going back, it has to be me. Dougal would kill you, and then it would all have been for nothing." He closed his eyes and waited. Sweat dewed his face, and his breath came short and frantic, but still he didn't fight.

Lugh's aura retreated and he rolled off of Raphael. Raphael just lay there, eyes closed, body tense. Lugh righted the chair he'd knocked over, then grabbed Raphael's arm, hauled him to his feet, and deposited him in the chair. Then he sat on the edge of the bed again and just stared until Raphael opened his eyes.

The staring contest seemed to go on forever. I had

no idea what was going on, what Raphael was thinking, what Lugh was thinking. But I watched through Lugh's eyes as Raphael's fear faded to puzzlement, then to understanding, then to fury.

"You *bastard*!" he spat, and it looked like he was holding himself in the chair by force of will alone. "That was some kind of test, wasn't it? A test of my loyalty?"

"If you're to be in my inner circle, if I'm to trust you, then I had to know for certain you're on my side."

To my shock, Raphael's eyes glittered with what looked like a hint of tears. "And that's what it took for me to prove my worth?" His voice was hoarse, and there was no missing the pain in it. I'd sometimes mistrusted Raphael's emotions in the past, never sure he wasn't just acting. This time, I was sure he wasn't.

Lugh reached out to pat his brother's shoulder. Raphael actually flinched from the touch.

"Ask yourself this, little brother," Lugh said. "Given everything that's at stake, would I have taken the risk of fighting you if I really thought you'd fight back? You may think me arrogant, but surely you don't think I'm so arrogant as to assume I'd win."

Raphael blinked and shook his head. "But then why . . . ?"

"Because I'm not the only one who needed to be convinced."

Well, shit. That whole show had been for *me*? I hadn't been Raphael's favorite person before, and this wouldn't do anything to endear me to him.

Raphael thought about that for a long time without saying anything. Then he nodded. "I can't say I appreciate your methods, but I understand. What happens now that I've passed your test?"

"Did you truly tell Morgan everything you know

about the Houston project?" I'm sure Raphael could hear the skepticism in Lugh's voice as well as I could.

Raphael's shoulders stiffened, but he answered civilly enough. "Yes, I did. There are at least thirty-five or forty facilities scattered throughout the world. I know very little about their day-to-day operations."

"Am I really supposed to believe that when you were so intimately involved with the project at The Healing Circle?"

Raphael visibly bristled. "I thought I'd just passed your test of loyalty. Apparently, I was mistaken."

"I believe in your loyalty," Lugh said with a sardonic smile. "Your honesty, however, is still very much in question."

To my surprise, Raphael laughed at that. "You'll make a good king if we can ever get you back on the throne," he said, and there was no longer any animosity in his voice.

"I'm glad you think so. Now, about the Houston facility..."

Raphael heaved an exaggerated sigh. "I'm telling the truth, hard though that might be for you to believe. The Healing Circle was something of a pet project for me."

"But you were overseeing the campaign to breed a better host," Lugh protested. "You were in charge of the whole thing!"

Raphael shook his head. "*Dougal* was in charge. I was merely his emissary to the Mortal Plain."

I didn't believe him, and I don't think Lugh did, either. But it seemed there was little point in pushing the issue any further. Raphael wasn't going to admit the lie. But I'm sure Lugh was as curious as I about just what his brother was hiding this time.

"All right," Lugh said, though I'm sure Raphael heard the hint of skepticism in his voice. "I'll accept that you don't know what was happening in the Houston facility. But you must have known who was in charge. Surely there was *some* communication between the facilities?"

"Why are you so interested in Houston anyway? Nothing that happened there is important in the grand scheme of things. What's important is figuring out how to outwit Dougal."

But Lugh shook his head. "Figuring out what he was up to on the Mortal Plain, and what progress he made, is also important to me. We've allowed ourselves to interfere with humans too much already while our monarchs have kept themselves blissfully ignorant. I won't allow that to continue during my reign. So contact some of your old friends in the breeding business and find out what was happening at the Houston facility. I want to know why Tommy Brewster is so important that a demon would take the risk of possessing him illegally under such suspicious circumstances."

"Aren't you forgetting something? I'm an outlaw at the moment, in as much danger from Dougal and his supporters as you are. My contacts have all dried up."

"Like hell they have. Or are you telling me that Dougal has the means and the desire to inform every demon on the Mortal Plain that you are no longer his sidekick?"

From the look of him, Raphael was about to explode with frustration, but he managed to keep it under control. "Fine," he said, his voice flat. "I'll see what I can find out, and I'll report back to you. Do you have any other orders, Your Majesty?" With that flat voice, it was hard to tell if the honorific was meant as sarcasm or as a term of respect. At least it was hard for *me* to tell. Lugh would know if it was traditional for his brothers to address him by title, but he wasn't letting on one way or another.

"Only to be kind to Andrew, no matter how much you dislike him."

Lugh stood up, and Raphael did, too. They had another one of their staring contests, and I had no idea what either one was thinking.

Um, Lugh? If you're all done, can I have my body back? I asked. I'd been interested enough in their conversation to forget for a while just how uncomfortable it was to have Lugh in control, but it was coming back to me fast. It took a lot of willpower to keep myself from trying to break free of his control.

Lugh didn't answer me, but he held out his hand. Raphael stared at him for another second, then shook the offered hand and nodded.

"I'm glad we had this little talk," Raphael said, and once again I couldn't tell if he was being sarcastic.

Lugh made a little snorting sound that could have been agreement, amusement, or disdain. Then he jerked Raphael forward and gave him one of those back-thumping hugs men are so fond of. Raphael stiffened for a moment, then responded in kind.

It was all very touching, but I was getting more and more antsy as every second ticked away. I wanted control back, and I wanted it *now*. I lost the battle against my nerves, and found myself trying to close my mental doors without any conscious will.

And then suddenly, Lugh was gone, and my body was my own once more. I could tell from the frost in Raphael's eyes that he'd noticed the difference immediately. He and Lugh might have made some kind of peace with one another, but that didn't mean things were all right between the two of us.

Raphael opened his mouth as if he was about to say something, then shook his head as he thought better of it. Without a word to me, he turned his back and strode out of the room. Seconds later, the front door slammed, and he was gone.

Chapter 19

After Raphael left, I fell back into bed and slept like the dead. When I woke up, the bruises had well and truly set in, and my entire body ached. I downed a handful of ibuprofen, then took the world's longest hot shower. I felt marginally better afterward.

While I was in the process of figuring out what to do with myself all day, I checked my phone messages from the office and discovered I wouldn't have to go looking for things to do after all. I was absurdly grateful to be able to schedule a routine exorcism for the middle of this afternoon. Maybe for just a little while, I could pretend my life was normal. At least, as normal as an exorcist's life ever is.

I caused a bit of a stir, showing up at the courthouse with my ostentatious bruises. I told anyone who asked that I got mugged. It was a whole lot simpler that way.

The guy I'd been hired to exorcize, one Jordan Maguire, had been a legal demon host for five years. He'd apparently run into trouble when he'd split with his girlfriend, with whom he had a two-year-old daughter. They'd been arguing—loudly, according to the neighbors. When the demon stormed out of her apartment, the girlfriend had called the police and accused him of assault. She even had the bruises to show for it.

If he'd been human, there would have been a protracted inquiry into what had happened. However, demons have few rights, and the legal system tolerates no hint of impropriety. I felt kind of sorry for the demon, who swore he hadn't hurt his girlfriend, that she'd been two-timing him with another guy and that it was the other guy who had hit her. But he'd already been convicted and sentenced, and I knew I was only sending him back to the Demon Realm, not killing him, so my guilt only went so far.

Maguire's demon was a bitch to cast out, but I managed it.

The guilt evaporated completely when the demon was gone. About eighty percent of hosts whose demons are exorcized end up as vegetables afterward, but every once in a while, it was even worse. This was one of those times. As soon as the demon was gone, the host's brain completely shut down, no longer capable of directing such vital bodily functions as breathing. He wasn't just brain damaged; he was brain-dead.

He was taken from the courthouse by ambulance, and would be admitted to the hospital until his family could be notified. Then they'd take him off life support, and he'd be dead. I shuddered to think what the demon must have done to him to make him shut down so completely. And I prayed Raphael wasn't treating my brother the same way.

Depressed as hell, I went to my office and filled out the paperwork. I hadn't heard from Adam, and, being the impatient sort, I tried calling him. I went straight to voice mail and didn't bother leaving a message.

I was in pain from the beating, depressed by the exorcism, worried about Dominic, and angry about being tossed off Tommy Brewster's case. It wasn't a good combination of emotions, and it left me with a burning desire to *do* something.

What I decided to do might have been reckless, especially given the very unequivocal instructions I'd been given to keep my nose out of Brewster's business, but I decided it was time to pay another visit to The Seven Deadlies. Shae and Tommy seemed to have become buddies—or at least accomplices. Perhaps I could "gently" persuade Shae to tell me what Tommy was up to.

The thought of giving Shae a hard time brought a smile to my face. The best part about it was that because she was an illegal demon herself, she wouldn't be able to report me to the police if I got a little…aggressive in my questioning. Adam had to play seminice with her, or his well of information might dry up. I was under no such restrictions.

I showed up at the club at nine, just when its doors were opening for the night. The same bouncer I'd haggled with last time was on duty. There was no question that he recognized me—I'm not one who blends into a crowd—but he also remembered that Shae had let me in last time. When I asked him to let Shae know I wanted to talk to her, he made a *sotto voce* call and then told me she'd be right down. I found a corner where I'd be out of the way and waited.

I wasn't shocked when Shae's definition of "right down" and mine differed significantly. I refrained from doing the pointed-stare-at-my-watch thing when she finally swept out of the Employees Only doorway.

Apparently, she favored the dramatic when it came to her wardrobe. Today, she wore a neon-orange silk tunic with frog closures and a mandarin collar over skinny black pants. I don't know how, but somehow she'd found a pair of stiletto heels that exactly matched the color of the tunic. She should have looked ridiculous, but, of course, she didn't.

Shae looked me over unabashedly, her gaze lingering on the bruises. I clenched my teeth, waiting for her to make a smart-ass comment about them, but she just smiled at me—the predatory shark smile I'd come to expect from her.

"What a pleasant surprise," she said, her eyes sparkling. "This makes twice in one week. Perhaps we should make you a member."

I suppressed a shudder at the thought. "Your doorman said you had a three-month wait list."

"I'd be willing to make an exception for you."

I'm sure we both knew that Hell would freeze over before I joined, but I played along with her anyway. Trying to reel in my prey. Or just trying to give myself time to change my mind and walk away.

I raised my eyebrows. "Why would you do that?"

I had to resist the urge to shrink back when Shae reached out and hooked an elbow around my arm. "Because you provide boundless entertainment," she said, trying to steer me toward the door into the heart of the club.

I dug in my heels. I didn't want to go in there again, especially not on Shae's arm. "Let's cut the crap," I said. "I have no interest is setting foot in your club again."

She narrowed her eyes at me. "You already have."

"You know what I mean. Is there somewhere quiet we can talk?"

She let go of my arm—thank God—and gazed at me curiously. I put on my blandest expression and hoped that I was getting better at hiding what I was feeling. Shae would have creeped me out even if I *didn't* know she was an illegal demon. There was just

something about her. Not evil, per se, but perhaps...
chaotic.

Whatever she read or didn't read in my face, Shae
seemed satisfied. She smiled at me once more and gestured to the Employees Only door.

"Come along," she said, heading that way. "We
can talk in my office."

I wasn't surprised the door was locked, but I was
a bit surprised to see it was key-carded. The card
reader was hidden in a particularly deep shadow, and I
hadn't noticed it before. I wondered if following Shae
through that door was a monumentally stupid thing to
do. My Taser was in my purse, but I'd learned through
hard experience that it didn't do me a whole lot of
good in there.

I grabbed the door, which was heavy and solid, but
didn't immediately follow. Shae turned back and
raised an eyebrow.

"Is there a problem?" she asked, and her smile told
me she knew exactly what the problem was.

"I'm expecting a call from Adam," I told her,
which was actually true. "I was just wondering if you
get cell phone reception in here. It looks kind of... for-
midable."

Yeah, okay, the "expected phone call" gambit was
a cliché straight out of about three thousand suspense
movies. Usually used to no avail, come to think of it.
But it was the first thing that popped into my mind,
and I didn't have enough time to come up with something better.

Shae laughed, but at least she was kind enough not
to berate me for my lack of originality.

"You'll have no trouble getting a signal," she assured me. "I use my cell in here all the time."

It was time for me to make up my mind. Was I following Shae into the nether regions of her club, away

from all possible witnesses, or would I play it safe, tell her we'd talk some other time, and get the hell out?

Playing it safe has never been one of my fortes, so of course I followed her.

I suppose I'd been expecting something mysterious-looking based on the key card entry. What I found instead was a hallway that could have been plucked out of any modest-sized office building in the city. On my right, a janitor's closet. On my left, a supply room. Just past that was Shae's office. At the very end of the hall, there was an unmarked door with a card reader beside it.

"What's in there?" I asked Shae as she pushed open her office door and gestured me inside.

"Just more offices," Shae answered, but I don't think she expected me to believe her.

What was behind that door was none of my business, I reminded myself. I was here to see what I could find out about Tommy Brewster, not poke my nose into the shadier sides of Shae's business.

Shae's office was as striking as Shae herself. The walls were painted black, and the floor was covered with black, industrial-style carpet. Her desk was gleaming black lacquer with silver accents, and her chair was black mesh with silver tubing. On each side of her desk was a shiny metal bookcase, filled with very boring-looking business titles, and the only adornment on the walls were some black and white photographs of cityscapes, each framed in silver.

I found the effect cold and forbidding. But then, it went well with its owner.

Shae gestured me into a guest chair, then took a seat behind her desk and leaned back, crossing her hands behind her head. Her eyes gleamed with interest and speculation as she watched me sit. Under the guise of checking my phone, I opened my purse and made sure I had a clear shot at the Taser. I also armed it and glanced at the battery indicator. It was ready to go, should I need it.

"So," Shae said, apparently impatient with my dithering, "what can I do for you, Ms. Kingsley?"

I had any number of suggestions, but I didn't think voicing them would be conducive to a productive discussion. "I was wondering if you could tell me a little bit about Tommy Brewster. I hear he's a frequent visitor to your club, and I gather that the two of you have some kind of a business relationship."

Shae blinked at me for a moment, then laughed—a deep, rich laughter that I'm sure many men would find sexy as hell. I merely found it irritating. But then, I'm sure that's what she intended.

"I see you put as much value in subtlety as I do," Shae said when she could stop laughing.

I shrugged, trying to look nonchalant. "Subtlety is highly overrated."

She controlled her laughter, although amusement still tugged at the corners of her mouth. "I couldn't agree more. So if we're going to dispense with subtlety, let me ask you what the hell makes you think I'm going to answer any questions about Tommy?"

I considered pulling the Taser to give her some instant motivation. Then I recognized the fundamental problem with that idea. Many demons enjoyed pain, and it seemed likely that a demon who owned a club that catered to the S&M crowd would be one of them. That made threatening her with pain pointless.

"Do you have any personal loyalty to Tommy?" I asked instead.

Shae gave me a droll look. "Honey, do I look like the kind of person who'd have personal loyalty to anyone?"

"Just checking," I muttered. "If it wouldn't offend

your delicate sensibilities, then, perhaps you and I can reach some kind of arrangement." She'd played both sides of the fence before. No reason to think she wouldn't do it again.

I could tell by the sudden glint in her eye that I'd sparked her interest, though her voice remained bland. "What kind of an arrangement did you have in mind?"

I'd never been involved in anything remotely resembling this kind of illicit negotiation, and I realized I didn't know how to play it. How much should I offer her? I didn't even know what a ballpark figure might be. When she'd helped me and Adam rescue Brian from Hell, she'd demanded way more money than I could afford, especially while I was still reeling from the financial impact of my house burning down.

When in doubt, lob the ball into the enemy's court. "How much do you want?" Maybe if I got her to throw out a figure, I could then negotiate her down.

Shae laughed again, and I wished I could stop giving her fodder for amusement. "You don't have the kind of money it would take to buy me," she said. "But I'd be willing to consider other forms of payment."

Remembering the "other form of payment" she'd demanded from Adam and Dominic in the past, I had to fight to suppress a shudder. Fat lot of good that did me, when my face insists on telegraphing everything I'm thinking.

"It all depends on how badly you want the information," Shae continued. Her eyes traveled up and down the length of my body, and I most definitely did *not* want to know what she was seeing in her mind's eye at the moment.

I pushed my chair back. This was a dumb idea. As dumb as coming to the club in search of Tommy

Brewster the first time. "Not that badly, I guess. Thanks for the chat," I said, turning to the door. My hand hovered near the opening of my purse, just in case.

She let me step out into the hallway and close the door about halfway before she stopped me.

"Don't leave angry," she said. "I'm sure we can reach some kind of mutually acceptable arrangement."

I stood in the doorway, hesitating. I had a feeling I was being drawn in like a fish on a hook. But I also had a feeling if I played my cards right, I'd get the information I wanted out of Shae. And really, what girl can't afford to lose a pound of flesh from somewhere on her body?

"If the arrangement involves me setting foot anywhere near Hell, then no, we can't."

Her smile now was almost pleasant. "Honey, I may be mercenary, but I'm not stupid. There's no point in bargaining for something I know I won't get. Now, why don't you shut the door and make yourself comfortable?"

Feeling very much like the fly to her spider, I shut the door. However, I didn't sit down, and I decided it was time for more blatant self-defense. I drew the Taser out of my bag, but I didn't point it at her. I tried my own pleasant smile, though I was glad there wasn't a mirror nearby.

"I think now I'm as comfortable as I'm ever going to be in your presence," I said. She might not mind the pain of being Tasered, but if I found myself needing to get out quick, I was prepared. Whatever she might think of the pain, the electricity would muck with her control of her host's body, and she'd be helpless for a good ten to fifteen minutes. If I couldn't get out in ten minutes, then I was already up shit's creek.

The drawn weapon didn't seem to faze Shae. "Suit yourself. You don't need the Taser. Violence isn't my style. But I don't expect you to take my word for that."

"Good," I muttered, "because I won't. Now, if my money's not good enough to buy information on Brewster, and if you know full well I'm not providing you 'entertainment,' then what exactly are you hoping I'll give you?"

"Information is a very useful currency. For every question I answer about Brewster, I get to ask you a question myself."

Why was it the idea instantly made all the little hairs on my arms stand on end? How much useful information could I possibly give her? What would I know that she'd care about? Certainly she'd be fascinated to know about Lugh and Raphael, but it wasn't like I was going to blurt anything out about them.

"How very Hannibal Lecter of you," I said as I tried to make sense of the request.

She didn't look insulted, which somehow didn't surprise me. "Here's how it would work. You ask me a question. Then I ask you a question. If you answer my question, then I answer yours. If you don't answer my question, then I don't answer yours, but you can ask a different one." She smiled broadly, her teeth looking suddenly very white and deadly against her ebony skin. "You see, I'm even giving you a choice as to which questions you're obligated to answer."

If it sounds too good to be true... "What's the catch?"

"There is no catch, save for the questions themselves." Her eyes glinted with amusement. "I'm not going to ask what your favorite color is."

I thought about it a long time, but I couldn't see any concrete reason not to at least give it a try. I could answer or not answer as I saw fit, and while I felt sure she'd go for some pretty difficult questions if I asked something she didn't want to tell me, at least I might be able to get a little bit of information out of her this way.

"Why do I have a feeling this is a bad idea?" I asked out loud as I once again sat in front of her desk. I kept the Taser out and ready, and I pushed my chair back enough to give me some reaction time if she decided to launch across the desk after me for some reason.

"Is that your first question?"

"Ha, ha." It was surprisingly difficult to figure out what my first question should be. After all, I wasn't really sure what I was fishing for. "What is your relationship with Tommy Brewster?" I asked, going for something vague and broad. Maybe she'd spill more than she meant to in answering that question. Hey, a girl can hope.

Shae gave me her shark smile. "What is your relationship with Adam White?"

That seemed like an almost innocuous question. I figured that meant I was going to get an answer as vague as my own question in return, but I might as well make an effort to play her game.

"Adam's my friend," I said, though I couldn't speak those words without squirming. Adam was many things to me, but "friend" wasn't one of them.

Shae arched a shapely brow. "I thought the point of this exchange of information was to get to the truth. If we're going to deal in falsehoods, then I'll say that Tommy Brewster is my long-lost cousin. Will that do either of us any good?"

I hate talking to people as sarcastic as I am, though of course she had a point. I squirmed a little more.

This was not a question I could answer with any degree of specificity, not without bringing Lugh into the picture, which I wasn't about to do. "All right," I said, "I guess he's not really a friend. It's a little hard to stick a neat label on him. I guess I'd call him an ally."

I had the sense Shae made more of that than I'd hoped, but it was too late to take it back. She nodded in satisfaction.

"Tommy Brewster is a business associate. Nothing more, nothing less."

Ask a vague question, get a vague answer. Score one for Shae. "What kind of business arrangement do you have?"

"Why does an exorcist need a demon ally?"

Yeah, I could definitely see how things could go very, very wrong if I didn't think carefully before I answered. I wasn't entirely sure what Shae could do with any information I gave her, but I *was* entirely sure I didn't want to find out.

I figured my best strategy was to give her stuff she already knew. "I've made a lot of enemies in my line of work, and most of them are demons. I need to have a demon on my side if I want to live to a ripe old age."

It was the truth, though hardly the whole truth. Shae regarded me with an expression that bordered on contempt. "You get what you pay for. Are you sure you want to stick with that answer?"

I met her eyes, trying to project the image of a woman with nothing to hide. "I answered your question, and I told you the truth. What more do you want?"

Shae snorted. "Fine. My arrangement with Tommy is that he gives me money, and I keep my mouth shut." When I glared at her, she said, "I answered your question, and I told you the truth. What more do you want?"

Yeah, I was definitely in over my head. I sure could use Brian's lawyer skills right about now. If I had him here feeding me the answers, I bet I'd be able to answer all kinds of questions in great detail without giving away anything. I briefly considered giving up and asking Adam to interrogate Shae, but I knew without being told that that would never work. Shae cooperated with Adam at times because she had no choice, and Adam cooperated with Shae because he needed her help to catch certain illegal demons. That didn't mean they would ever cooperate with one another when not forced, and there was no missing the deep-seated animosity between the two.

"I suppose asking you to tell the *whole* truth would be overly optimistic of me, huh?" I said, stalling a bit to give myself more time to think.

"Do I need to remind you again that this is a trade? You give me the whole truth, I give you the whole truth. You give me the tip of the iceberg, and..."

It made sense, but I wasn't in a position to give her the whole truth. "Why do you want to know this stuff anyway?" I was still stalling. She probably knew that, but she didn't call me on it. I didn't expect her to answer, but she surprised me.

"I've managed to stay on the Mortal Plain for more than eighty years," she said, which of course made me wonder how many hosts she'd gone through in that time. Certainly her current host wasn't eighty years old. "If there's one thing I've learned, it's that information is the most valuable currency anywhere in the world. And the funny thing is, you never know exactly what information is going to come in handy in the future. Obviously, I know you have enemies in high places. Knowing the full story behind it may turn out to be absolutely useless to me." Her eyes glittered. "Or maybe it won't."

It was the latter possibility that made me hesitate. What did I dare tell her? How badly did I need to know whatever it was she could tell me? Lugh shot me a brief stab of pain through the eye, but it was hard to determine what he was trying to communicate. Maybe I'd been better off when I could hear his voice in my head, after all.

I concentrated as hard as I could on a question for Lugh. *Should I take some chances in what I reveal in order to maybe learn more about Tommy? Give me one stab for yes, two for no.*

I guess he heard my question. Not being a masochist, I was glad his answer was yes. *Let me know if you think I'm about to say something I shouldn't.*

I took a deep breath and then forced myself to meet Shae's eyes. "All right," I said. "I'll tell you the whole truth. But the information you have on Tommy had better be worth it."

"Fair enough." She leaned forward in her chair, and I'd swear the look on her face was almost lust. "So tell me, what is your relationship with Adam White?"

"Like I said, we're allies. He's one of Lugh's lieutenants, and I would very much rather see Lugh on the throne than Dougal."

Shae was better at masking her expression than I was, but she couldn't entirely hide her surprise. I would have thought she'd known that I was somehow involved in the war of succession after Dougal's minions had paid her to hold Brian hostage. I had to remind myself once more that she was a mercenary. A mercenary who could be persuaded not to ask "why" if the price was high enough.

"You look surprised," I told her, hoping to press my advantage. "Do you expect me to believe you knew nothing about any of this?"

She recovered her composure much more quickly than I'd have liked. The smile was back, sharp and cold as ever. "That sounds almost like another question."

I scowled at her. "Just tell me what your deal is with Tommy Brewster. It's late, I'm tired, and I want to go home."

She gave me a long, piercing, probing look before she answered. I suspect she was trying to determine if she could wring anything else out of me. She must have come to the correct conclusion.

"You might say I'm serving as his matchmaker," she said with a wry twist of her lips that might have been a smile.

"Huh?" I responded intelligently.

Shae stood up, and my hand tightened on the Taser. She held both her hands up, her eyebrows arching. "Now, now," she said. "Don't shoot me before I give you the information you want."

I kept the Taser pointed at her as I eased out of my chair. "You can talk just fine sitting down."

"If you want the answer to your question, you'll follow me and I'll show you. You can keep your Taser handy if I make you that nervous."

Her condescending tone suggested I was somehow being a coward for insisting on the weapon, but I didn't feel any particular sense of shame. As far as I was concerned, it was an entirely practical safety measure.

I kept a wide distance between us as Shae walked to the door, her hands still in plain sight. But when she stepped through the door out into the hallway, I followed.

I wasn't sure where we were going, but I suppose I wasn't all that surprised when she headed toward the mysterious door at the end of the hall. The door that led to "more offices." The door opened with a beep when Shae swiped her card. I had to get closer to her than I'd have liked to catch the door before it slammed shut behind her.

There were indeed a couple of other office-like rooms behind that door. However, of far greater importance was the massive, space-age security center that Shae showed off with a flourish.

There were at least a couple dozen screens, each displaying a different image of the club. And not all of them were of the main room. My stomach twisted as my eyes finally focused on one screen and I realized what the two men and the one naked woman were doing. I jerked my gaze away, only to find myself looking at an even more unsettling image—a woman wearing nothing but a black hood that covered her entire head except for her mouth down on her knees with her hands cuffed behind her as she fellated the disgusting no-neck man who'd tried to pick me up the other night. It was all I could do not to hurl.

Shae reached up and tapped her finger on one of the other screens, drawing my eye once again. And there was good old Tommy Brewster, his naked ass pumping as he fucked a pretty young woman who was bound spread-eagled on the bed. The look on her face told me she wasn't there against her will. If that wasn't already more than I wanted to know, I could see two more young women, both blond, naked, and eager-looking, watching the proceedings, apparently waiting their turn.

I'm nowhere near a good enough actress to hide my disgust and embarrassment, so I didn't bother trying. Instead I focused on Shae's face and tried to convince myself I had no peripheral vision.

"Isn't there some kind of law against videotaping people having sex without their knowledge?"

Shae grinned. "How do you know it's without their knowledge?"

I knew that most people who frequented this club would find me prudish in the extreme. I also knew that there was no way they were all so uninhibited that they didn't mind being taped in the act. But what was I going to do about it? I sighed as I came to the inevitable conclusion: nothing.

I wanted to cross my arms over my chest, my favorite defensive gesture, but that would mean hindering my Taser hand, and I wasn't about to do that.

"What does this have to do with anything?" I asked. "I already knew Tommy was into the kinky stuff, and I really don't give a shit."

"I told you I was his matchmaker," Shae said. Once more she tapped a nail against the screen, three times, once for each girl. "I handpicked these for him."

I shook my head. "Why does he need you to pick his girls?"

"Those girls are all regulars here. Real groupies. They'd do just about anything a demon wants them to do."

I hate to imagine what kind of face I must have been making. "I still don't see why this is relevant."

"As you may have noticed, I'm in the information business. Among other things."

I gave her a keep talking motion.

"So let's just say I know a lot about my regulars. Things that they wouldn't usually share with their one-night stands."

"Like what?" I asked, still making absolutely no sense out of what she was saying.

"Like, for instance, their family medical history. Tommy's particularly interested in girls who have a family history of cancer. And he also likes those who put a little too much faith in condoms."

"What the hell...?" I muttered. "Why?" I asked out loud.

"Which of these screens turns you on the most?" Shae asked with a sweeping gesture to indicate the bank of monitors that showed the sickening "play-rooms" from Hell. "And don't tell me none of them, because I'll know that's a lie."

I was about to voice an indignant objection, until my brain caught up and realized this was her quid pro quo question. I also realized that I didn't need her to tell me why Tommy was targeting these particular girls. I bet I could come up with a perfectly good guess myself.

For reasons I yet had no clue about, Tommy was continuing the Houston breeding project. Only he was taking his genes out into the general human population.

I shook my head yet again. I didn't know exactly what he was up to. I didn't know what would happen to these chicks if they happened to get pregnant. I didn't know what would happen to their children. What I did know was that none of this could possibly be good for the human race.

Tearing my eyes away from the monitors, I gave Shae my best sneer. "If I weren't worried that too many people had seen me come in here, I swear I'd shoot you full of juice and exorcize you so fast..."

"Sticks and stones, sugar. Now, I think we've concluded our business here, don't you?"

I couldn't have agreed more.

Chapter **20**

It was late when I got home, and my body and mind were both complaining that I hadn't recovered from my sleep deprivation yet. Working almost on autopilot, I checked my answering machine, wondering why I hadn't heard from Adam yet. Had he chickened out about approaching Dom? Or had he gotten an answer he didn't like? Right now, I wasn't sure I wanted to know, but there was no way I could go to sleep with three unplayed messages on my machine under the circumstances.

The first call was an immediate hang-up. The second call was from a reporter, of all things. He wanted me to call back and talk with him about this afternoon's exorcism. I couldn't imagine why he'd be interested. It had been a long time since exorcism had been considered newsworthy. He left a number for me to call, but I just laughed. Like I needed the press in my life!

I thought surely the third call would be from Adam. I really wish I'd been right.

The caller ID told me it was from an unknown number, and at first I thought it was going to be another hang-up. My finger was halfway to the Delete button before a voice started talking. A chill ran down my spine from the first digitally-altered word.

"You'd better pray Jordan Maguire lives," the message said, the voice so garbled I couldn't tell if it was male or female. "If he dies, you die, too. This is your only warning."

I closed my eyes and pinched the bridge of my nose. Once upon a time, a threat like this would have had me . . . well, not exactly in a panic, but at the very least in a state of high alarm. Tonight . . . it scared me a little, but after all I'd been through since Lugh came into my life, it seemed almost more of an annoyance than a cause for serious concern. Oh, for the days when a death threat on my answering machine was the worst problem in my life!

The "right" thing to do at the moment was call the police. Usually, when I'm reading a book or watching a movie where the heroine fails to call the police when she's threatened, I berate her as an idiot. But my life had been far too eventful lately, and I'd had too many brushes with the law. Adam had extricated me from my most awkward moments, but I had to be setting off police warning bells everywhere. If I called them now, it might remind certain people to dig out the files about my arrest for illegal exorcism, or about Brian's kidnapping, or about my father's death in the "car accident," or about the break-in and subsequent attack at my parents' home while I just happened to be there.

Maybe if I thought the police could actually help me, I'd have made the call anyway. But I seriously doubted someone who was thinking ahead enough to digitally alter their voice would make a call the police could trace, so what would the police do? Except make me wait up for them a few hours and subject me to suspicious looks and leading questions.

I gnawed on my lip. What was the deal with this Jordan Maguire guy, anyway? Who felt strongly enough about him to threaten me, and why had a reporter called? Since I'd been hired by the state, not his family, the only details I had about him were those directly pertaining to his conviction. Perhaps I should have inquired about his background before taking the case, but that wasn't part of my routine.

I really wanted to just fall into bed and forget all about it, but I supposed that wasn't one of my options. So instead I did an Internet search on Maguire. I didn't find out much about the guy I'd exorcized, but I did find out that Jordan Maguire Sr. was rich enough to endow his son's high school with a new multimillion dollar athletic facility, start up a mega-grant program for underprivileged artists in his daughter's name, and fund a new wing of Pennsylvania Hospital. That made Jordan Jr. somewhat of a local celebrity—hence, the call from the reporter—and Jordan Sr. a potentially powerful enemy.

I cursed loud and long. I didn't need any more enemies! I'd had no idea Jordan Maguire was anything out of the ordinary when I'd agreed to do the exorcism. I'd known when he'd come out the other side brain-dead that his family wouldn't be happy, and it wouldn't shock me to find out they were blaming the exorcist. There was a small, but vocal, minority who thought hosts who came out of an exorcism brain-dead—as opposed to "merely" brain damaged—were the victims of incompetent or malicious exorcists. I guess it's always nice to have someone to blame.

There'd been a few lawsuits that had made the news, but since there was no way to *prove* that the exorcist did anything wrong, so far none had been successful. Of course, in a country where McDonald's can be successfully sued for serving hot coffee, I guess it's not surprising that lawyers with dollar signs in their eyes still hoped to find a way to hold exorcists responsible.

With a sigh of resignation, I turned off the computer and told myself that Maguire was no longer my problem. Whoever had left the death threat had probably gotten the vitriol out of their system and things would calm down in the days and weeks to come.

But I did a lousy job of persuading myself. I made sure to take my Taser to bed with me that night. I'd already seen how porous my building's security was.

Despite the anxiety that rattled my brain like a set of maracas, I managed to fall asleep. I probably would have slept until noon if the phone hadn't rung at eight in the morning. It was the reporter again, asking me if I had any comment about the Maguire family's decision to pull the plug this afternoon. I had some comments for him all right, but they weren't about the exorcism or Jordan Maguire.

I tried to go back to sleep, but the phone rang again at eight-thirty. I was prepared to give the reporter the kind of comments that might get me arrested, but when I checked the caller ID I saw that it was Brian.

I seriously considered letting my answering machine take the call. Not because I didn't want to talk to Brian, but because I didn't want to talk to him about the Maguire situation. I figured there must be something in the newspaper about it, and Brian would want to gallantly support me in my time of trouble. I wasn't up to dealing with him in knight-in-shining-armor mode. Yes, I'm really bitchy in the morning before I've had my coffee.

Virtue won out over expedience, and I actually picked up the phone.

"If you mention Jordan Maguire, you're not getting laid again for at least three months," I said.

Brian chuckled. "Guess you haven't had your coffee yet."

Why does everyone have to find me so goddamn amusing? "I was sound asleep, so no." So I hadn't been sound asleep for at least a half hour. What was a little exaggeration among friends?

"Sorry to wake you," Brian said. "But I don't think this can wait. I'm coming over. I'll be there in about half an hour."

"Huh?" I glanced at the clock again. "What's going on? Don't you have to be at work?" Actually, if he'd been following his usual routine, he'd have been at work a half hour ago. Suddenly, I was feeling much more awake, and that wasn't necessarily a good thing.

"It's not something I can explain on the phone," he said. "Get some coffee in your system, and I'll see you soon."

To my surprise, he hung up. It wasn't like Brian to be cryptic.

Giving up my illusion that I might be able to get some more sleep, I rubbed the grit from my eyes and got out of bed. I started a pot of coffee, and by the time I emerged from a quick shower, the heavenly brew was ready for me. I burned my tongue on the first swallow, but it was worth it.

I was still in my bathrobe when Brian arrived. A girl has to have priorities, and coffee came before clothes for me any day of the week.

I hadn't expected this to be a social call, of course, but that didn't mean I wasn't unnerved by the grim look on Brian's face. And that was *before* he got a look at my bruised and battered face.

"What happened?" he asked, sounding appalled.

"It's not that big a deal," I answered, hoping I

could somehow miraculously avoid a big, dramatic scene. "A couple of Tommy Brewster's pals thought I should lay off him, and I didn't agree. But really, I'm fine. And yes, I reported it."

He stared at me in silence for a moment before he spoke again. As I'm sure he intended, the silence made me squirm, but I refrained from blurting out anything I shouldn't have.

"This is the case you insisted wasn't dangerous, right?" he asked. "The one you told me you'd handed off to Adam."

"If you're going to scold me, then you might as well turn and get your ass out of here before things get ugly. I'm just not in the mood for it."

His shoulders lowered, and he looked slightly less like he was about to explode. "Old habits die hard. But I really can't leave right now."

I remembered how grim he'd looked even before he got a good look at me and knew this couldn't be good. I served him a cup of coffee just to put off hearing what had put that look on his face. But I couldn't put it off for long.

"Okay," I said with a resigned sigh. "Tell me what's going wrong now." I cupped my hands around my second cup of coffee and tried to brace myself for whatever bad thing was about to rear its ugly head.

Brian put his coffee down and leaned his butt against the kitchen counter. I think he was trying to look calm and normal, but he wasn't pulling it off very effectively.

"When I came down to the front desk to get my paper this morning," he said, "there was a message in my mailbox. The night man said it was delivered by a young woman, but he had no idea who she was or where she'd gone."

This didn't sound good at all. "What was the message?" I asked.

He didn't answer, instead reaching into his jacket and pulling a plain white envelope from the inner pocket. He handed the envelope to me, and I saw my name typewritten on the front. The envelope was still sealed.

I closed my eyes for a moment as I fought a wave of self-pity. Wasn't there enough shit going on in my life already? Did I really need mysterious letters delivered through Brian?

"If someone wanted to give this to me," I mused, "then why did they leave it at *your* building?"

"Beats me," Brian answered, looking worried.

I stared at the envelope, trying to guess what might be inside. I guess I stared a little too long, because Brian prompted me.

"Well? Are you going to open it?"

"Back off," I snapped, then wanted to slap myself silly for killing the messenger. "Sorry. I just can't imagine there's anything good in here, and I'm not in a big hurry to add to my problems."

Brian smiled faintly. "Lawyers get to be the bearers of bad tidings on a regular basis. I'm used to being underappreciated."

"Ha, ha," I said, though I'm not sure that was supposed to be a joke. "Can you give me a minute?" I didn't want him looking over my shoulder while I read, just in case . . . Well, just in case.

He raised his eyebrows. "I've done my messenger duty, and now I'm dismissed?"

I fought the urge to snap at him again. "I'm not dismissing you. I just want a quiet moment to open this and read it. Is that too much to ask?"

He gave me a reproachful look, but he pushed away from the counter and stomped out of the kitchen. Even after he'd gone, I still had trouble forcing myself to open the envelope, but there was only so long even I could procrastinate.

Trying to steel myself for all possibilities, I slid a finger under the flap and ripped the envelope open.

Inside, there was a photograph, along with a neatly handwritten letter. The photo was the one Claudia had showed me at the restaurant, the one of her adopted daughters.

The letter was from Claudia.

Ms. Kingsley,

They have my daughters. I'm sorry I wasn't able to tell you the truth about why I wanted you to drop the case, but I was told in unequivocal terms that I am to act as though nothing were wrong. Still, while I don't know you very well, I imagine you're the kind of person who would be unwilling to drop the case just on my say-so, so I felt I had to take the risk of contacting you.

They are watching my every move, and most likely yours, too. I can't contact you personally, but I will try to get this letter to you in a roundabout fashion that will avoid detection. I just hope it doesn't reach you too late.

I love my son, more than I can say. I desperately wish there were something I could do to save him. But I can't risk my daughters. They are helpless children, and I can't bear to do anything to endanger them. The kidnappers have pointed out that with two hostages, they can afford to kill one as a message if anyone "misbehaves," as they put it. Please, Ms. Kingsley. Drop the case. Don't ask any more questions. These are very bad people, and I believe they won't hesitate to hurt the girls. Don't give them an excuse.

Claudia

My heart dangled somewhere around my knees. Just what I needed. A hostage crisis. And after I'd spent last night questioning Shae about Tommy. Please, God, don't let the bad guys retaliate against those children!

My throat knotted up, and I swallowed to try to loosen it. There was nothing I could do to change the past, and if Tommy's friends had found out what I'd been up to last night, then at least one of those children might already be doomed. Tears stung my eyes, and I cursed Tommy Brewster and all his demon friends. While I was at it, I cursed Raphael for having enabled the whole breeding program and for whatever information he might be withholding at the moment.

I heard Brian turn on the TV in the living room and wondered if I should show him the note. Would he have any better idea what to do about it than I did? I let out a heavy sigh and closed my eyes. This was Mr. By-The-Books I was talking about. His natural reaction to seeing this letter would be to call the police. He and I rate on opposite ends of the cynicism scale. Most likely, he'd believe the police could actually help in this situation. Myself, I believed the police would get those kids killed. Which meant I couldn't tell him.

Your Mr. By-The-Books helped me arrange your father's death, Lugh's voice whispered in my mind, and it was all I could do to suppress a groan. Obviously I was reaching stress overload, since my subconscious firewall appeared to be failing me.

Stay out of my head, Lugh, I thought furiously at him. I had the faint impression of laughter, but he didn't otherwise respond. Maybe that had been just a momentary fluke, a glitch in my defenses.

He was right about the tarnish on Brian's suit of shining armor. But that didn't mean Brian wouldn't go to the police about this. He'd helped Lugh with my father out of a desperate desire to save me when all other hope had failed. In this situation, he was much more likely to put his hope in the police than in me.

The TV clicked off, and I heard Brian's footsteps approaching. I guess he'd gotten tired of waiting. Wishing I could calm the racing of my heart, I folded the photographs back into the letter and stuffed the letter into the envelope just as Brian rounded the corner into the kitchen.

We engaged in a long staring contest that ended in what I interpreted as a draw. Brian's eyes were shadowed with pain.

"You're not going to tell me what this is all about, are you?" he asked, and the hurt in his voice was almost more than I could bear.

"I'm sorry," I said, my voice thick with genuine regret. I wished I trusted him enough to tell him the whole story. It seemed patently unfair, even to me, that I should love him this much and still not be able to give him my trust. But part of what I loved about him was his basic goodness. I loved that he was always willing to do the right thing, even when it wasn't in his own best interests. I loved his sense of honor and decency, even though sometimes I cursed him for it. I loved his faith in mankind's goodness, even though I didn't share it.

Brian's gaze dropped to the kitchen floor, and he shook his head. "Why do I bother hoping?" he muttered to himself, and the words hurt like a stab to the heart.

"Brian—" I started, reaching out to him, but I couldn't think of anything to say to make this better.

He twitched away from my reaching hand. I flinched at the rejection, then flinched again when he put on his damn lawyer face. Even so, I forced myself to meet his eyes.

"I guess I know you better than you know me," Brian said.

I frowned in puzzlement. "What the hell does that mean?" I asked, hoping to come off angry instead of hurt. I think I succeeded, but if Brian knew me as well as he claimed, he'd see right through it.

He folded his arms over his chest, still meeting my gaze, still hiding his feelings behind his lawyer face. "Was it because you were trying to 'protect' me again, or was it because you're afraid I'll go to the police? I couldn't decide which it would be."

I'm capable of being pretty dense at times, but now I had no trouble figuring out what he meant. The fake anger turned into real anger.

"You opened the letter, you asshole!"

Brian unfolded his arms, then covered his eyes with one hand as he barked out a bitter laugh. "You're absolutely priceless, you know."

"What?"

"It's amazing how you can turn any situation into an opportunity to get mad at someone no matter what you yourself have done."

I scowled at him. "If you're just figuring this out, then you don't know me as well as you claim."

He nodded sagely. "Right. So we're going to have a big blowup about me reading the letter, and we'll just gloss over the fact that once again you decided to shut me out of your life."

I love Brian to death, but right now, I wanted to smack him. "Don't be a drama queen about this. There are a couple of children whose lives are in imminent danger, and you want to argue about the lack of openness in our relationship? Get a sense of proportion already." He puffed up indignantly, and no doubt if I'd let him get a word out he'd have put me right in my place. So I didn't let him get a word out.

"I didn't want to tell you because yes, I was afraid you'd want to go to the police, and yes, I think that's a piss-poor idea. If I'm wrong and you'd never dream of calling the police, then by all means please, continue to tar and feather me. Otherwise, stuff a sock in it."

His lips quirked into a grin that seemed completely out of place given the situation. "May I use your stove?"

"What?" I asked, wondering if he'd suddenly misplaced his mind.

"To heat up the tar."

I opened my mouth to say something, but my brain went on strike and refused to feed me any pithy replies.

"Here's my suggestion," he said, and I swear even though he was pissed at me he was enjoying my discomfiture. "Since you're such bosom buddies with the Director of Special Forces, you call *him*. I suppose technically that's calling the police, but he'll probably be able to make a better judgment on whether to take this on in an official capacity or whether to keep it off the books."

Once again, I couldn't think of a good reply—unless it was duh! Maybe the sleep deprivation had stolen more brain cells than I realized. Or maybe I'd just been picking a fight, because hey, I'm ornery that way.

"You still shouldn't have read it," I said, but there was no heat left in my words.

"Are you going to call Adam, or aren't you?"

I wanted to ask what he would do if I said no, but I was too chicken. I was pretty sure he'd say he'd call Adam himself, and that would lead to more arguing. For once, I wasn't up for that.

"Yeah, I'll call him."

Chapter **21**

I should have known better than to expect Brian to trundle on home like a good little lawyer. I hoped he was sticking around for the reason he stated—that he wanted to help me—not because he didn't trust me to make the call. Not that I had any room to throw stones where trust was concerned.

I hated the idea of calling Adam when he and Dom were in the middle of their own personal crisis—assuming Adam had done as he'd said and let Dom know about the crisis. But Claudia Brewster's daughters couldn't wait until the love boat sailed on smooth waters, so I picked up the phone and dialed his number.

No one answered, and this wasn't exactly the kind of message I could leave on an answering machine. I figured he was probably at work, so I called his cell phone, but that went straight to voice mail. I bit my lip. It seemed silly, and maybe even a bit hypocritical, to worry about Adam. If there was anyone more capable of taking care of himself than Adam, I didn't know him. I left a terse message for him to call me ASAP, then decided to try his office number. I hated calling his office. Everyone who'd ever answered the phone there was an asshole—including Adam, now that I thought about it—but I called anyway.

"He called in sick today," said the man who answered the phone. He had a nasally voice that made everything he said sound like a whine, though so far he'd been perfectly polite.

I held the phone away from my face for a moment and stared at it as if it were somehow responsible for the crap I'd just heard. "He's a demon," I said with forced patience when I decided the phone wasn't to blame. "Demons don't get sick." One of the fringe benefits that went with being possessed, though giving up your entire life seemed a bit too much to pay.

"No," the officer whined, "but they do get sick days. And Director White took one. I'll put you through to his voice mail."

"No, that's not—" But he'd already hit the transfer button. Like I said, assholes all. "...necessary," I finished, hanging up the phone. This was a shitty time for Adam to go AWOL. He was probably at home, just ignoring the phone. I *so* didn't want to go there in person looking for him. If he and Dom were in the Dreaded Black Room, they probably wouldn't even hear the bell.

However, I didn't have any better ideas, and I was all too conscious that the clock was ticking. I didn't know what the chances were that the kidnappers were ever planning to let those kids go, but I figured that as with all missing persons cases, our best hopes of finding them were in the first forty-eight hours.

"Road trip," I said to Brian, and he followed me without question.

When we got to my car, I found I had a flat tire—a nuisance I *so* didn't need right now. I didn't feel like taking the time to change the tire, so we took a cab to

Adam's place. It was past rush hour, so it didn't take long to snag one, and since the cabbie drove at somewhere around the speed of light, we were at Adam's practically before we left my apartment. A peek at the small parking lot across the street showed me that both Adam's and Dom's cars were in residence.

Ever the gentleman, Brian paid the cabbie—which was probably a good thing, since I didn't think I had any cash on me—and together we climbed the steps up to Adam's door. I pressed the doorbell, but I didn't hear any sound. I pressed again, harder. Still nothing. Great! A broken doorbell reduced the chances of anyone hearing me from about twenty percent to about zero.

I grabbed the knocker and gave it a few heavy thumps. The sound was gratifyingly loud, but after a good sixty seconds of waiting, no one came to the door. I tried again, with the same result.

"I guess no one's home," Brian said.

"Their cars are in the lot."

He shrugged. "It *is* actually possible to get places in this city without driving."

"Remember, *I'm* the smart-ass. *You're* the nice guy."

He grinned. "Oh yeah. Sorry, forgot about that."

I rolled my eyes at him, then backed down the steps and craned my head upward. There didn't appear to be any lights on in the house, but then it was the middle of the day.

"You don't happen to know how to pick locks, do you?" I asked. Brian just gave me a look that said I was crazy. It was my turn to shrug. "Never hurts to ask."

Any moment now, Brian was going to decide it was time to give up on Adam, and I felt sure his next suggestion would be a call to 911. I couldn't let that happen.

If you let me in, I can break the door, Lugh whispered in my head.

I hesitated. The fact that I could hear him at all meant my defenses were already weak. Weak enough for me to voluntarily let Lugh take over? A shiver crawled down my spine then back up again. I grabbed Brian's arm and dragged him around the corner. I didn't want too many people watching us as we cased the place. The last thing I needed was some Good Samaritan calling us in as suspicious loiterers.

"Let's go sit down for a moment," I said, jerking my chin toward a bus stop half a block down. A bus was just pulling away, so the bench was empty when we got there.

"Okay," Brian said slowly, watching me suspiciously. But he didn't press until we'd both sat down. "What's up?"

I took a deep breath and ordered myself not to panic. "I'm going to try to let Lugh take over so he can break the door down."

Brian's eyebrows shot up in almost comical surprise. "That's ridiculous! They're almost certainly not home, and I doubt Adam would appreciate having you vandalize his house."

"Not me, Lugh. And I'm pretty sure they're home."

"They can't be. You knocked loud enough to raise the dead."

Brian had been in Adam's house once before. He'd even been on the second floor, but I didn't know if the door to the black room had been open at the time.

I cleared my throat. "When you were in Adam's house, did you see his, uh . . ." I didn't know what to call it. I supposed "dungeon" was the proper term, but

I couldn't make myself say it. I cleared my throat again. "Did you see the black room?"

"Black room?" Brian asked in a voice that told me the answer was no.

I stared at the pavement, trying not to remember too much about that damn room. "Yeah. At the head of the stairs. It's where Adam keeps his, uh, S&M stuff." I'd never told Brian about what Adam had done to me in that room, what I'd *let* him do to me. I didn't want him to feel guilty about the hell I'd gone through to get Adam to help me rescue him.

"What about it?" Brian asked softly.

"I think they're in there now. And I think I could shoot a cannon through the front door and they wouldn't bother to come check it out."

"Oh," Brian said. Thankfully, he left it at that.

"Wish me luck," I mumbled, then let out a deep sigh and tried to relax. I closed my eyes and visualized opening the doors of my mind. The wail of a siren broke my concentration, and my eyes popped open in time to see a police car zoom down a cross street.

I closed my eyes again and ordered myself to focus. Which lasted about ten seconds. Then a pimpmobile cruised by with its stereo blasting rap loud enough to make the sidewalk vibrate. After that, I was distracted by the roar and stink of a bus traveling in the opposite direction.

All typical city sounds. Sounds that I ignore with ease every day of the week. But each was an excuse to let my mind shy away from what I asked it to do. Just this once, I cursed the strength of my subconscious defenses. I tried reminding myself that the lives of two innocent children might lie in the balance, but although stress had helped erode the barriers of my mind before, it wasn't working now.

Sorry, Lugh, I thought. *I just don't know how to let go.* He didn't answer me, which was just as well.

Regretfully, I opened my eyes. "No dice," I told Brian. He probably gave me a reproachful look, but since I was staring off into space, I didn't see it.

"So what's plan C?" he asked.

I was about to admit that I didn't have a plan C, but then I realized that I did.

The only reason I'd tried to let Lugh take control was because I needed a demon's strength to break Adam's door. There was nothing to say it had to be *my* demon's strength.

"I guess I call in the cavalry," I said, though in my case the cavalry wore very black hats. Trying not to clench my teeth too hard, I fished out my phone and called Raphael.

"Morgan or Lugh?" he asked as soon as he answered.

I was severely tempted to say it was Lugh, thinking perhaps Raphael would be more willing to help if he thought he was getting orders from his king. I managed to resist the temptation, though, not sure if I could pull it off.

"It's Morgan," I said. "I need your help."

"Where are you? Are you in trouble?"

The alarm in his voice might have been gratifying if I thought it had anything to do with concern for *me.* "No more trouble than usual," I assured him. "But I need your help just the same. How fast can you make it to the corner of Twenty-Second and Walnut?" His apartment building was only about five blocks away, so I figured it would be pretty fast.

"I'm on my way now," he said, and I could hear his hurried footsteps. "I'll be there in ten minutes, tops."

He hung up before I had a chance to say thank you. Not that I'd been going to thank him anyway, not until after he'd actually helped me. I figured he might be a bit peeved when he got here and found out what I wanted him to do. And why. Somehow I doubted he'd be anxious to play the white knight and rescue those little girls. In fact, he'd probably blow a gasket when he found out what I'd been up to.

For all his many faults, I didn't think Raphael would like the idea of any harm coming to those children. His moral compass was severely bent, but I didn't believe it was completely broken. However, he would consider protecting Lugh a higher priority, and making any attempt to rescue the children was bound to put Lugh in some kind of danger. I just had to get him to break that door down before he knew why I wanted him to.

I was planning out my argument when my cell phone rang. When I saw the call was from Adam, I felt a rush of mingled relief and irritation.

I answered the phone, practically shaking with outrage. "Isn't there some kind of rule that you have to be available by phone at all times?" I snapped. Saying hello is highly overrated.

"I am," he said simply.

"I've been trying to reach you for hours!" An exaggeration, but it sure felt like hours.

I could almost hear him shrug. "My office has my emergency number."

I reminded myself to stop by his office and thank the whining asshole who'd answered the phone for all his "help." "Where are you? I need to talk to you. *Now*."

"I'm at home. I'll be at your place in twenty minutes."

"No, I'll be at yours in two. I guess you didn't hear me knocking."

"Oh. That was you?" He cleared his throat. "Sorry. I was, uh, busy."

"I'll bet," I muttered. "How's Dom?"

Adam hesitated. "He's fine," he finally said, but there was something funny in his voice.

I wanted to ask what was wrong, but there was no reason to talk about it on the phone when I was right around the corner. "Whatever," I said, figuring I'd grill him about it in a couple of minutes. "I'll be there in a few. And just so you know, I'll have Brian and Raphael with me."

"Wonderful," he said sourly. "I'm in the mood for a party right now."

"Don't get pissed at *me*! If you'd answered your phone when I first called, this would have been a lot simpler."

"Whatever," he said, and I guessed that funny voice was supposed to be mimicking mine. His impersonation could use a little work.

I couldn't think of anything else to say, at least nothing that wasn't so snarky it would get us off on even more of a wrong foot, so I just hung up and waited for Raphael.

Raphael must have been alarmed by my call even though I'd told him I wasn't in any more trouble than usual. He showed up in less time that it would take me to cover *half* the distance. People had gathered at the bus stop, and though like typical city dwellers they were all pretending they were the only people around, I knew full well we couldn't afford to talk about the situation in anyone's hearing. So when Raphael strode toward me with the obvious intention of giving me the third degree, I jerked my thumb toward the corner.

"We're going to Adam's," I said, and started moving before he had a chance to reply. I felt his eyes boring into the back of my head, but I did my best to ignore it. Brian fell into step beside me, and moments later, I heard Raphael hurry to catch up.

"You gonna tell me what's going on?" Raphael asked when he reached my other side.

I wished Adam's call had come just a couple minutes earlier so I could have avoided Raphael's company, but I supposed if he was to serve as one of Lugh's advisors, it was for the best that he come along. Besides, if he'd been following Lugh's orders, maybe he'd found some more information about the Houston facility. And maybe the information *I'd* gotten could fill in some of the gaps.

"When we get inside," I answered. I still felt like Raphael was staring holes in me, but I refused to confirm my suspicion by looking at him.

Adam was waiting for us when we arrived. I didn't even have to knock. It looked like he'd dressed in a hurry. His T-shirt was only haphazardly tucked into his jeans, his feet were bare, and his hair was mussed. He gave Brian and Raphael each a long look, then opened the door wide enough to let us in.

When Dominic was playing hostess, any conversations that took place in this house happened in the kitchen, usually accompanied by food. But there was no sign of Dominic now, so Adam directed us to the living room instead. I hoped Dom was upstairs wrapped in blissful post-coital slumber. However, Adam seemed pretty tense, and I worried about what that might mean.

Much though I wanted to ask about Dom, he couldn't be my first priority at the moment. So instead, I forced myself to stay on topic and explain to Adam and Raphael what had happened.

I wasn't surprised when there was a long silence after I'd finished. I sure wished I could read their minds like Lugh could read mine. And I sure hoped Adam was enough of a cop to want to help Claudia's daughters, even if sticking his neck out for them might not be in Lugh's best interests. After all, Lugh didn't seem to have any objections to the idea of mounting a rescue. Or if he did, he wasn't stupid enough to think he could bully me into keeping out of it.

The silence went on a little too long, and like an idiot I rushed to fill it.

"I didn't find out about all this until this morning," I said, then squirmed a bit, knowing no one was going to like hearing what I had to say next. "All I knew last night was that Claudia had 'fired' me and that some goons thought beating me up would make me back down."

Adam fixed me with one of his black looks. "What did you do?" he asked, and I tried not to wither under his preemptive disapproval.

"I, um, stopped by The Seven Deadlies."

Brian looked vaguely ill at the mention of the club; Raphael looked worried; Adam, predictably, looked furious. I wondered if talking fast and loud would keep the boys from letting me know what they thought of me right now. I decided it wouldn't hurt to try.

"I figured Shae knew more than she was telling us, so I had a little chat with her." Adam looked like he was about to kill me, so angry I caught the faint glow in his eyes that meant his demon was shining through. I kept talking, though my instinct for self-preservation suggested now would be a good time to run like hell. Adam has a very effective death glare.

"I found out that Tommy's been paying her to procure women for him."

That surprised Adam enough to dim the glow in his eyes. "Come again?"

There seemed to be more oxygen in the room now

that he wasn't glaring at me like that, and I heaved a sigh of relief. "She apparently can get a great deal of information about her regular customers. Tommy wanted her to find him women whose families have a history of hereditary cancer. And it sounded like he specifically selected ones who might be a bit careless about their birth control." Out of the corner of my eye, I watched Raphael, seeking any clue that this meant something to him. Unfortunately, he has an effective poker face, unlike mine.

"She doesn't know why, but I can make an educated guess." This time, I faced Raphael full on. "Care to tell me *your* theory?"

He lifted one shoulder in an elegant shrug. "I haven't gotten any new information since we last spoke, if that's what you're asking. But it does seem pretty obvious that Tommy's trying to spread his genes." He looked thoughtful. "My guess would be that Houston had more success with their project than I'd realized. Tommy must be a pretty valuable specimen."

"He's not a specimen!" I snapped. "He's a human being. And don't give me any bullshit about how he's not human because you demons have been mucking with his DNA."

Raphael held up his hands in a gesture of innocence. "I wasn't going to. What we call him doesn't matter. What *does* matter is that the Houston project was successful enough that they want to spread his genes in the human population."

"Are you sure that's what it means?" Brian asked, startling us all, I think.

"What do you mean?" I asked, turning to face him.

"I'm just wondering...They're keeping their human subjects captive in or around the facility somewhere. Even if they're keeping them in the most inhumane conditions, they'd need a lot of room to have a viable breeding population. Maybe now that they've had some success, they need to introduce a little more genetic diversity."

Raphael was nodding. "You could be right. We definitely had trouble with that at The Healing Circle. We tried to manipulate the DNA as much as possible to counter the effects of inbreeding, but it got progressively harder with each new generation."

My lip curled with distaste. "So what you mean is they're sending out Tommy to act as a stud, and most likely if any of those women get pregnant, they're going to suddenly disappear, never to be heard of again." Bad enough that the demons were raising humans as lab rats. At least those humans wouldn't know any better. But to snatch some unsuspecting pregnant chick and stick her in some kind of sick breeding facility . . . I shuddered and gave Raphael another glare of disgust. His lips thinned, but he had no answer for my accusation.

"So what about the cancer?" I asked. "Why does Tommy want girls with cancer in their families?"

"I don't know," Raphael answered, "but I can take a guess. It may be that they're trying to harness and accelerate the rapid cell division that comes with cancer. If they can make the cells divide at super speed, then maybe they can heal faster." He shrugged. "It's sort of what we do when we heal our hosts now, only we're limited by what the human body is capable of."

I shook my head. "Remember when you were trying to tell me how breeding these hardier hosts was actually to those hosts' benefit?"

Raphael squirmed a bit and didn't look at me. "I could be wrong. I'm just guessing what the significance of the cancer is."

"Doesn't matter! There's no way it's good for

anyone to have their chances of getting cancer genetically increased. We are *so* exorcizing that damn demon." I no longer cared if it was illegal. If it was the last thing I did, I was sending that creature back to the Demon Realm. It sure would be nice if I could just kill it, but much as I disapproved of Tommy's life choices, I wasn't ruthless enough to burn him to death to kill the demon.

Adam shook his head. "No, we are not."

I shot to my feet, an indignant response on my lips. Brian, who was sitting next to me on the couch, grabbed my arm and hauled me back down. I was so surprised I just sat there and stared at him.

"I doubt jumping up and down and yelling is going to be very effective," Brian said reasonably, though far be it from me to be reasonable when my dander was up.

I wasn't sure who I was most pissed at right now, Brian or Adam. I chose Adam. I stayed in my seat as I prepared to ream him out, but he beat me to the punch.

"If Tommy suddenly shows up sans demon, who do you think is going to be the prime suspect?" he asked, sounding as reasonable as Brian.

I clenched my teeth. I already knew that, had already made the same argument to Claudia. But, damn it, I couldn't just sit back and do nothing! I had to stop that demon from making any number of women into broodmares with cancer-riddled children. And I had to stop his buddies from hurting Claudia's daughters.

My heart pounded with my fury, and my nails dug into my palms as I tried to think of an argument that would convince Adam and company that it was okay to perform an illegal exorcism. After we gently convinced Tommy's demon to tell us where the children were, that is.

"So maybe he shouldn't show up sans demon," Raphael said, and we all turned to him. His expression was studiously neutral, but I thought I detected a hint of excitement in him.

"Explain," Adam urged.

But I was pretty sure I knew what Raphael was about to say, and it was hard to hear him over the sudden pounding of my heart.

"I agreed to move out of Andrew if I felt safe enough to do it and if we could find me another host. I believe Lugh and I have reached a formal peace, and that Morgan wouldn't kill my host just to send me back to the Demon Realm. It therefore occurs to me that Tommy could fulfill the latter requirement for me. After all, considering his rather extreme prejudices, I expect he is not faring well with his current demon and is unlikely to be intact after an exorcism."

No one said anything. I don't know about the rest of them, but my mind was yammering at me nonstop. I could save my brother and save Tommy's herd of broodmares all in one fell swoop. All I had to do was give up a God's Wrath fanatic who would cheerfully burn me at the stake if he had a chance.

Brian put a comforting hand on my back, and, despite my audience, I leaned into the touch. There were so many problems I could solve just by letting Raphael take Tommy. And yet my conscience balked at it. I wanted to scream in frustration and confusion. Then Adam went and made things worse.

"There is another demon we've been hoping to find a host for," he said, and I couldn't suppress my groan.

My head felt too heavy to hold up, so I lowered it into my hands. This wasn't fair! Sure I was a control freak, but it was only *my* life I wanted to control. I didn't want to have to make life or death decisions for Andrew, or Tommy, or Dominic. And yet even with my head buried in my hands, I felt the weight of everyone's expectations.

I don't know whether it was merely because I was hosting Lugh, or whether it was because I was so naturally bossy, but somehow all three of these strong, decisive, confident men had handed the reins of leadership to me. How was I supposed to make a decision like this? *Lugh?* I pleaded. *A little guidance, maybe?* Of course, I didn't hear a peep out of him. Either he, too, considered this my decision to make, or my subconscious had once again shored up my defenses.

"I seem to have missed a memo," Raphael said, interrupting my pity party. "Who is the other demon in need of a host?"

I'd forgotten Raphael wouldn't know about Lugh's decision to summon Saul to the Mortal Plain. Luckily, Adam saved me the discomfort of having to explain.

"Ah," Raphael said when he was finished. "So my brother would have both me and Saul serving on his council. Well, it certainly won't be boring." He answered my question before I even opened my mouth to ask it. "Let's just say that Saul and I don't get along and leave it at that, shall we?" Adam made a sound between a cough and a choke, and Raphael gave him a quelling look. "And because of your attachment to Dominic, you don't wish Saul to return to him. Is that the situation?"

"Yes."

I heard the edge in Adam's voice, so I forced myself to sit up straight and get ready to intervene should things get ugly.

"I would have expected you of all people to put your duty above your own personal desires," Raphael said to Adam.

I laughed. I couldn't help it, though the laughter took on an edge of hysteria. Both Adam and Raphael glared at me. Brian, my rock, simply rubbed my back in silent support. I bit my tongue to stave off the hysteria.

"Sorry," I said. "But you've gotta admit, Raphael pontificating about duty and self-sacrifice is pretty damn funny."

Adam made a snorting sound that might have been agreement, laughter, or a burp. Raphael stuck with the death glare. Okay, so maybe it wasn't funny to *him*.

"It's not Adam's decision anyway," I said, meeting Raphael's glare. "It's Dominic's."

"So you would prefer to summon Saul into Tommy, when he already has a demonstrably compatible host available to him, and leave me in your brother? And here I thought you cared."

I was about to snarl at him, but Brian startled me into silence.

"Aren't we getting ahead of ourselves?" he asked. "Perhaps we should worry about what to do with Tommy *after* his demon's been exorcized—and after we've figured out what to do about the children."

Ouch. I guess I shouldn't lecture Raphael about being self-centered after all.

Adam visibly relaxed, stepping away from the edge of battle. After a moment, Raphael did the same, and some of the weight lifted off my chest. The issue wasn't going away, and I felt sure I would have to face it again soon. But "soon" was better than "now."

I looked at Adam. "May I assume you agree that we're better off handling this off the books?"

He waved a hand dismissively. "Of course."

"And may I also assume that you're not going to argue we need to sacrifice those kids for the greater good?"

"I don't think the 'greater good' is at issue. *You*, of course, will stay far away from Tommy and his pals so Lugh isn't at risk. *I'll* see what I can do about finding the kids."

I swallowed the protest that tried to crawl out of my mouth. If Adam thought I'd sit idly by and let him take care of everything, then he didn't know me very well.

He smiled at me suddenly, his eyes glowing with a spark that had nothing to do with his demon. "I know I've mentioned this before, but it bears repeating. You *really* need to work on your poker face. You leave me with no choice but to make an executive decision. You're going to stay here while I go have a talk with Tommy, see if I can find out where he and his friends are holding the children."

Damn it, damn it, damn it! When was I going to learn how to control my facial expressions? I began sliding my hand to the side, though I figured the chances of me getting to my Taser, arming it, pointing it, and shooting before someone stopped me were approximately zero.

I was right. Brian grabbed my hand and gave it a squeeze. He made it look like it was just a gesture of support, but I knew he'd read me as easily as Adam had. I glanced at Raphael, wondering if there was any chance I could convince him to take my side, but that was a stupid idea. Raphael would never agree to let Lugh take any "unnecessary" risks.

I jerked my hand from Brian's and crossed my arms over my chest. "Fine!" I said, sounding sulky even to my own ears. "I'll sit on my ass while you go out and play hero." Adam gave me a knowing look, and I gritted my teeth. "Don't look at me like that. I got the point. You're going to lock me up."

Beside me, I felt Brian start. There was a lot he didn't know about the water under Adam's and my bridge. I supposed I should fill him in on some of it someday. But not now.

Raphael rubbed his hands together. "So Adam is going to play policeman, Morgan's going to twiddle her thumbs, and I presume Brian's going to resume his usual daily activities. Do I have an assignment, or may I follow Brian's lead?"

Instinct told me there was something off about Raphael's voice, but I just didn't have the energy to think about it right now. "I doubt you want to hear the instructions I have for you," I muttered, loud enough for everyone to hear. Raphael didn't seem to find it as funny as the others did.

Our impromptu council meeting broke up after that. Brian had been a bit startled when he discovered Adam planned to lock me up, but instead of arguing for clemency, he offered to keep me company. I imagined it would have been fun, but I was way too surly to be in the mood for fun.

"You'll keep her safe?" Brian inquired of Adam, which, naturally, pissed me off.

"I'll keep my own damn self safe!"

Adam shook his head at Brian. "I can't imagine how you could actually *want* to be in her presence." Lucky for him he'd been smart enough to confiscate my Taser already.

I could have hoped that Brian would take offense that Adam was insulting me, but he just shrugged. "I can see behind the prickly exterior," he said, then ignored Adam and fixed me with a pointed look. "Call me if there's any news, or if there's anything I can do to help."

I agreed, and Brian, visibly reluctant, left.

The room Adam locked me in was right next door to the Dreaded Black Room. The door was closed when Adam led me by, and I wondered if Dominic was in there. I was too pissed off that Adam saw through me so well to ask, however. And so by lunchtime, on a day when my instincts screamed at me to act, to fight, to move, I found myself a prisoner in a comfortable little guest room with convenient iron grillwork covering the windows. Yup, another peachy day in the life of Morgan Kingsley, exorcist.

Chapter **22**

I paced the "guest room" for about an hour. Probably I should have been taking advantage of this period of forced inactivity to catch a few Zs, but I didn't think I'd have much luck falling asleep. I was starting to get hungry, my stomach protesting my failure to eat either breakfast or lunch, when I heard footsteps in the hallway. I smelled food, and my stomach immediately let out a howl that would have been embarrassing if I thought anyone could hear it. I guessed that meant my visitor would be Dominic, not Adam, and I had a momentary urge to rush the door and see if I could escape in a moment of confusion. But for all I knew, Adam was sitting downstairs, and I'd get my ass handed to me if I tried anything.

The first thing I saw when the door opened was Dominic's back, because his hands were full and he was using his butt to hold the door. When he turned toward me and let the door go, his head was bowed, and I thought at first he was keeping an eye on the bowl of soup that rested on the tray he carried. But then he turned to put the tray on a desk, and a beam of light illuminated the side of his face.

I gasped when I saw his ostentatiously black eye. His Adam's apple bobbed, and he let out a sigh as he turned to face me. He crossed his arms over his chest, and his body language screamed that he wanted to be left alone. I doubt he was surprised I ignored it.

"How'd you get the shiner?" I asked, though I knew from his discomfort who must have given it to him.

He grimaced. "Adam. And no, he didn't do it on purpose, so quit looking at me like I'm some battered woman."

I tried to picture Adam hauling back and punching Dominic, and I just couldn't do it. I realized with a little start that despite Adam's aggressive and overbearing personality, I'd never once seen him and Dominic fight. Oh, they grumbled at each other occasionally, but even then it was with such affection it was obvious they didn't mean it. And it wasn't because Dominic was a doormat, either. He stood up to Adam in situations that would have had me running for the hills.

Come to think of it—and this was a really scary thought—theirs was probably the healthiest romantic relationship I'd ever seen.

Dominic's shoulders were tight with tension, and his jaw worked like he was grinding his teeth. Everything about him screamed defensiveness, and I realized he was braced for an argument. I let go of my own tension and flashed him a rueful smile.

"Relax, Dom. I believe you." He blinked in surprise, but with my stomach reminding me once again that I was hungry and that there was food nearby, I decided questioning Dominic could wait, so I took a seat at the desk and dug into the bowl of soup. I let out a moan of sensual pleasure when I tasted it. I'd never been a huge fan of minestrone, but I now saw the error of my ways.

Dominic got that pleased look he always gets when someone compliments his cooking, then took a seat on the recliner and waited in silence for me to finish eating. It didn't take long.

"Would it be terribly uncouth of me to lick the bowl?" I asked, wanting to see his smile. I got my wish.

"You don't need to go to such drastic measures. Seconds are available."

I patted my full tummy. "I'd love to spend the rest of the afternoon stuffing my face, but I've got to watch my girlish figure." That won me another smile.

Dominic reached for the tray, but though I'd have liked to let him leave on a high note, I just didn't have it in me.

"So, are you going to tell me what happened between you and Adam?" I prodded.

The smile faded and his shoulders drooped. If I read the look on his face correctly, he was seriously contemplating leaving without answering me. I'm not sure I would have blamed him if he did, but he's not as likely as I am to run from conflict. He set the tray back down and returned to the recliner.

"He told me everything," Dominic said. "About Saul, and about what he does at The Seven Deadlies."

I winced. There was such a thing as too much honesty. I wished Adam had kept the last part to himself, at least until we'd gotten Saul another host—however we were going to manage that.

"Did you decide anything?" I asked, then practically held my breath as I awaited the answer.

He nodded. "A number of things, actually." He started counting off on his fingers. "One, that Adam's a prick."

I couldn't help a snort of laughter. I would have felt

bad about that if the corner of Dom's mouth hadn't twitched upward ever so slightly.

"Two, that he's an *insecure* prick. And three, that I'm a mean little bastard for not immediately reassuring him that I don't want to host Saul again."

For reasons I didn't want to examine, I rose from my chair and gave Dominic a quick, awkward hug. "I'll agree with your assessment of Adam, but if you're a mean little bastard, then I'm Miss Sunshine-and-Roses."

He laughed and visibly relaxed. "Thanks for the vote of confidence. But I really was pretty mean to Adam earlier. I wish he'd had enough faith in me to tell me about The Seven Deadlies from the start, but I understand why he didn't."

"And have you told him yet that you're not going to take Saul back?"

He shook his head. "I was too busy brooding, and now he's gone off to talk to a hostile demon who inhabits a superhost who may have abilities of which we are not aware. I feel like shit."

"I'm sure he'll be fine," I said, and I meant it. It was hard to imagine Adam getting into any kind of trouble he couldn't handle. Perhaps I was overestimating him, but his combination of competence and confidence made him seem almost invulnerable to me.

"Do you have any idea where he's gone?"

I shook my head. "No. Why?"

Dom's lips pressed together in a tight line, his eyes narrowed in pain. "Because I'm worried about him. I hurt him, and I'm worried he'll be distracted by it, get himself in trouble..."

I thought I understood what Dominic was trying to say, even though he didn't come right out and say it. "You want me to go look for him?"

His brilliant smile lit up his face. "Would you? He's

turned his phone off, and I don't know how to reach him. I want to make sure he knows I'm staying before he faces Tommy."

I almost took him up on it without thinking, but every once in a while I surprise myself by considering the consequences of my actions. "You know he's going to be pissed at you for letting me go."

Dom's smile turned into a grin. "Do you think I'm afraid of him? It won't be the first time I've pissed him off, and it won't be the last, either." He sobered and looked at me gravely. "Sometimes he has trouble understanding that people have a right to decide things for themselves, even if he doesn't like their decisions."

I had a feeling he was talking about more than my own situation. Had Adam tried to bully Dom into not taking Saul back? That would explain why Dom hadn't rushed in to reassure him.

"All right," I said. "I'll go see if I can find Adam and make sure his head is in the game where it belongs. But first you have to tell me about the black eye." I believed him when he said Adam didn't do it on purpose, but considering they'd obviously argued, I felt like I *had* to know the circumstances before I could get near Adam without killing him. "Were you fighting?"

Dom stared at his hands in apparent fascination. "We were play-fighting, though we both should have known better. You don't do any kind of BDSM play when you're angry. At least, you *shouldn't*." I must have looked horrified, because he hastened to reassure me. "We weren't throwing punches or anything, just wrestling. Of course, I don't stand a chance of winning a wrestling match with a demon, so usually I don't try very hard. But I was angry, so I fought harder than usual, and I managed to break his grip." A wry smile twisted his lip. "I was as surprised as he was, so I lost my balance. You've seen the bed next door."

Yes, I had. It was a massive king-sized black iron bed that looked heavy enough to fall through the floor.

"I ran into it face-first. Adam managed to catch me or it probably would have been much worse."

If it were anyone else, I might have thought this story equivalent to the "I bumped into a door" story that's the staple of battered women everywhere. But I believed Dominic, and that meant I could go off in pursuit of Adam without wanting to kill him.

I don't know what was to stop Adam from dragging me right back to my civilized little prison cell the moment I found him, but I'd worry about that later. I smiled at Dom to let him know I bought his story.

"Do you happen to know where Adam stashed my Taser when he confiscated it?"

"No, but I'm sure we can find it."

Picking up the tray, he led me out of my cell.

I can't tell you how relieved I was to get out of that house, though I felt a little like I'd escaped under false pretenses. I'd promised Dominic I'd look for Adam, but I had no real hope of success. Philly is a big city, and I had no idea where he'd gone. Naturally, I tried stopping by Tommy's place, but no one, not even his slimy roommate, seemed to be home. I then tried Adam's office number, even though I doubted he'd officially gone back to work on his "sick day." I was right.

Other than The Seven Deadlies, I didn't know where else Tommy was likely to hang out. It was now three o'clock in the afternoon, and the club wouldn't open until nine. I tried Adam's cell phone on the off chance he'd turned it back on since the last time Dom had called, but no dice. I even tried calling Claudia, but she was in a meeting—not with Adam, because I asked—and couldn't be disturbed. I declined to leave a message. I'm sure the kidnappers had commanded her to go about her day as if nothing were wrong, but I hoped the fact that she was in a meeting meant the children were okay.

It was almost five when I admitted defeat. Until The Seven Deadlies opened, I had no clue where to find Adam. I called Dom to let him know I was going back to my apartment, and he confirmed that Adam still hadn't returned any of his calls. The worry in Dom's voice was contagious, but neither one of us could come up with any brilliant ideas. I gave Dom strict orders to call me if he heard from Adam, then headed home.

My day was not improved when I found a reporter for the *Philadelphia Inquirer* camped out in the lobby of my building. Not the same reporter who'd been calling me on the phone, but I recognized her as press—perhaps because of the whiff of brimstone that clung to her—as soon as she sprang up out of her chair and strode toward me.

If I ran for the elevator, would I be able to get in and get the door closed before she caught me? With my luck, that would be a big no. So instead I turned to glower at her, arms akimbo, body language screaming "get the fuck away from me."

She couldn't possibly have missed the message, but I suppose reporters were used to ignoring hostility, since she came right up to me anyway and stuck out her hand.

"You must be Morgan Kingsley," she said with a polished smile. "I'm Barbara—"

My smile was so polished the edges could cut

through diamond. "I don't care who you are. I have no comment, and I want you to stay out of my hair."

Her shapely eyebrows rose. She held out a press badge for me to examine. I ignored it and turned toward the elevators. Barbara What's-Her-Name followed, her businesslike black pumps making clicking noises as she tried to catch up. Naturally, both elevators were near the top of the building. I hit the Up button with more force than necessary.

"You know," Barbara said as she settled in to wait beside me, "I'm from the *Philadelphia Inquirer,* not the *National Enquirer.* There's no reason to be so skittish."

I tried to pretend she wasn't there. With all the crap I was going through in my life, you'd think the universe would give me a break once in a while! But no, why would anyone think that?

"So you have no comment about the death of Jordan Maguire Jr.?"

I stared at the blinking lights above the elevators, wishing the damn things weren't about a hundred years old and slow as tortoises.

Reporter Barbie was undaunted. "What about Jordan Maguire Sr.'s threats to file suit?"

I blinked. This was the first I'd heard of it, and I groaned internally. Just what I needed—more trouble. One of the elevators was still at floor twenty, but the other one was making its way down steadily. Fifteen, fourteen, twelve—because this was an old building and had no thirteenth floor—eleven, ten... And then the damned thing stopped, and I almost howled in frustration.

"Is there anything you'd do differently if you had a chance to do it all over again?" Barbie continued, as if I'd been answering her questions all along.

The elevator stayed on floor ten, and I decided

enough was enough. I walked back into the lobby and caught the doorman's attention. He was a big black guy built like a linebacker, but he was one of those gentle giants who wouldn't hurt a fly. I'd talked to him just enough to know he was a starving artist who worked the door to keep food on the table while he pursued a career as a painter. Still, Barbie didn't know any of that.

"Hey, Mike," I said with a big smile, "is there any chance you can help me get rid of an unwanted visitor?" I jerked my thumb at Barbie.

He returned my smile. "Sure thing," he said, then looked at Barbie. The smile gave way to a politely blank expression. "Ma'am, this is a private building. I'm afraid I'm going to have to ask you to leave."

Reminding myself to slip Mike a generous tip later, I pivoted back toward the bank of elevators. Barbie started to protest, but Mike was firm. I breathed a sigh of relief when the elevator doors closed behind me. I felt a little less relieved when I remembered the death threat on my answering machine last night. Great to know everyone and their brother was gunning for me!

I half-expected there to be another death threat when I finally let myself into my apartment, since the universe seemed to be piling it on right now. The fact that there were no messages made me practically cheerful. Yeah, welcome to my life.

I scrounged up a dinner, if you could call it that, of a toasted frozen bagel and dry cereal. I hadn't had much chance to hit the grocery store lately. Then I spent the rest of the evening alternating between trying Adam's cell phone number and checking in with Dom. I decided *not* to call Brian. He thought I was safely locked up in Adam's house, and he'd probably feel it his duty as my knight-in-shining-armor to come "protect" me if he knew I was alone. I'm not very good at accepting help even when I need it, but I seriously didn't think the bad guys were going to storm my building. I'm sure they could get past security if they wanted to—obviously, they'd done it once already—but they'd still have to get through my door. I kept my Taser in my pocket just the same.

I was really starting to get pissed off at Adam. If he was in trouble, I'd feel guilty about it later, but right now I figured he was probably just sulking over his little spat with Dom. I didn't think members of Lugh's council should be allowed to sulk. Except me, of course. I could sulk all I wanted.

When I still hadn't heard anything from Adam by nine o'clock, I decided it was time for me to put in yet another appearance at The Seven Deadlies. Unless he was in trouble, he was bound to be there, staking the place out, looking for Tommy. We had never really discussed what would happen if he found him, but I felt pretty sure Tommy wouldn't enjoy the encounter.

This time, I didn't particularly care if I fit in with the crowd, so I dressed in jeans and a plain white button-down. The only nod I made to the Seven Deadlies crowd was to wear a single skull and crossbones earring with bright, genuine rubies in the eyeholes. Brian had bought it for me as a semi-joke, though it looked too expensive to be relegated to the junk drawer. I put an assortment of gold and silver studs in the remaining holes, then stared myself in the eye in the bathroom mirror and tried to convince myself I was ready.

I wasn't ready, and I knew it. But other than washing my hands of the whole situation, I had no other choice, so I guessed that meant I was going.

I still hadn't bothered to deal with the flat tire, so I called a cab to take me to South Street. It was well past ten when I headed for the club. Still pretty early for the Friday night club scene, but then I'd rather get there before the place was completely packed with demons and their groupies. Making sure the cabbie couldn't see me past the partition, I opened my purse and re-arranged everything so that the Taser was in a compartment by itself. Easier to grab that way. All the other pockets were full to bursting, making for un-sightly lumps, but oh well.

As soon as I closed the purse, it rang. Great. My cell phone was buried at the bottom by now. I dug through all my junk and reminded myself I had to clean out my purse someday. I finally got my fingers wrapped around the phone, and I knew it was seconds before the call would go to voice mail. I answered just in time, but I hadn't had the chance to check caller ID yet.

"Hello?"

"Dominic tells me you're not where I left you," Adam said, and though my hackles immediately rose, I couldn't deny the relief that surged through me. I was glad Adam couldn't see me. I had the feeling I'd never hear the end of it if he thought I'd been worried about him.

When uncomfortable, get angry, that's my motto. With Adam, it was never a hard one to live by. "Where the fuck are you?" I asked, too loudly. I saw the cabbie glance at me in the rearview mirror. Like about ninety percent of the cabbies in Philadelphia, he wasn't born in the good old U.S. of A. By the looks of him, he'd been born in a place where they cut out a woman's tongue if she let such a filthy word leave her mouth. I lowered my voice, and vowed to edit my language.

"Dom and I have both been trying to reach you for hours!"

"So I heard. Let's just say I needed a little me-time."

"When those children—" I stopped myself before I

finished the sentence. The driver was obviously listening, so it seemed prudent for me to be a tad more discreet.

"I was explaining why I had the phone turned off," Adam growled. "I don't mean I've been gazing at my navel. I've presently got a good friend of ours passed out in the backseat."

"Oh." The good news was, I wouldn't have to go back to The Seven Deadlies. The bad news was... Well, I wasn't sure what the bad news was yet. All I was sure of was that there would be some seriously bad news soon. "How did that happen?" I asked, because demons don't just have attacks of the vapors.

"He had a little too much to drink."

"Oh," I said again. A brilliant conversationalist, that's me. Demons are as capable of getting drunk as humans, although they usually metabolize the alcohol faster so their drunkenness doesn't last long. Still, it seemed awfully careless of Tommy, especially if he had any inkling that Adam was investigating him.

"I helped him along a bit," Adam explained. "We're on the way back to the house now. I thought you might want to meet us there."

No, I wanted to tell the driver to turn around and take me home. But I supposed that would be irresponsible. I sternly ordered myself not to think about what would happen to Tommy when whatever knockout drops Adam had given him wore off. I didn't think it was going to be pretty.

"I guess I have to," I said. I didn't actually mean to say it out loud.

"Yes. We might need Lugh."

I closed my eyes for a second, wondering just what Adam thought we might need Lugh for. To exorcise Tommy's demon? I supposed it was in the realm of possibility that whatever demon had taken Tommy was beyond my ability or Adam's ability to exorcize. But I suspected that wasn't what Adam meant. We would need to know Saul's True Name if we wanted to summon him, and the only people who would know it were his close family members . . . and his king.

"I'll be there soon," was all I said. I hung up abruptly, because I didn't want Adam to hear anything suspicious in my voice. Then I gave the driver Raphael's address and braced myself for one very nerve-wracking phone call.

Chapter **23**

Convincing Raphael to come with me to Adam's wasn't exactly difficult. Even over the phone, I heard what I could swear was repressed excitement. I knew he and my brother didn't get along, and if he really was treating Andy better this time around, it meant he had to interact with him more than he'd like. Perhaps he was just excited at the thought that he might find a new, more enjoyable host. But I didn't think that was it.

No matter how loyal Raphael might be to Lugh, I had to agree with Lugh's assessment of him: he was a liar. He knew more about the Houston project than he'd admitted, and for some reason he was very, very eager to have Tommy host him.

What was it about Tommy that made demons everywhere fall over themselves in order to acquire his body? I suspected I wouldn't know unless and until one of Lugh's allies ended up in possession of Tommy's body.

And therein lay the crux of my moral dilemma. Could I really stand to let anyone, even a fanatic like Tommy Brewster, be possessed against his will?

Demonic possession had been my own worst nightmare, and though I had learned to live with it to some extent, I still longed for the days when I was alone in my body. And not only was I a hell of a lot more compatible with Lugh than Tommy would be with Raphael, but I also still had control of my body. It wouldn't be the same for Tommy, and he would suffer. *If* I let this happen.

I hadn't reached anything that resembled a conclusion by the time the cab pulled up in front of my brother's apartment building. Raphael was waiting at the curb and quickly slipped in while the car behind us honked in indignation at the delay. Gotta love Philadelphia drivers. Always so polite and understanding.

I gave the cabbie Adam's address, and we were off again.

"Does Adam know I'm coming?" Raphael asked.

I grimaced. "In this case I decided to adopt your philosophy of asking forgiveness rather than permission."

He looked like he was about to say something, but then his gaze darted to the driver and his mouth thinned into a hard line. I, of course, was not at all unhappy to have our own personal censor available. I didn't want to talk about what I was contemplating. I'd put off deciding what to do for as long as I could manage it. And maybe even longer.

We rode the rest of the way in silence. I wished Adam lived farther away, though I don't suppose having more time would have made me any more prepared. I gave the driver a generous tip, which I couldn't afford, and then stood on the pavement for a long moment, staring at Adam's house, not wanting to go in yet.

Raphael had no such problems, and before I was ready, he'd hurried up the steps and rung the bell. My throat felt tight with panic, but I fought it off as best I could.

It was Dom who answered the door. I supposed Adam was keeping an eye on our prisoner. Dominic raised his eyebrows when he saw Raphael, but didn't comment.

"Come on in. The party's just getting started." There was a hint of strain in his voice. He was too nice a guy to like Adam's interrogation methods, but though he disliked them, he didn't seem inclined to protest. Then again, maybe he already had.

"Adam's not going to be happy to see you," Dom said to Raphael as soon as the door closed.

Raphael shrugged. "Doesn't much matter. I'm a member of your merry band now whether you want me or not."

Something sparked in Dom's eyes. He looked like a man about ready to take a swing at a rival. I guess that meant he was *really* having a hard time with Adam's methods. He'd always been the calm one in the face of Adam's or my temper before.

Raphael went on the ready, his shoulders drawing up and back, his posture stiffening. I rolled my eyes and laughed, hoping to defuse the tension.

"If one of you guys starts pounding his chest and yodeling, I'm outta here."

Dominic laughed suddenly, and Raphael lost the aggressive body language. Just your average, everyday peacekeeper, that's me.

"Are they . . . ?" I asked, tilting my head toward the ceiling over which the black room loomed.

The laughter faded quickly from Dom's eyes. "Yeah. Do you, uh, need me up there?"

I stared at him a long moment. I pitied the misery that showed on his face. But not enough to let him off the hook. "You don't get to hide your head in the sand

and pretend nothing bad is happening," I told him, though I kept my voice as gentle as I could manage. "I know you don't want to see Adam showing his true colors. I don't, either. But we're both going to have to suck it up."

A hint of fire flared in his eyes again. My, he sure was touchy tonight. I guess knowing your lover was going to torture someone could do that to you. But there was truth in my words, and even Dominic had to admit it. Or at least he couldn't find a way to argue it.

Looking grim but determined, he headed toward the stairs without another word. Raphael and I followed.

Déjà vu plagued me as I climbed those stairs toward the black room. I remembered a frantic rush up the stairs, a desperate desire to stop Adam from hurting my best friend. I remembered Val's screams, and I remembered the sound of her neck breaking. I hadn't been able to stop Adam that time. And this time, I wasn't even sure I wanted to. The realization did not sit well in my stomach.

Dominic took a deep breath, then opened the door.

Adam and company were waiting for us. Though I'm not sure Tommy knew he was waiting—he looked like he might be passed out still. Or again.

Adam caught sight of Raphael, then turned to glare at me. I tried to look innocent. I suppose the expression doesn't sit well on my face, since Adam kept glaring.

Dominic stepped into the room and closed the door behind him, drawing Adam's attention. I let out the breath I hadn't realized I was holding.

"Why don't you wait for us downstairs," Adam said, and at that moment there might as well have been no one in the room except him and Dom.

To his credit, Dom refused the opportunity to

shove responsibility for his presence on my shoulders, even though that was where it belonged. He kept his gaze locked with Adam's, not even flicking the briefest glance in my direction.

"I'm not going to hide downstairs," Dom said. "We've decided we're going to be open with one another, haven't we?"

Adam looked remarkably uncomfortable. I guess it was kind of tough for him to torture someone when his lover was looking on. Not that Dom didn't already know how ruthless Adam was. He did, and loved Adam anyway. But knowing something and seeing it are two different things. I almost convinced myself to tell Adam why Dom had decided to stay and to let Dom escape, but not quite. It just didn't sit well with me to condone Adam's behavior but then not be willing to bear witness.

"Are you sure?" Adam asked.

Dom crossed his arms over his chest and shivered. But he nodded.

"Fine," Adam said, a hint of sharpness in his voice. "Just keep out of the way." Adam turned his attention away from Dom, and I followed his gaze.

Tommy lay on the floor, not moving. A heavy stun belt circled his waist.

"Since you're here, you might as well make yourself useful," Adam said to Raphael, shoving something at him. "I may need to use both hands."

I saw that he'd handed Raphael the trigger device for the stun belt. Raphael nodded his agreement, and Adam went to squat in front of Tommy.

"Time to stop playing possum," he said. "I know you're awake in there." Tommy didn't move, and Adam let out a huff of exasperation. "If you're going to start being difficult already, this is going to be a very long night. When I asked around about you at the club, everyone agreed you're much more into giving pain than taking it. So I can either prove you're awake by breaking a finger and listening to you scream, or you could just sit up."

By this time, even I could see that Adam was right and that Tommy was awake. Although his eyes were still closed and his breathing steady, his muscles had visibly tensed. Finally, he swallowed hard and opened his eyes.

"Good boy," Adam said with a sneer.

Tommy didn't seem to like that much. He snarled, baring his teeth.

"Behave," Raphael said, holding up the stun belt trigger.

Tommy suppressed the snarl and struggled up into a sitting position. "You're all going to fry for this," he said, setting his face into a petulant expression that was probably one of the human Tommy's favorites. "I'm a legally registered demon, and you can't—"

"*You're* the one locked in my room with a stun belt around your waist."

Tommy seemed about to retort, but then it must have occurred to him that if we were all so blatantly breaking the law it must mean we thought it didn't matter.

"You're going to exorcize me," he said, sounding stunned. He looked at me, eyes wide. "You're going to jail for the rest of your life for this!"

"No one here's going to jail," Adam said. "*You're* going back to the Demon Realm, though." Tommy started. "Yes," Adam confirmed, "everyone here already knows exorcism doesn't kill us."

Tommy's lip curled again. "If you know it's not going to kill me, then you know I'll be back someday and kill everyone here."

"You can try. You might find it a little harder than

you imagine. But that's beside the point. What's important is that you can either go back quickly and painlessly, or you can go back after I've shown you what an amateur you are at inflicting pain."

Tommy's eyes narrowed. "And what would I have to do to get this quick and painless exorcism?"

"Tell us who has the children and where they are."

Tommy's jaw dropped, and those narrowed eyes widened. "Children? What children?" Then he suddenly screamed and collapsed.

It took me a second to figure out what had happened, but when I did I turned to look over my shoulder at Raphael, who was smiling as his finger hovered over the trigger.

"Should I give you another jolt just for fun?" he asked. "Don't lie to a liar. We're far too good at picking up each other's tells."

All Tommy could do at the moment was glare. The electricity fucks up a demon's control of the nervous system so badly they're essentially helpless. Unfortunately, it meant his tongue wasn't functioning too well, either, so we had to wait until he'd recovered before we could get anything but drool out of him.

Eventually, he regained control and managed to sit up again. There was a glint of fear in his eyes, but his face was set in stubborn lines. "I have no idea what you're talking about," he said.

Adam held up his hand in a gesture obviously meant to stop Raphael from zapping Tommy again. "If we have to wait ten minutes for him to recover every time, this is going to take all night," he said. "Just zap him if he tries anything."

"Sure thing, boss," Raphael said dryly.

Adam paid no attention to him, instead piercing Tommy with a look that should have left him bleeding. "If you think the stun belt hurt, you ain't seen nothing yet. Now, would you like to reconsider your answer?"

Tommy firmed up his resolve, getting that stubborn, mulish expression on his face once more. I tensed, and out of the corner of my eye, I saw Dominic tense, too. Neither one of us wanted to see whatever Adam was going to do now. We both stood with our arms crossed over our chests. I seriously considered not watching, but that seemed like cowardice, especially when I had guilted Dom into being here.

I held my breath as Adam casually reached for Tommy. I had no idea what he was going to do.

And I didn't get to find out, because, before he laid a hand on Tommy, there was the distinctive pop of a Taser, and Adam went completely limp.

Chapter 24

It was Raphael who'd Tasered Adam. Why was I not surprised? Raphael seemed to make a habit of Tasering his allies.

It was only by force of will that I was able to sound relatively calm. "I'm having déjà vu," I said to Raphael as Dom rushed to Adam's side. "This is the part where you change sides again, isn't it?"

He smiled at me. "No. This is the part where we cut through the bullshit and get this over with in something less than five years." He put the Taser away. He was still holding the trigger for the stun belt, so Tommy wasn't going anywhere, though I'm sure he must have been enjoying this evidence of dissension in the ranks.

Dominic, after confirming that Adam wasn't injured, took a menacing step toward Raphael. I grabbed his arm, but he was a lot bigger than me, so I wasn't stopping him if he was determined to play macho man. It wasn't typical behavior for him, but he was as capable of going Tarzan as anyone when his lover was hurt.

Raphael snorted. "Trust me, Dominic. You don't want to start something with me."

"Come on, Dom," I said, pulling on his arm. "Let's not make this any worse than it already is." I noticed suddenly that Lugh hadn't made an effort to surface, which he usually would have done the moment there was even the slightest hint of danger. I wondered if that meant he knew where Raphael was going with this and didn't object. I hoped so.

Raphael turned to Tommy once more. "We haven't been properly introduced. My name's Andrew Kingsley, and I used to host Raphael." Tommy's face paled at the mention of Raphael's name. "Let me lay it out for you simply. These folks," Raphael said, jerking his thumb in our general direction, "may be badasses in the torture department, but I make them look like pussycats. Raphael taught me everything he knows, as it were. And as you're probably aware, he knows a hell of a lot. Dominic, do you have a fire extinguisher in your kitchen?"

"What the—"

"Just answer me!" Raphael snapped.

Dom's olive skin had paled more than I would have thought possible. "Yes." Of course he did—his kitchen was practically professional grade, except for the pedestrian appliances that came with the house.

"Get it."

Dom looked to me for confirmation. I nodded, and Dom hurried out.

"Now," Raphael said, turning his attention to Tommy once more, "you might be wondering why I need a fire extinguisher. Let me clear that up for you real fast." Still holding the stun belt trigger in one hand, he fished a flask out of his pocket. Man, he'd really loaded up for this. You could tell he'd worked in a lab before, because he had no trouble twisting the cap off the flask with one hand.

Smiling evilly, Raphael blew over the mouth of the flask, spreading the distinctive scent of gasoline throughout the room. I'd thought Dominic was pale; Tommy looked like he was auditioning for a part as an albino.

Dominic returned to the room, fire extinguisher in hand. His face went from white to green when he sniffed the air.

"You might want to get Adam out of the way," Raphael said. "We don't want him getting singed."

Please, God, let this be a bluff. Only I knew Raphael too well. He wasn't bluffing. I could see it in his eyes, and I bet Tommy could, too.

Dominic looked like he wanted to argue, but one look from Raphael banished whatever he'd been about to say. He put down the fire extinguisher, then grabbed Adam under the arms and pulled him away from Tommy.

"I'm sure if they thought they could take me, Morgan and Dominic would try to stop me from lighting you," Raphael said to Tommy. "Adam would even have been able to do it, but he's not available to come to your rescue just now. So here's the deal: you tell me where those children are, who's holding them, and how many of them there are, and I'll let Morgan exorcize you.

"Otherwise, I start toasting marshmallows and lead Dominic and Morgan in a rousing rendition of 'Kumbaya.' Which would you prefer?"

Tommy didn't answer immediately. I think he was on the verge of hyperventilating. It seemed he hadn't been prepared to face threats of death.

Raphael splashed some gasoline out of his flask

onto Tommy's lap. Tommy yelped and tried to get away, but Raphael held up the trigger.

"I wouldn't if I were you. Who knows? The stun belt might not react well with gasoline. Now tell me where the kids are. If I have to ask you again, I'm going to light you."

Tommy was trembling, and I didn't think all the liquid that stained his jeans was gasoline. "If you kill me, you'll never find those children," he said through chattering teeth.

"If you're willing to let me kill you rather than tell me where they are, you're no good to us anyway." He splashed out a little more gas, and Tommy started to cry.

"Okay, okay!" he said, and it was practically a scream. "I'll tell you. Just don't—"

"Don't waste time telling me you're *going* to tell me. Just tell me."

"They're in the basement of Claudia's house."

Raphael laughed. "Yeah, right. Try another one."

"They *are*!" Tommy insisted, white showing all around his eyes. "We took them to a safe house overnight, but none of us wants to take care of a couple of screaming, sniveling brats. So we went back to the Brewsters' place with them. That way Claudia can feed them and clean up after them while we keep them...contained."

Raphael looked skeptical, and Tommy's voice rose even higher. "I swear, I'm telling the truth! We've got a hostage to spare, so if Devon or Claudia try anything stupid, they know we can kill one without losing our leverage. They wouldn't dream of risking those kids' lives."

"Hmm," Raphael said, still not looking entirely convinced. "Just how long are you planning to keep them there, anyway?"

Tommy swallowed hard. "Three months."

"What happens in three months?" I asked, though I already knew it wouldn't be anything pleasant.

Tommy didn't answer immediately, so Raphael splashed out a little more gas. That loosened Tommy's tongue.

"After three months of Claudia seeming to accept me as legal, there won't be so much of a spotlight on me."

"That's not what I asked," I said.

Tommy wouldn't meet anyone's eyes. Maybe that meant he felt some remorse. "We were going to shut them up permanently. There was going to be a fire at the house. Since Claudia and Tommy would have been on seemingly good terms by then, no one would suspect me, especially when we left evidence that Tommy's God's Wrath buddies had targeted him."

If Raphael felt any moral outrage at the plan, he didn't show it. "How many demons are in that house?"

"There'll be at least two or three demons in there with them at this time of night. If you try to rescue the girls, you'll just end up getting them killed."

Raphael sneered. "That's not so big a deterrent when you've already admitted that you and your friends are going to kill them anyway. But thanks for the advice. You've been most helpful."

It sounded exactly like what the bad guy would say before he carried out the threat he'd promised not to. Apparently Tommy thought so, too, because he closed his eyes and sobbed.

"Don't you dare!" Dominic said from across the room. He was sitting on the floor with Adam's head on his lap. He'd have to dump Adam back on the floor if he wanted to get to the fire extinguisher.

Raphael chuckled. "Don't worry, I'm not going to

light him. He might be helpful in getting to those kids."

Tommy snorted, amusing Raphael even more.

"Oh, *you* won't be in him when he does. Morgan will take care of that." He frowned. "I suppose we might want to get you out of those wet clothes. Morgan uses candles for the exorcism ritual, and I think that might be a bad idea just now."

Actually, I used vanilla-scented candles, and I didn't exactly carry them around with me at all times. I wondered what the chances were that Adam and Dom had some lying around, but I figured they were slim. I bit my lip, wondering if I'd be able to get into the necessary trance state without my traditional trigger.

I averted my eyes as Tommy took off his wet clothes. My eyes landed on Adam and Dominic. Adam was beginning to regain control of his limbs, but Dom wasn't letting him sit up yet. If Adam wasn't strong enough to fight Dom's restraint, then he wasn't ready to sit up.

"Someone should get a trash bag for Tommy's clothes," I said to no one in particular. Raphael was busy menacing Tommy, Adam was still too weak, and Dominic wasn't about to leave his lover's side, so I slipped out of the room.

I made an educated guess as to where I might find trash bags and headed for the kitchen. It wasn't until I tried to open the cabinet under the sink that I realized my hands were shaking. I supposed Raphael had saved us a lot of time—and, in a strange sort of way, saved Tommy a lot of suffering—by his methods. That didn't mean I liked them. I shuddered and tried not to think about what it would have been like in there if Raphael had lit the fire.

I found the trash bags, but then took a minute or

two to splash some cold water on my face and pull myself together as best I could. Yeah, I was a real badass, all right.

By the time I got back to the room, Adam had recovered enough to sit up. Dom helped him to his feet, and Adam struggled over to the big black bed, sitting down heavily when he reached it.

"You going to be okay?" Dom asked, and Adam nodded.

Dom took the trash bag from my hand, stuffed Tommy's clothes into it, then took the bag away. The room still reeked of gas, and I wasn't sure lighting candles would be a good idea, even if Adam and Dom had the requisite vanilla.

"We discussed logistics while you were gone," Raphael said. "Dom's going to get the candles."

"I don't suppose you've got vanilla," I muttered at Adam.

He looked a little woozy from the Taser shot still, but he managed to smile at me. "Actually, we do. Candles can be a lot of fun, and vanilla's an erotic scent."

I must have looked as clueless as I was, because, of course, Adam had to elaborate.

"Think of it as a kind of erotic hot wax treatment," he said, then waggled his brows at me.

Predictably, my face went hot. I admit I'm pretty naive where the practices of S&M are concerned, and I'd have been perfectly happy to stay that way. Dominic returned with the candles, saving me from having to think of the perfect reply.

"Move away from the wall," Raphael ordered Tommy.

Tommy didn't seem to have any fight left in him. He just did as he was told. Without me having to ask, Dom started laying out the candles in a circle around

Tommy. The circle isn't really necessary for the ritual, but I knew this was going to be a particularly tough exorcism, and I was happy to fall back on tradition.

I wasn't overly concerned that I wouldn't be able to exorcize Tommy's demon. It was what would happen next that had my stomach tied into knots.

Would I really give Tommy over to another demon? In a rare flash of insight, I realized part of the reason I'd been so desperate to exorcize Tommy's demon was my inability to exorcize my own. If I couldn't be free of the demons, at least I could free one other lost soul.

Take one problem at a time, I advised myself, but I'm lousy at taking advice, even my own.

Considering what scum the demon who'd taken Tommy was, in all probability, he'd come out the other end of this exorcism brain damaged, maybe even brain-dead. Would it really be so wrong of me to let Raphael or Saul take him then? If he was going to be a prisoner in his own body anyway . . .

The scent of vanilla drew me out of my tumultuous thoughts, and I saw that Dom had started lighting the candles. Needing to *do* something, not just stand still and think, I took over the candle-lighting duties. Though I dragged my feet a bit, all too soon the last candle was lit.

Everything was ready for me. The only question was, was I ready myself?

Hell, no. But that didn't stop me.

Trying to still the clamoring of my mind, I sat cross-legged facing Tommy. He looked much younger now than he had before, with his red-rimmed eyes and pale skin. He'd drawn his knees up to his chest and wrapped his arms around them, whether because he was cold or because he was trying to cover his nakedness, I didn't know. I felt a tug of pity, then shook my head.

This wasn't Tommy Brewster. This was a demon who'd taken over Tommy's body. And I wasn't going to hurt the demon—more's the pity—I was just going to send him back to the Demon Realm.

Taking a deep breath and hoping my nerves would steady, I let my eyes slide closed. The warm scent of vanilla enfolded me, and I felt my muscles begin to relax—a conditioned response for which I was very thankful at the moment. It took me longer than usual to get myself into the trance and open my other-worldly eyes, but I managed it.

In my otherworldly vision, I can see only the living. They show up as patches of bright, primary colors in a never-ending sea of black. Demons glow bloodred, and I had a moment of primal terror as I cast my vision around the room and saw the three red auras that hovered so close to me. Only Dominic showed up in the human blue that I thought of as "normal."

I shook off that moment of fear and concentrated on the aura I knew was Tommy's. I gathered my will, my power, whatever it was that gave me the ability to exorcize demons, waiting until I'd drawn in every ounce I could find.

Every exorcist has an image he or she uses to help visualize casting out a demon. Mine is wind. I gathered that will into my body, and then all at once released it in a great gust of gale-force wind. The wind of my will slammed into Tommy's demon-red aura.

For a moment, the aura clung stubbornly. Then the pressure of the wind became too much. The red aura shattered and was swept away, leaving only a very human shade of blue behind. Letting out a breath of relief, I opened my eyes.

But then I looked into a pair of hate-filled, obviously sentient eyes that bored into mine.

Tommy Brewster wasn't brain-dead, or even brain damaged. And boy, was he ever pissed.

To show his great gratitude to me for freeing him from the demon, Tommy launched himself across the short distance that separated us. I'd been expecting a vegetable, not a homicidal maniac, so I was completely unprepared for the attack. Before I'd even managed a squeak of alarm, he'd knocked me flat on my back and wrapped both his hands around my throat. He started to squeeze, his eyes wide and hysterical-looking as he shouted Bible verses. It didn't take a Biblical scholar to notice he was mixing and matching verses at random, but then most of his concentration was focused on the important task of choking me to death. I was starting to see spots by the time he suddenly screamed and went limp on top of me.

Holding the stun belt trigger, Raphael came to stand over the two of us, looking disgustingly amused. "You make a lovely couple," he said, and I remembered that Tommy was naked. I shoved him away from me, and though he was conscious and tried to keep his hands on my throat, he was too stunned to manage it.

I lay there on my back and breathed. I was going to have yet another set of bruises if I didn't give Lugh a chance to fix things. Tommy was shouting so loud I could hardly hear myself think. Something about hellfire and brimstone.

If he'd kept that up, I might have been happy to give him to the demons just to shut him up. As it was, the invective gave way to sobs, and pity reared its ugly head. I didn't know what Tommy had just gone through in the clutches of that demon, but clearly it hadn't been a good time. It seemed like something of a miracle that his mind had survived. Perhaps his child-hood trauma had left him stronger and more resilient than your average human. Or perhaps his fanaticism had served as some kind of shield. After all, there's a reason we call people like him "closed-minded."

"I am unclean," I heard him hiccup among the sobs.

At first I thought he was talking about the gas and piss on him. Then I remembered what I knew about the World According to God's Wrath. They hated human hosts as much as they hated the demons, because they believed that only a corrupt soul would allow a demon in. It even made a little sense, when you're talking about legal demons. After all, they're "legal" because they've been invited. But God's Wrath hated even those who were taken by force, and despite his convictions, Tommy would never be able to return to them.

Fingering my aching throat, I sat up and stared at Claudia Brewster's son. He'd faced more hardship in his twenty-one years than most people faced in a lifetime. Could I really condemn him to a lifetime of possession now that he was free? I wished he'd attack me again, or at least start raving like the lunatic that he was so I could stop feeling so goddamn sorry for him. But he didn't. He just lay there on the floor in the fetal position and wept.

Raphael, still holding the trigger, squatted down to meet my eyes. I found I couldn't look away.

"Let me take him," he said softly, and only the dilation of his pupils gave away how eager he was. "He's the only person in this room who could walk right into Claudia Brewster's house without causing a raised eyebrow. He can get us in there, and we can get those children out."

"You're not doing this because you want to save

those children," I said. I didn't know what Raphael really wanted, but he didn't do much of anything out of the goodness of his heart.

"He'd be just as able to get us in there if he was hosting Saul," Adam said.

I hadn't heard him approach, but he was standing practically on top of me. I didn't think this was a decision I should make sitting down, so I forced myself to my feet. Both Adam and Raphael tried to help steady me, but I snarled at them until they let go.

"Take a good look at him," Raphael said, and we all did. He hadn't let up on the sobbing yet. "Do you really think you can get him to speak the incantation to summon Saul?"

I narrowed my eyes at him. "You got *me* to summon Lugh!"

"Because I drugged you and knew you well enough to get through your defenses. Tommy wouldn't be that easy, and you know it. How much time do you think those kids have? Enough time for me to break Tommy and to make him speak the incantation? I doubt the demons will keep them alive long when Tommy goes AWOL on them."

"Shut up! You've made your point."

"Besides, I bet we can find a good host for Saul." He looked up at Adam. "Surely you can find someone at that club you're so fond of. Someone who's too homely to be a host, but would really like to be. And who shares Saul's unique tastes."

Adam didn't say anything, but I could tell he was thinking it over. It seemed Tommy would not be Saul's host. But it remained to be seen whether he would be Raphael's. Raphael didn't need an invitation to take him over. Once on the Mortal Plain, a demon can transfer from one host to another through physical contact. All it would take was the slightest brush of skin against skin, and Tommy would be gone once more. And my brother would be back.

"You have to decide, Morgan," Raphael urged. "And the sooner you decide, the sooner we can get those kids to safety."

I hated this. I was going to hate myself, whatever I decided. "Is this what Andy wants?" I asked, meeting Raphael's gaze and wishing his face were as open as mine.

Raphael blinked as if startled by the question. Then he shrugged. "He would never admit to wanting it. He's far too noble for that." In Raphael's mouth, "noble" sounded like a dirty word. "But down beneath his civilized exterior, he wants it quite desperately."

I supposed that had been rather a silly question. Whatever Andy might choose if he actually had a choice, it was inevitable that deep down inside he would wish for freedom. So much for my attempt to put this decision on Andy's shoulders.

I took another look at Tommy, tried to imagine what his life would be like if we just let him go home now. Then I shook my head at myself. It didn't matter if his life would suck or not. I could justify this till the apocalypse, and it wouldn't change the reality. When faced with the choice between my brother and a stranger, I was going to choose my brother—even if I thought my choice was morally wrong. I reminded myself to apologize to Brian for not fully understanding his decision to help Lugh kill my father.

I couldn't force any words out of my mouth, but I managed a nod. My eyes burned, and I was gritting my teeth so hard my jaw ached.

Obviously, Tommy had been too sunk in misery to listen to our conversation or realize that it had to do with him. When Raphael came to squat beside him, he didn't move.

"Wait!" I cried as Raphael reached out to touch him. I could see him fight the urge to ignore me, and was actually rather impressed when he dropped his hand away from Tommy's bare flesh.

"I just want to remind you—if Andy comes out a vegetable, I'm going to skin you alive, and damn the consequences."

Raphael's shoulders drooped with relief. He must have thought I'd changed my mind. "Have no fear," he said, his hand moving toward Tommy once more. "He's fine. As he'll tell you in a moment."

My conscience screamed as Raphael's hand brushed over Tommy's shoulder. Instantly, Tommy stopped his sobbing. Andy looked up at me, and it was my brother whose eyes met mine, not Raphael. I guess I was relieved Raphael had been telling the truth for once, but I felt too guilty to rejoice. Andy, not looking any happier than I felt, lowered his gaze to the floor.

Raphael unfolded Tommy's body and rolled to a sitting position. He didn't seem to care that his new body was naked, but Dom said, "I'll go see if I can find you something to wear."

"Thanks," Raphael said, and he flexed his hands experimentally, familiarizing himself with his new anatomy. He and Andy shared a look I couldn't interpret, and then Andy stood up and backed away from him.

I wanted to run to Andy, to throw my arms around him and welcome him back, but he wouldn't even look at me. I suppose his conscience wasn't feeling too frisky, either. I didn't know what to say, so I just stood there in brooding silence and waited for Dom to return with the clothes.

"Mind if I take a quick shower?" Raphael asked Adam.

"Suit yourself," Adam replied. The look on his face was not a happy one, but he wasn't as pissed off about being Tasered as I would have been in his position. "Bathroom's down the hall on the left."

"What happened to your desperate hurry to rescue the children?" I asked, and I didn't give a damn how suspicious I sounded.

It didn't seem to matter what face Raphael wore. He was always good at the marrow-chilling glare, the glare that always made me think there was something evil behind those eyes. "I think it would be a tad suspicious if I showed up at the house smelling like gas and piss, don't you?"

He had a point, but hell if I was going to admit it.

Chapter 25

Our rescue plan was hardly to my liking, but then nothing ever is these days. Raphael would take me to Claudia's house, under the pretext that he'd taken me prisoner because I was getting too close. Adam offered to provide handcuffs to lend some verisimilitude to the scenario, but I flat out refused.

When we got to the house, Raphael would insist I be taken downstairs into the basement with the children. That was about as far as our plan went. We didn't know what we would find when we got there, didn't know if the children would be restrained, didn't know for sure how many demons would be there, didn't know how careful they might be. If we could get to the girls before the demons did, and if it seemed likely we could extract them without too much danger, we'd just go for it. I'd seen Raphael fight before, and I had every confidence he could hold off the bad guys with ease while I spirited the children away.

But what were the chances the demons would make it that easy for us? With the way my life was going these days, we'd be lucky not to find an entire demon regiment camped out at that house. If it turned out we couldn't get to the girls without endangering them, we'd have to wing it.

I found myself wishing that it would be Adam by my side for this adventure rather than Raphael. True, I didn't like Adam. But I trusted him, which was more than I could say for Raphael. It seemed like a bad idea to wing it with someone I didn't trust, but that was my only option.

I gave careful consideration to the idea of calling Brian before I left. I'd already more than broken my promise to call him if there were any new developments. I told myself I didn't want to worry him, but in reality I just didn't have the emotional energy to deal with all the explaining I'd have to do—nor did I have the courage to listen to his objections, of which he was sure to have many. After all, everyone else did.

No one liked the idea of me being directly involved in the rescue, even Raphael, who'd come up with the plan in the first place. Anything that involved risk to me involved risk to Lugh. But it seemed unlikely Raphael could manage a rescue all by himself. Not to mention that I didn't trust him enough to let him go alone. For all his seeming hurry to launch the rescue, I *knew* there was something else behind it all. I wished I knew what, but he wasn't telling, and guessing wasn't helpful.

Raphael rummaged through Tommy's memory until he discovered where his car was parked. He had to fish Tommy's wallet and keys out of the trash bag, but though he made prissy faces about it, he took them.

Adam and Dominic saw us to the door, Andy following behind them looking a little like a lost soul. I didn't like the way he looked, wished I had time to talk to him. Maybe we could help each other deal with our consciences. But that would have to wait.

Adam drove Raphael and me to Tommy's car, then

dropped us off with stern instructions that Raphael keep me—actually, Lugh, but we were one and the same at the moment—safe. Tommy's car turned out to be an aging black Corolla sporting an impressive collection of dents and scratches. It wouldn't have looked out of place up on cinder blocks on a redneck's lawn, and I wasn't looking forward to riding in it. I leaned against the passenger door as Raphael unlocked it, my suspicions about him gamboling playfully in my chest.

"Can you find out from Tommy how he ended up 'volunteering' to be a host?" I asked.

He shook his head as he walked around the front of the car to the driver's side. "He was definitely already possessed when he arrived at the courthouse. Some guy brushed against him one day when he was standing in line at Starbucks, and before he knew what hit him, he was on his way to file the paperwork."

I suppressed a shudder. It was so damn easy for a corporeal demon to take a new host! Everyone was vulnerable. Except me, of course.

I was about to get into the car when there suddenly came a spike of pain through my eye. I winced and hissed. It let up immediately. I knew Lugh was trying to tell me something, though I didn't know why he didn't just come out and say it. He seemed to be able to do that much of the time lately. Of course, perhaps my less-than-happy thoughts about demons had put my subconscious back on alert.

Raphael, who'd already gotten into the car, leaned across the seat and looked up at me. "What's wrong?"

"I don't know," I answered, scanning the area for anything that might have upset Lugh.

We were in a small private lot on Lombard Street, near The Seven Deadlies. It was getting pretty late, and although South Street was just a block away, here on Lombard it was pretty quiet. Which made it a little easier for me to spot the source of Lugh's concern.

"Shit!" I said, then said it again, just because.

"What?" Raphael asked, getting out of the car and looking alarmed.

I jerked my chin toward Reporter Barbie, who exited her car now that she'd been spotted. "We've got company," I said grimly. "She's a reporter."

"In the mood for a nice car chase?"

I bit my lip, tempted to agree. We could get into the car and put the pedal to the metal faster than Barbie could get back into hers. Maybe we'd be able to lose her immediately. But maybe not.

I sighed heavily. "I don't think drawing that much attention to ourselves would be a great idea," I said. "We'll just have to get rid of her somehow."

"I'm sure we'll manage something."

I glanced at him sidelong and shivered. I didn't like the way he was looking at Reporter Barbie, but before I had a chance to warn him to behave, she'd caught up to us.

Barbie smiled, looking for all the world like she expected me to be happy to see her.

"Give me one good reason why I shouldn't call the police and report you as a stalker," I growled at her.

She blinked. "There's no need to be so hostile. I'm just doing my job."

Ah, yes, the excuse of sleazy reporters everywhere. Not that I had any reason to believe Barbara What's-Her-Name was a sleazy reporter. She hadn't really done anything *that* obnoxious—yet—and not all reporters are sleazy. Just like Brian reminds me every once in a while that not all lawyers are sleazy. But old stereotypes die hard, especially when they're in the process of inconveniencing me.

"I'm not answering your questions, so go do your job elsewhere."

Barbie's glance flicked to Raphael, who was doing a great job of mimicking Tommy's sullen look. Then she looked back at me and raised her eyebrows. "You seem to have become exorcist to the rich and famous. Care to comment?"

I'd forgotten that Tommy's father was old money, putting him in the same league as good ol' Jordan Maguire Jr. Crap. I imagined this would be a fascinating coincidence to anyone with a journalistic mind.

"I'm a legal, registered demon," Raphael said calmly. "And clearly Ms. Kingsley is not exorcizing me or we'd be in the basement of the courthouse and I'd be in lots and lots of restraints."

I wished he'd kept his mouth shut. Engaging Reporter Barbie in conversation of any kind was a bad idea. But too late now.

"But there were some questions that arose at the time of your summoning. Claudia Brewster alleges that you have taken her son against his will. And I know that she has hired Ms. Kingsley to look into the case."

This was just getting better and better. I knew denying it wasn't going to do any good, but my reflexes kicked in. "She didn't hire me to do anything." I sounded pissed even to my own ears, which was not a good thing. It let Barbie know she was getting to me, which would just make her more curious. I made a concerted effort to calm my voice. "She consulted with me to see if I could find any evidence that Tommy was taken against his will. I told her I couldn't, and that was that."

"Then what business do you have with Mr. Brewster at the moment?"

A perfectly logical question—and evidence that I'd

been right in my conviction that both Raphael and I should keep quiet.

I was still struggling to find an answer when Raphael took a step forward, invading Barbie's personal space. His new host wasn't quite as tall or imposing as most demon hosts, but he was able to look down on her from a significant height advantage.

"*Our* business is none of *your* business, Ms. . . . ?"

"Paige," she supplied. "Barbara Paige. I work for the—"

"I don't care who you work for." Raphael's voice was outwardly calm, but still intimidating as hell. "You're getting on my nerves, and that isn't in your best interests."

Raphael radiated so much menace any sane person would have tucked her tail between her legs and bolted. Barbie apparently wasn't sane. She held her ground, and didn't even look particularly uneasy.

"I don't think threatening me is in *your* best interests, Mr. Brewster." She put her fists on her hips and met his glower with a blandly calm expression.

Raphael blinked, startled that she'd called his bluff. He stared at her for a moment, then looked over at me.

"Get in the car," he said.

It sounded suspiciously like an order, which of course made me want to dig in my heels and refuse. Common sense prevailed, however, and I turned my back on Barbie and opened the door. Raphael had already gotten in, and Barbie had started running back to her car. Luckily, she was wearing businesslike pumps that weren't optimal running shoes.

Raphael stomped on the gas pedal before I even managed to close the door behind myself. He peeled out of the parking lot with a squeal of rubber, the car jouncing hard over one of Philly's ubiquitous potholes.

I struggled to get my seat belt on as he blew through a red light.

The expression on his face was grim, and he didn't slow down, even when I looked back over my shoulder and told him I didn't see Barbie's car following us.

"Take it down a notch," I said, bracing my hands on the dashboard as another pothole threatened to break the POS into bite-sized pieces. "We've lost her, and I doubt she's going to be willing to break as many traffic laws as you are."

"She's not a reporter," he said, screeching the car around a corner.

"What?"

"She's not a reporter," he repeated. "I was thinking it was strange that she was being so aggressive over such a nothing story. I thought it was even stranger that she didn't bat an eyelash when I started crowding her." His lips thinned. "Then when she put her hands on her hips, I got a glimpse of a shoulder holster under her jacket."

"Oh shit."

"Yeah. I don't know who she is, or what she wants, but I'd say staying away from her is a really good idea."

"I agree," I said as my stomach decided it objected to the rough handling it was getting as we bounced and rocked down the street at warp speed. "But if you don't slow down, we're going to get stopped for speeding, and that could give her time to catch up with us."

To my immense relief, the car slowed to near the speed limit. But I couldn't help noticing he kept a watchful eye on the rearview mirror as we made our way out of town.

Chapter 26

Devon and Claudia Brewster lived out past the Main Line, which marks the boundary between the city and the suburbs. Their neighborhood was chic and obviously expensive. Most cars were discreetly tucked away in garages, but those that weren't tended toward the Mercedes and BMW end of the luxury scale. I wondered whether Tommy drove a POS because his parents were cheap, or because it was some kind of fashion statement. Of course, the way he usually dressed, he'd have looked like a car thief behind the wheel of a Mercedes. Raphael's outfit of well-worn jeans borrowed from Adam and navy blue sweatshirt borrowed from Dominic looked like black-tie attire compared to Tommy's usual wardrobe. I hoped that wouldn't make the bad guys suspicious.

"That's the house," Raphael said, pointing briefly before pulling the car to the curb two houses down. He left the engine running, but put the car in park and turned to face me. He surprised me by reaching out to grab my wrist. If I'd had an inkling he'd been about to touch me, I'd have been out of the car before he'd moved five inches.

"Let go of me!" I said, giving my hand a yank for emphasis. Of course, he didn't let go. "What are you doing?" Did I mention I didn't trust Raphael one bit?

He grinned at me. "I'm keeping you from bolting if you don't like my next suggestion."

"I already don't like it. Now get your hands off me or things'll get ugly."

"Let Lugh surface."

I jerked on my hand again, but when a demon's got a grip on you, you aren't getting free. "That wasn't part of the plan."

"Yes, it was. I just didn't mention it before."

Raphael had hold of my left hand, but I'm right-handed. I reached for the Taser that was strapped to my belly with adhesive tape, where it was hidden by my oversized sweatshirt. Another loaner from Adam. Raphael grabbed my right hand before I got to the Taser.

"What if they don't buy it, Morgan?" he asked. "What if we get down into that basement, and they figure out I'm not Tommy's original demon? I can mimic Tommy just fine since I have access to his mind, but he wasn't paying enough attention to what his demon was doing in the real world to give me any clue who his allies are. We'll go down there, and everyone will expect me to recognize my so-called friends."

My heart sank, and some of the fight went out of me. He was right, damn him. There were plenty of ways this rescue attempt could go wrong. And puny human me wouldn't be much help in a fight against demons.

"You've had trouble letting him in the past," Raphael continued, "even in extenuating circumstances. Do you want all hell to break loose in there and then find out you can't let him in? Or would you rather go in there prepared?"

"You can let go of me now," I said, in what I hoped was a calm voice. "You're right, and I have to find a way to let him in. It's just ... I haven't had much success."

Raphael let go of my right hand, but kept hold of my left. I guess he didn't trust me any more than I trusted him. I was sure he was keeping a careful watch on me in case I went for the Taser again.

"You let him in the other night when I woke you up."

I grimaced. "Yeah, but I'd already let him in while I was sleeping. All I had to do was keep the doors open."

"So try to do the same thing now. Try to do whatever it was you did when you kept the doors open."

"I don't—"

"Would you rather I clock you and let him take over while you're unconscious?"

The grimace turned into a scowl. He was right-handed, too, and his right hand was busy holding on to me. However, I didn't doubt he could turn my lights out just as easily with his left.

"Bastard," I mumbled.

"Your choice."

"Fine! I'll try to let him in. Don't you dare hit me!"

He didn't say anything, and I knew he'd do whatever he damn well pleased. This wasn't what I'd call the optimal situation for achieving the kind of relaxation I thought I'd need to let Lugh take control. Especially since Raphael still had hold of me and wasn't going to let go anytime soon.

"Close your eyes," Raphael said. "Try pretending you're going into the trance state."

"I don't suppose you carry vanilla candles with you?" I said, but I closed my eyes and leaned back in my seat, trying to ignore the disquieting feel of his hand on my wrist.

I drew in a deep breath and told myself that the scent of vanilla filled the air, and that the orange glow that lit my eyelids was a plethora of candles, not a streetlamp. Sometimes, I can lie to myself with great skill, like when Lugh first possessed me and I tried to deny all the evidence that I wasn't alone in my body anymore. I seemed to have lost my touch, however, because I remained very much aware that I was sitting in a car in the middle of the night with a man I didn't trust, trying to let a demon take control of my body.

Frustration curled my fingers into fists. I didn't want Raphael hitting me! It probably wouldn't really hurt, because I probably wouldn't be conscious long enough to register the pain, but I'd been beat up enough lately.

"Visualize what you did with Tommy tonight," Raphael said in what I'm sure was supposed to be a hypnotic voice.

I cracked one eye open to look at him. "Do me a favor and shut up. Hearing your voice does *not* relax me."

He shut up, and I closed my eye again. Despite the fact that I'd grumped at him, I actually did as Raphael suggested and mentally took myself through the events of earlier tonight. I visualized arranging those vanilla-scented candles in a circle around Tommy, then remembered what it had felt like to light each one. Adam and Dom didn't have a lighter, so I'd been forced to use matches.

The sensory memory became stronger, and I remembered the acrid after-scent of burning matches and smoke. I sat my imaginary self down across from Tommy, closed my imaginary eyes, and took a very real deep breath. If I didn't know I was making this all up in my head, I would have sworn I caught the scent of vanilla.

The orange glow faded from behind my closed lids, and my otherworldly eyes opened. Beside me glowed Raphael's crimson aura. I'd done it! I'd reached the trance state. Now all I had to do was let Lugh in.

I felt tension building in my muscles as I contemplated opening those mental doors, and before I even had the chance to try, my eyes popped open. I tried to curse in frustration, but my mouth wouldn't open and my throat wouldn't form the words.

Raphael smiled. "How kind of you to join us, brother," he said.

I snorted. Actually, *Lugh* snorted. *I* tried not to panic.

I hadn't opened my doors yet! I protested to Lugh.

"Your defenses go down almost entirely when you're in the trance," Lugh responded, using my own vocal cords to speak to me. Have I mentioned how much I hate it when he does that?

So anytime I do an exorcism, you can just waltz on in? He didn't answer, but then he didn't need to.

I really like Lugh. I think he has a good heart, and I admire his ideals. He can be a good friend, when he wants to be. But he is one manipulative son of a bitch. Always for a good cause, but still . . .

Were you ever planning to mention this little tidbit to me?

"Not if I didn't have to." Well, at least he was honest, unlike his brother.

"Are you talking to me? Because if you are, you're making no sense," Raphael said.

"I was talking to Morgan. But it's time for us to go rescue a couple of children, don't you think?"

Raphael nodded. "You and me playing hero together. Who would have believed it?"

Not me, I said, still fighting my subconscious, which really wanted to kick Lugh out and take control of my body again. *Raphael is up to something. There is no way he'd have been so all-fired eager to put on the white hat.*

I know, Lugh agreed, keeping the conversation just between the two of us for now. *He's my brother, remember? He might not be quite so bad as I once thought, but I know rescuing children isn't one of his major goals in life.*

Do you have any idea what *he's up to?*

Raphael started the car, heading toward the driveway of the Brewster residence.

I think your guess before was right. I think he knows more about the Houston project than he's saying, and I think he wanted Tommy Brewster as a host very, very badly. Any pretense at an urgent need to save the children was just a way to get you to agree to let him take Tommy.

Alarm trickled through my system. *But he's going to go through with the plan, right? He's not going to drop the pretense now.*

He'll go through with it, Lugh assured me, and his mental voice held more than a hint of steel.

It sounded like there was a threat behind his words, but I didn't think it did much good if Raphael didn't hear it. Still, we were pulling into the driveway, and if Raphael were planning to back out, he would have done it by now. At least, I hoped that was the case.

It was almost midnight, but there were plenty of lights on in the Brewster house. I suppose it's hard to sleep when there are demons holding children hostage in your basement. Raphael parked in front of the garage, the car coming to a stop with a squeal that set my teeth on edge. Before we got out, Raphael reached into his back pocket and pulled out a pair of handcuffs. I was pretty sure those were the same ones Adam had offered earlier. Shows how much good my refusal did.

We're not going down there in handcuffs! I protested.

I can break out of them easily, Lugh reminded me.

Yeah, but what if I lose my nerve and end up back in the driver's seat? I can't break them.

Then don't lose your nerve.

I wanted to strangle him, but my body was useless to me. Lugh allowed his brother to cuff his hands behind his back. Raphael then grabbed my arm in a brutally tight grip, stuck a gun in my side—had he been carrying that all along?—and dragged me toward the side door, where there was less light.

My body's heart was thumping along steadily, pulse not even elevated. But that didn't stop me from feeling like my heart was in my throat, making it hard to breathe.

Raphael moved the gun from my side to my head, then let go of my arm to fish through his jeans pocket for a set of keys and open the door. Instead of escorting me in, he grabbed my arm again and threw me in so hard I crashed into the trunk of one of the Brewsters' Mercedes. Lugh considerately blocked out the pain. With his demon strength and agility, he probably could have kept his feet, but since he was pretending to be just little ol' me, he keeled over sideways.

Who the hell is he putting on a show for? I complained, wishing Lugh would turn his head so I could give Raphael the dirty look he deserved. *There's no one here to see!*

Perhaps he's getting into character, Lugh's mental voice said, a hint of humor in it. *Or perhaps that was just a cheap shot because he and I still have issues. It doesn't matter. I won't allow him to hurt you, and I can tolerate the pain.*

You're not one of those demons who enjoys pain? I asked, then mentally slapped myself upside the head. Like we needed a distraction right now! And like I really needed to know Lugh's sexual preferences!

Not particularly, he answered, though I'd have preferred he just ignore the question. *But as I said, I can tolerate it. Even if things get a lot rougher.*

Oh joy! I didn't want to think about things getting rougher.

Raphael hauled me to my feet. Lugh swayed back and forth as if woozy from the impact with the car. Raphael didn't give us much time to recover, grabbing my arm again and half-dragging me through a laundry room and into the main house. He had to pause to enter a code in the alarm, but with Tommy's memories at his fingertips, that was a piece of cake.

The laundry room opened out into the kitchen, which then opened into an enormous, two-story living room with a cathedral ceiling and a chandelier so high off the ground you'd need an oxygen tank to change the bulbs.

Claudia Brewster sat on the uncomfortable-looking antique sofa. She'd traded in the power suit for a velour tracksuit, her hair was loose around her shoulders, and she wore no makeup. It would be the relaxed, weekend-at-home look, if it weren't for the tension in her shoulders, the bloodshot eyes, or the blue-gray shadows beneath them.

Beside her, holding her hand, sat an older man with salt-and-pepper hair and laugh lines around his eyes.

Despite the laugh lines, he didn't look any happier than Claudia, and I figured he must be her husband, Devon Brewster III.

The man sitting across from them was much younger, probably no more than twenty-five. He was classic demon-fodder, with the athletic build and the generic good looks the Spirit Society favored as hosts for the "Higher Powers." He'd apparently been reading a magazine when we entered, though we immediately had his undivided attention. Another demon entered the room from the hallway on the opposite end.

Tommy's demon had told us there would be two or three demons on duty tonight. It seemed there were *at least* three, since I didn't imagine they'd left the children unattended.

Unless the children were already dead.

For once, I was glad Lugh was in control and not me. If it were me, I'm sure my face would have gone white, and I might even have been sick to my stomach.

If they'd killed the children, Lugh said, *they wouldn't still be here. And I doubt the Brewsters would still be alive.*

That made a reassuring amount of sense, so I relaxed a little.

The demon across the room looked me over from head to toe then glowered at Raphael. "What do you mean by bringing *her* here?"

"She was being nosy. I thought it was time to put a stop to it."

The demon's glower shifted to Claudia, who wilted under that angry, frightening gaze. "I believe I made it quite clear what would happen if you didn't call off your bitch."

Oh shit! If we ended up getting one of those kids

killed just by showing up at the house, I was never going to forgive myself!

"Please!" Lugh said, and he had my inflection just right. He even managed to sound like begging hurt him, which is probably how I would have sounded. "It's not Claudia's fault. She told me to lay off, and I promised her I would. But I just couldn't let it go. She had no idea I'd started poking into it again."

The demon crossed the room, coming so close he invaded my personal space. I tried to take a step backward, but Raphael was behind me and grabbed hold.

I felt almost like I was the one driving my body, because Lugh was doing exactly what I would have done in the situation. He momentarily struggled, as if on the verge of panic, then forced himself to stop and put on the usual mask of bravado. He met the demon's gaze.

"When the state calls me in to exorcize you, I'm going to pretend to fail, and you'll go straight to the cremation ovens."

You're freaking me out, Lugh. That's exactly what I would have said!

I know. That's why I said it. Now hush. I can't carry on both conversations at once.

The demon backhanded me, and only Raphael's iron grip kept me from falling. Yup, I was really glad I didn't have to feel that. It would have sucked, big time.

Lugh let my body go limp in Raphael's arms. Raphael scooped me up in a fireman's carry. "I'm going to dump her in the basement. Who's on guard duty?"

"Alex," the demon replied. "But give me one good reason why we shouldn't just kill her. She's already proven she's going to keep digging, no matter what."

"We have to find out what she knows and who

she's told before we kill her," Raphael said with exaggerated patience.

The other demon didn't seem to like that much. All I could see from my ignominious position over Raphael's shoulder was his butt, and to tell you the truth, it wasn't much to look at. But there was no mistaking the anger in the other demon's voice.

"You'd better watch your tone of voice when you talk to me, *Tommy*," he growled. It was that deep, growling, almost animalistic sound that demons seemed to be able to make, even though humans lacked the proper vocal equipment for it.

"Sorry," Raphael said. "It's been a long day."

"Aww, did the big, bad exorcist make you miss your nightly fuck-fest?"

Raphael was used to being in charge, used to outranking everyone around him—except Lugh. He was obviously supposed to be subordinate to this other demon, but that might be a hard act for him to pull off for long, especially when he was being goaded.

Lugh seemed to agree, choosing that moment to pretend to wake up and start struggling.

"Hold still or I'll make you sorry you were born!" Raphael snapped, and I stopped struggling. It was the first time Lugh acted differently from how I would have. No way I'd have been intimidated by such a second-rate, cliché threat.

"Another reason not to kill her," Raphael said as if the angry exchange hadn't happened, "is that colon cancer runs in her family." He chuckled. "I guess that's why she's such a pain in the ass."

Groan. Bad enough to be a helpless passenger in my own body, did I also have to listen to cliché threats *and* bad puns? Talk about your cruel and unusual punishment.

Big Cheese Demon seemed to find it funnier than I did, and he and Raphael shared a bit of a laugh at my expense.

"There's a spare bedroom upstairs, if you want to give her a test drive," Big Cheese said when he'd stopped laughing. Apparently I would be allowed to live if I had the potential to be a good broodmare. Lucky me.

"Nah," Raphael said. "She's on the pill. Need to let that work its way out of her system before she's likely to take."

"That doesn't mean you can't have a little fun."

God, I hate demons. Yeah, yeah, I know, there are plenty of humans who are just as bad. I just don't have to deal with *them* on a daily basis.

Raphael snorted. "You try doing it as many times a night as I do, see if you still think it's fun." He shifted me on his shoulder like I was heavy, which of course I wasn't for a demon. "Can I take her downstairs now? I'm sick to death of dealing with her today."

Big Cheese hesitated a moment, thinking it over. I mentally held my breath, praying he would go for it. And for once, something actually went my way.

"Yeah, sure," he finally said. "It's late, and I don't feel like dealing with her tonight, either." I heard him turn around, though I still couldn't see anything except Raphael's ass.

"Here's a little something for you two lovebirds to think about tonight," he said, addressing the Brewsters in a nasty voice. "Someone's got to pay for your inability to stop the exorcist from poking her nose where it doesn't belong. In the morning, you're going to tell me which kid you like better, and you'll get to keep her. You do that, and I'll take care of the other one quick. But if you make *me* pick, it will be very, very slow, and you'll get to watch every minute of it."

Even Raphael had trouble swallowing that threat. I could feel him tense beneath me.

I started struggling again as Claudia burst into sobs and Raphael carried me out of the room.

Chapter **27**

Raphael carried me down a long hallway, then opened a door and stepped through into a dimly lit stairwell. In my peripheral vision, I could see Big Cheese and the other demon following. No way we'd get lucky enough to be allowed into the basement without an escort.

My body jounced against Raphael's shoulder as he carried me down the stairs. Then, instead of just setting me down on my feet, he slung me off his shoulder and let me fall to the floor. The hard, cement floor, I might add. Once again, I was glad to have Lugh blocking out the pain.

Lugh managed to wriggle around until we could see the room into which we'd been deposited.

I'd known the hope that we could just snatch the kids and run with minimal risk was very low. But even that tiny hope faded when I looked around.

An unfamiliar demon—Alex, I presumed—sat on a straight-backed chair near the stairs, holding the younger girl on his lap. She was fast asleep, and though in her disheveled state she wasn't as cute as she'd been in the photo, her vulnerability brought out maternal instincts I hadn't thought I had. I wanted to snatch her from that demon's arms and make him pay for touching her.

The other girl was wrapped up in a blanket on the floor. She, too, was asleep, her thumb stuck in her mouth, her knees curled to her chest. I suppose if you're young enough, and tired enough, you can sleep anywhere, even on a cold cement floor while being held hostage by demons.

We couldn't make any aggressive moves while the demon had his hands on the little girl. She'd be dead or possessed as soon as we tipped our hand.

The situation went from bad to worse when I noticed the air bed and the cot set up just to the right of the stairs. Big Cheese and his crony were heading for them, and I realized they all slept down here with the kids. As if one of them couldn't handle a three-year-old and a five-year-old with ease! Hadn't they ever heard of overkill?

Raphael stood there for a moment, assessing the situation. His face didn't give away much, but he had to be coming to the same grim conclusion I was: this was not going to be a piece of cake, and we were now into the "winging it" stage of our plan.

"I presume you don't need me anymore?" Raphael asked Big Cheese, who'd sat down on the air bed and started stripping off his sneakers and socks.

Big Cheese sneered a bit, not looking up from his task. "I didn't need you in the first place."

Raphael shrugged. "Well then. Good night, all."

And he started plodding up the stairs. I wondered what the hell he was up to. My only guess was that he was going to turn around at the last moment and try to shoot the demon that was holding on to the little girl. He was our biggest, most immediate threat. But that still left two demons and two children for us to take care of. The kids would probably wake up and panic when they heard a gunshot. If the demons were smart, which I was betting they were, they'd immediately go for the kids and use them as hostages. *Then* what would we do?

But Raphael didn't turn, didn't even look over his shoulder. He just marched to the top of the stairs, opened the door, and stepped out. I held my breath, still expecting him to make a surprise attack. But he didn't.

Big Cheese came to squat beside me so he could meet my eyes. "If I hear so much as a peep out of you, the girls are going to pay for it. Got it?"

I didn't respond, and Big Cheese punctuated the point with a vicious kick to my rib. I heard something snap, and Lugh stifled a scream.

"That ought to give you some extra incentive to stay still and keep quiet," Big Cheese said. Then he left me lying there and flopped onto the air bed. Cronyman had already stretched out on his back and folded his hands behind his head. Making himself nice and comfortable.

And still no Raphael. My spirits sank, and I cursed both myself and Lugh for fools.

We should never have trusted him, I said bitterly. *We should have known he'd never risk his ass for a couple of kids. He just used them as an excuse to get Tommy, and now that he's got what he wants, to hell with you and me.*

Maybe he would have followed through on his promises if the rescue had looked easy enough. But when he'd seen the odds were against it, he'd decided to cut his losses and abandon us here. After all, he had what he wanted, didn't he?

Don't give up on him yet, Lugh said. *He may well have something up his sleeve.*

Yeah, the knife he's using to stab us in the back!

I lay there stewing, wondering how the hell Lugh and I were going to get out of this without getting the children killed, for about five minutes, my rage increasing with every tick of the clock. Then I heard the sound of angry voices upstairs. I recognized one of them as Claudia's. The other was Tommy's, which made me hope Raphael hadn't abandoned us after all.

The angry voices came closer, and I realized it wasn't just anger I heard in Claudia's voice—it was hysteria. Tommy bellowed something, but the basement was just deep enough that I couldn't hear his words clearly. Claudia's voice rose to a scream.

Big Cheese and Crony had both sat up and were staring at the ceiling. Crony looked amused, but Big Cheese looked pissed off. I guess the commotion was interfering with his beauty sleep. Alex still sat like a statue with the sleeping girl on his lap.

The door at the head of the stairs crashed open. Both Big Cheese and Crony leapt to their feet. Alex tightened his hold on the girl, who woke up and immediately started crying. Her sobs woke her sister, who cried in chorus, curling up into the smallest ball she could manage and pulling the blanket over her head.

Tommy, his face red with rage, eyes glowing with demonic fury, started down the stairs. Claudia followed behind him, grabbing uselessly onto his arm and screaming.

"Don't! Please!" she begged, but she couldn't hold him off any more than she could a speeding train. He dragged her all the way to the base of the stairs.

"What's going on?" Big Cheese demanded.

"Bitch!" Tommy shouted, and flung Claudia away

from him. She hit the wall beside the stairs with a cry of pain, then crumpled to the floor.

"What's—" Big Cheese started to repeat, but Raphael cut him off.

"We're not waiting until tomorrow to settle things!" he snarled, striding across the room toward the screaming little girl on Alex's lap.

A part of me knew this had to be just an act. If Raphael were betraying us, he'd simply have left us here, and we never would have heard from him again. Certainly he'd have had no reason to pick a fight with Claudia, whom he didn't even know. But distrust dies hard, and watching him stride across the floor toward that helpless child with murder in his eyes inspired a kind of horrified terror I hoped never to feel again.

Lugh rolled over onto his side, ostensibly to watch what was happening. But by rolling over, he made it so his cuffed hands were hidden from view. I felt him use my own fingers to jerk open one of the bracelets, the lock no match for a demon's strength.

Raphael snatched the screaming child from Alex's arms. Her little arms and legs flailed wildly, and my heart ached with pity for her even as I finally recognized what Raphael was doing.

"Calm down, Tommy!" Big Cheese snapped. "We have better things to do with that hostage."

From across the room, Raphael met my eyes briefly, flicking his glance toward the other little girl, who cowered under her blanket. Lugh and I both got the message loud and clear.

Lugh surged to his feet, launching himself across the room until he was between the girl and the room full of demons. At this point, it was finally dawning on Big Cheese and company that all was not as they'd first assumed. But it was too late.

Keeping his body between the child he held and the other two demons, Raphael lashed out with his right fist, catching the gaping Alex right under the chin. The punch landed with a sickening crunching sound, and Alex immediately went limp, probably dead.

Lugh reached under my sweatshirt and ripped the Taser off my belly. He would fight as if he were no more than human unless forced by necessity to use his demon strength. It wouldn't do to have any of these demons return to the Demon Realm with news that I was possessed. Too many people would guess that meant I was still hosting Lugh.

He used his body to keep the child pressed up against the wall, out of harm's way, while he fired the Taser at Crony. His aim was good, and Crony went down with a shriek.

I wasn't sure what we were going to do about Big Cheese. It would be hard for Raphael to attack him while still protecting the child, and I doubted Lugh'd have had the time to reload the Taser even if I happened to have another cartridge on me, which I didn't.

But before I had time to put too much thought into it, the deafening blast of a gunshot echoed against the basement's stone walls. Blood exploded from Big Cheese's chest, and the life had left his eyes before he hit the floor.

I turned to see Claudia, standing with her back against the wall by the staircase, both arms held out in front of her as she braced one hand with another, the barrel of her gun following Big Cheese's body as it slumped to the floor. Her eyes were wide and ringed with white, but her hands were steady, her jaw set with fury and determination.

Even with Lugh controlling my body, my ears rang from the sound of the gunshot. But even through the ringing, I could hear Tommy's voice as he turned to Claudia while still holding the struggling, screaming child.

"Nice shot," he said with a sardonic lift of his brow. "But you can put the gun down now."

Claudia visibly swallowed hard and stayed in her shooter's stance. "Put my daughter down first!"

"Believe me, Claudia," he said as he followed her orders, "I wouldn't have given you my gun if I had any intention of hurting your children." He stood up slowly, hands away from his sides.

So, the whole screaming argument had been an act, on both their parts. I wasn't surprised that Raphael could be so convincing, seeing as he seemed to spend half his life lying and deceiving people, but Claudia's performance had been pretty impressive.

The little girl ran to her as soon as her feet hit the ground, throwing her arms around her mother's leg and bawling against her thigh. Claudia lowered the gun with a sigh of relief, her free hand stroking her daughter's hair.

Behind me, the other girl finally gave up hiding under her blanket, wriggling free and running to join her sister in Claudia's embrace. Still moving slowly and carefully, Raphael approached the tearful trio.

"May I have my gun back?" he asked. "That way you can use both arms to hug them."

Claudia gave him a look that said she trusted him about as much as I did. But hugging two little girls while holding a gun was a bit awkward, so after a moment of hesitation, she handed it over.

Thank you, Morgan, Lugh whispered in my head.

For what?

For not panicking. For letting me take control. For letting me stay in control. For trusting me.

Strangely moved by his words, I didn't immediately answer. And by the time I did, I was back in control.

"You're welcome," I said, so softly no one but Lugh could hear me.

Chapter **28**

That had been the longest Lugh had ever been in control while I was conscious and aware, and it felt kind of strange to move my own limbs. My chest ached where Big Cheese had kicked me. I'm pretty sure he'd broken the rib, though Lugh had at least partially healed it. Nausea roiled in my stomach, most likely from stress overload. My legs were none too steady as I crossed the room to Raphael. Actually, I felt kind of like I'd just gotten back to land after six months at sea, and I swayed on my feet when I came to a stop.

"What's the story?" I asked Raphael out of the corner of my mouth. Claudia was still busy hugging and comforting the children, and she paid no attention to us.

"I told her I was a friend of yours," Raphael answered. "You exorcized Tommy and had me transfer from my usual host to him for this rescue. All highly illegal, of course, but I doubt she's going to complain when our actions saved the kids."

"And what about Tommy?"

His voice lowered to a near whisper. "I told her I'd

transfer back into my original host and send Tommy back to her, though I warned her his psyche was not in good shape."

I still had plenty more questions—like what was Raphael *really* going to do—but the Tasered Crony was starting to regain control of his limbs. Raphael gave me a little push toward Claudia.

"Why don't you all go upstairs," he suggested. "Get the children out of here." He indicated the bloody battlefield with a sweep of his arm. "They're in for enough nightmares already."

"Yes, of course," Claudia agreed. She scooped up the three-year-old, and took the other girl's hand to lead her up the stairs. But it turned out both girls wanted to be carried, and neither Claudia nor I had the heart to deny them.

So I ended up carrying a still-sniffling, clinging five-year-old girl up the stairs, leaving Raphael alone in the basement. My conscience wasn't entirely happy about it. I knew Raphael was going to kill Crony. The demon deserved it, but it wasn't the demon who would die, it was his host. That really sucked for his host, who might have been totally unwilling to participate in this plot. But we couldn't let him live, couldn't have him testifying to his version of what had happened down in that basement. Hell, I wasn't sure *what* the legal ramifications of this night's work were going to be. I didn't think I'd like them.

"Where's your husband?" I asked Claudia when we emerged from the basement. Yes, it took me that long to wonder why Devon Brewster III hadn't come running at the sounds of the argument or at the gun-shot.

"He went to bed," she answered. I must have made some kind of face, because she hurried to clarify. "He hasn't slept in two days." A faint, exhausted smile lifted the corners of her mouth. "Neither have I. But I talked him into taking a sleeping pill tonight, so I expect it would take more than a little shouting and the sound of a gunshot in the basement to wake him."

"You should take one, too," I said as I followed her through the living room and up another flight of stairs. The children's sniffles were calming, though both still clung with arms and legs.

"I will," she assured me. "After I've put the girls to bed."

I followed Claudia into what was perhaps the girliest bedroom I'd ever seen. Everything was pink, and it looked like a lace factory had exploded inside. I suppose to a three- and a five-year-old girl, the place looked like the absolute height of femininity and romance. Myself, I felt immediately like a barbarian invading the royal palace.

I was very happy to have played the hero and saved the children, but I was now more than ready to go home. Claudia set her charge down on a ruffly, cloud-pink bed, then pried the other girl out of my arms.

"I'll take things from here," she said with a smile.

Yup, my poker face was working as well as ever.

"We'll talk again tomorrow," Claudia continued, her eyes misting with tears. "I don't know how I can ever thank you, how I can ever—"

I held up my hand to cut her off, even more uncomfortable now. "Please. I just did what I thought was right. No thanks are necessary."

She looked like she wanted to argue, but then one of the girls pulled on the leg of her tracksuit, demanding attention.

"We'll talk again tomorrow," Claudia repeated, then sat on the bed and gathered both children into her arms again.

Not if I could help it, though I wasn't sure it was

possible. Surely we'd have to get our stories straight! A frown puckered my face.

"Um, what about the bodies in the basement?" I asked.

"Your friend said he'd take care of everything," she responded without even looking at me, her attention riveted on the girls.

I had no idea how Raphael planned to "take care of everything," but it was clear Claudia wasn't inclined to discuss it just now, so I backed out of the room and closed the door softly behind me.

I made my way downstairs just as Raphael emerged from the basement. He held up his car keys.

"I'm going to pull my car into the garage. We'll have to see if we can fit all the bodies into the trunk."

I looked at him skeptically. These were all demon hosts we were talking about, which meant none of them was exactly tiny. "I don't know if we could fit *two* of them in the trunk, much less three."

Raphael shrugged. "We'll take two cars if we have to. I've got a key to Claudia's Mercedes." His gaze darted to something behind me, and his eyes widened.

Because I still didn't trust Raphael, I had the feeling I was falling for the oldest trick in the book when I looked over my shoulder. But I wasn't. Devon Brewster III was descending the stairs, fully clothed, his hair showing no signs of having encountered a pillow, his eyes too clear to be those of a man under the influence of a sleeping pill.

"Mr. Brewster?" I asked. "Claudia said you were asleep." And if you weren't asleep, why are you coming downstairs instead of hugging your children and helping your wife put them to bed?

Brewster smiled, but it wasn't a nice expression. "My wife is mistaken. In many things."

Belatedly, I saw the Taser he'd been concealing by holding it slightly behind his leg.

"Get down!" Raphael bellowed, and for once, I followed orders without hesitation. I was about halfway between Brewster and Raphael, and from my vantage point on the floor, I had a decent view of the showdown.

Raphael drew his gun as Brewster raised the Taser. Raphael was just a hair faster, and for the second time tonight, the sound of a gunshot split the air. The bullet slammed into Brewster's forehead. There was a squirt of blood as a small, circular hole appeared right in the center of his forehead. He grunted in pain, but didn't immediately crumple to the floor as he should have.

Brewster blinked a couple of times. From upstairs, I could hear the renewed screams of the children, and I hoped like hell that Claudia was staying up there with them, protecting them. Surely she wasn't the kind of heroic fool who would come running *toward* the sound of gunshots!

I was still waiting for Brewster to collapse, but he just stood there blinking. Raphael, still pointing the gun in Brewster's direction, reached my side and hauled me to my feet. Neither one of us took our eyes off of Brewster, and we both gasped when the edges of that hole in his forehead pulled toward each other and then knitted together.

"Oh shit," Raphael said, which I thought was the understatement of the century.

Raphael got off another perfect shot, but this time Brewster didn't let a little thing like a bullet wound to his head distract him. The Taser popped, the probes digging squarely into Raphael's chest. Raphael went down with a choked cry of pain.

Brewster and I faced each other. He ejected the cartridge from his Taser, but didn't seem to have another one handy. Not that that would be much of an inconvenience for him. I'm sure he Tasered Raphael because he wanted to preserve Tommy's precious body. He had no reason to do the same for me. He also didn't need a weapon to break me in half, so I couldn't take any comfort from the fact that his Taser was empty.

Pain stabbed through my eye. Lugh, trying to take control again.

Wait, I ordered him. Imagine, me giving orders to the demon king!

But—

Wait, I repeated. *I'll let you in if I need you, but I'd rather keep you hidden if I don't.*

He could have tried the same argument Raphael had used on me in the car, could have tried to convince me that if I waited until I needed him, it would be too late. But that argument didn't fly, and he must have known it. If I could voluntarily let him in right this moment, then I could voluntarily let him in when I determined once and for all that I needed him.

Brewster took a couple of steps down the stairs. I could still hear the children crying, and I realized that whatever was going to happen, I had to get Brewster out of this house before Claudia couldn't stand it anymore and had to investigate. Or before Brewster realized he could use those kids as hostages against *me,* just as his "friends" had.

So, I did what many would agree was the most sensible thing at a time like this: I ran like hell.

Demons have superhuman strength and agility, and they're able to control their host's bodies well enough to run with great efficiency. However, the human body has its limits, and an experienced human runner can actually outrun a demon in an untrained body, for a time, at least.

I wasn't a trained runner, but I was naturally athletic and had long legs, so I was out the front door with a bit of a lead. My lead improved when Brewster made an ill-advised attempt to tackle me. I dodged and pulled farther ahead when he belly-flopped onto the driveway.

Raphael had the car keys, so if I was going to escape Brewster, I was going to have to do it on foot. I briefly wondered if I was better off trying to attract attention by going for the main road and flagging down passing cars, or avoiding attention by running through darkened backyards.

I didn't know what Brewster's story was, didn't know how he'd come to be possessed, didn't know why he'd been able to heal a bullet wound to the head as if it were no more than a minor inconvenience, but I didn't want to risk innocent passersby being hurt by him in a fight, so I chose the darkened backyard option.

Being past the Main Line, we weren't in the city proper, but we weren't exactly in the country, either, so there was plenty of light to see by, even in the semi-wooded backyards of the wealthy.

I sprinted across a beautifully maintained lawn that could have been plucked straight from the fairway of a golf course, and had just enough light to see and jump over the croquet wicket that jutted from the grass. Behind me, I could hear Brewster's heavy footfalls as he relentlessly pursued.

The coast ahead of me looked pretty clear for a stretch, so I diverted a little of my attention to grabbing and arming my Taser. Unfortunately, I didn't have a spare cartridge on me, but the Taser could still work like a stun gun if this came down to hand-to-hand combat. I didn't really want Brewster to get close enough to me for me to use the Taser, but though I could outrun him in the short term, his demon would give him more stamina than I had on my own.

Let me in, Lugh urged.

Not yet, I said again. *I trusted you enough to leave you in control before. Now it's* your *turn to trust* me.

I didn't think he liked it much, but Lugh didn't try to take over by force.

I glanced over my shoulder and saw that Brewster was catching up. I guess I was starting to slow down, though I was still running as fast as I could. My breath burned in my throat and chest, and my heart slammed against my rib cage.

The next yard I tried to cross had motion-sensing lights that came blazing to life as soon as I set foot on the lawn. Worse, there were lights on in the house, which meant someone might look out to see what had activated the sensor in the yard. I was still worried about innocent bystanders—or overprotective landowners, as the case might be—so instead of continuing my sprint across the lawn, I veered toward the patch of overgrown woods that edged the property.

The lights of the backyard had killed my night vision, so the moment I plunged into the trees, I felt like I'd gone blind. Which really sucked, because I wasn't kidding when I said the woods were overgrown. I hadn't taken two steps before my feet tangled with some particularly aggressive underbrush and I crashed to the ground.

Somehow, I managed to keep hold of the Taser, and without even thinking about it, I rolled violently to my right, just avoiding Brewster's next pounce. I hoped his night vision was as impaired as my own. If he couldn't see the Taser, which I was doing my best to conceal, then I might be able to take him by surprise.

I came to a painful stop against a fallen tree, its

bark soft and crumbly with rot. I was probably acquiring all kinds of hitchhiking nightlife.

I squinted in the darkness. My eyes were beginning to adjust, and I could see Brewster's silhouette as he pushed to his feet, about five yards away from me.

I sucked in as much air as I could, and for the first time, I could hear something other than the pounding of my heart and the thud of pursuing footsteps: barking dogs. *Loud* barking dogs. As in, barking dogs that had probably just been let out of Overprotective Landowner's house and were now on their way to deal with the trespassers.

Brewster didn't seem to care about the dogs. He started coming toward me, slowly, stalking, ready for me to leap to my feet and make another run for it.

If he jumps you, he could break your neck before you even have a chance to pull the trigger on the Taser, Lugh said, his voice urgent in my head.

I knew he was right. But if I moved with demon quickness to avoid the strike, then we could end up sending Brewster's demon back to Hell—okay, the Demon Realm, but right now Hell sounded like a better option—with the knowledge that I wasn't alone in my body. Unacceptable.

The obvious conclusion was that I couldn't let him jump on me. I could try to dodge, but if this ended up taking too much longer, those dogs would make an appearance, and I didn't think I needed any more complications.

So I did the one thing Brewster couldn't possibly expect from a human woman who'd been fleeing from him in apparent terror. I attacked.

With a battle cry to give me courage, I launched myself at him, Taser held before me, finger squeezing the trigger even before I made contact. He almost reacted in time, almost managed to grab hold of my arm before I shoved a fistful of Taser in his belly. But you know what they say about horseshoes and hand grenades...

Brewster collapsed into a pile of what I hoped was poison ivy—not that I could see diddly squat—just as two large, snarling masses of fur and teeth burst through the bushes.

I was out of breath and overloaded with adrenaline, and my Taser was running low on battery power. Plus, I wasn't in the mood to be mauled. So with only the briefest of efforts, I let Lugh take control.

Don't you dare hurt those dogs, I warned. *They're just doing their job.*

But apparently, their job involved a whole lot of intimidation and not much else. Instead of leaping for me and going for my jugular, they merely came to a stop and stood there between me and their home, teeth bared, neck fur ruffled, very intimidating snarls rising from their throats.

Moving slowly, keeping a wary eye on the dogs, which now that my eyes had finally adjusted all the way to the darkness I could see were a pair of German shepherds, Lugh bent to pick up Brewster's limp body. The dogs snarled a little louder, but still refrained from attacking. In the background, I could hear a man's voice calling to them, asking them what they'd found. I laughed to myself. Did the guy expect them to answer?

Backing away carefully and quietly, Lugh carried Brewster deeper into the weed-choked patch of woods, and the dogs didn't follow.

Chapter **29**

I wanted to take control back immediately, but Lugh pointed out that I wasn't strong enough to lug Brewster all the way back to the house, and I had to concede the point. To our mutual surprise, we ran into Raphael when we were less than halfway back.

While the chase and the final confrontation had felt like it had taken hours, I doubted more than about five or ten minutes had passed since I'd started running for it. Raphael should still be curled into a quivering ball on the Brewsters' floor, not practically colliding with Lugh and me in the woods.

Lugh apparently came to the same conclusion. He dropped Brewster's body and put his fists on his hips. The gesture was so typical of me I had to laugh. Of course, I *didn't* laugh, because I wasn't driving and *couldn't*.

"You have some explaining to do, brother," Lugh said.

"Not now," Raphael answered with a negligent wave of his hand. "We've got other things to worry about at the moment." He dropped to his knees beside

Brewster. "I gather you Tasered him?" he asked, then continued without waiting for an answer. "It won't hold him very long, and, as you might have noticed, he's a bit hard to kill."

He grabbed Brewster and rolled him over onto his stomach, pinning his arms behind his back, though at this moment Brewster couldn't put up a fight.

"Morgan, you need to exorcize him, fast." He gave me a pointed look, which I interpreted as "Don't let on you're not Morgan at the moment, even if you did just call me 'brother.'"

I wanted answers to my questions as badly as Lugh did, but Raphael was right. I might be able to get one more effective jolt out of my Taser before the battery died, but it wouldn't hold Brewster for long.

Lugh seamlessly slid into the background. I was back in control, but I didn't feel too hot. Maybe it was all that running, maybe it was the fading adrenaline high . . . I didn't know what was wrong, but my knees felt weak, my stomach twisted unhappily, and my head ached. Not the ice-pick-in-the-eye sensation that was Lugh trying to take control, but an allover pounding that felt almost like a hangover.

Now wasn't the time to moan about feeling sick, though. We had to get rid of the demon that had possessed Devon Brewster III before he became a danger once again. I sat on the ground in front of Brewster—an act for which my weak knees thanked me—and closed my eyes.

It was hard to concentrate on anything but the queasiness and the pounding in my head, but I tried to reproduce the calm, tranquil trance state I'd achieved in Tommy's car despite all the nerves that had troubled me. My gorge rose, and I had all I could handle trying to fight it down.

"Hurry up!" Raphael urged, and I wanted to give him a swift kick in the ass. Putting more pressure on me wasn't going to make relaxing any easier.

I almost blurted out that he should do it himself if he was in such a hurry, but remembered just in time that humans weren't supposed to know demons could perform exorcisms. I didn't know what Brewster's demon might make of my forbidden knowledge, but I didn't want to find out.

I could hear Brewster starting to struggle. Weakly, to be sure, but he wouldn't stay weak much longer. I had to fight past the sickness and get this done.

When I managed to conjure the scent of vanilla in my mind, I almost hurled. Food smells and queasy stomachs don't go well together. I was on the verge of panicking, when Lugh said, *Here, let me,* and took control of me for the third time this evening.

Instantly, my body steadied, and strength returned. Lugh mimicked my ritual with no trouble, and he was more than powerful enough to cast the demon from Brewster's body. He put me back in control as soon as he was done.

I felt even worse than I had before, and this time I couldn't stop myself from being sick in the bushes.

"What's wrong?" Raphael asked, still pinning the now-human Brewster to the ground.

My hands were shaking, and my skin felt clammy. And I hadn't the faintest idea what was wrong with me. And why Lugh hadn't fixed whatever it was after he'd done the exorcism?

I think your body is having an adverse reaction to the continued changes of control, Lugh said in my mind. *I tried to fix it, but I think I just made it worse. Sorry.*

Great! Just when I'd gotten almost comfortable

with the ability to let Lugh help out when necessary, there was another reason not to.

"Can I get up now?" Devon Brewster asked, his voice surprisingly calm after all he must have gone through.

Raphael rolled off him, and Brewster raised himself to a sitting position. Despite my misery, it was almost funny, the three of us sitting here on the ground in a clump of mangy woods in the dark, but no one seemed in a huge hurry to get up.

"How are you feeling, Mr. Brewster?" I asked, trying to take the focus off how I, myself, was feeling.

Brewster blinked at me. "My name is Dick."

I was pleasantly surprised to discover his mind was intact. Rarely did two exorcisms in a row turn out so favorably for the host. But I wondered if he was suffering from some kind of shock after the exorcism. "Is 'Dick' your nickname?"

"What?" Devon/Dick said.

"Is 'Dick' a nickname for 'Devon'?" I asked, speaking slowly and carefully.

His forehead furrowed with concentration. "I don't know."

What the hell was the matter with him? Maybe he had some kind of weird brain damage after all. Maybe the demon hadn't thoroughly healed those gunshot wounds. I was trying to remember one of those simple questions you're supposed to ask people who might have concussions, but Dick/Devon spoke again.

"Am I supposed to know?" he asked, and there was no missing the anxiety in his voice. "I'm sorry." He sounded even more agitated. "I'll do better next time!"

"Hush," Raphael said quietly. "No one's upset with you."

Dick/Devon looked enormously relieved, then broke out into a goofy smile. "My name is Dick," he said with renewed confidence.

Thinking of those gunshot wounds to his head made me think of how impossible what I'd witnessed had been. Those wounds would have killed any normal demon host. And then I remembered the bits and pieces of information Raphael had reluctantly coughed up about the Houston project's goals. Goals like accelerated healing.

My stomach gave an unhappy lurch, but luckily I had nothing left in it or I'd have been puking in the bushes again.

Dick was one of the Houston superhosts, and if this was his real personality we were seeing right now, he must have been possessed for a long time. Certainly throughout the course of his marriage. But it made no sense! It *couldn't* be a coincidence that two Houston superhosts ended up living in the same house. And if Dick/Devon was a superhost, then what the hell was he doing living the life of the idle rich?

I turned to glare at Raphael. He was trying to act as baffled as I felt, but he looked too nervous to pull it off.

"What the hell is going on?" I asked him.

"I want to go home," Dick said plaintively.

But how could we take him back to Claudia and the girls like this?

"We'll take you home," Raphael promised, "but we have some things to take care of first."

"Yeah, like you telling me—" I began, but of course he cut me off.

"I'll explain later. Right now, let's figure out what to tell Claudia and get out of here."

"We can't take him home to Claudia like this!" I insisted.

Raphael grimaced. "That's not what he means by 'home,'" he said cryptically. "I promise I'll explain, but right now we have to get back."

I wanted the full explanation *now*. But Claudia was probably still terrified that the demons were going to come for her children again. I couldn't leave her like that while I satisfied my need for answers. "All right," I agreed reluctantly. "But what are we going to tell her?"

Biting my tongue until I could have some quality alone-time with Raphael was one of the hardest things I'd ever done. Especially when I felt like I had three cases of flu all at the same time.

I let Raphael do all the talking when we got back to the Brewster place. He was, after all, a consummate liar. He told Claudia that her husband had been possessed, and that he'd attacked me and then run off when Raphael had come to my rescue. Naturally, Claudia was devastated, and I would have felt sorry for her if I weren't so busy feeling sorry for myself. Dick—who'd shown no indication that he thought of Claudia's house as his home—lay on the backseat of Tommy's car, keeping out of sight, while we tied up loose ends. I'd have been worried about him running off, if it weren't for his childlike—and guilt-inducing—faith that Raphael and I would help him get home.

Deciding to pin the three dead bodies all on Brewster's demon, Raphael called Adam and asked him to come "investigate." He and I and the mysterious "Dick" headed out of there before Adam arrived. Sometimes, it's useful to have the Director of Special Forces in your pocket when you're constantly finding yourself at crime scenes.

When we were a few miles from the house, Dick sat up in the backseat. "Will you take me home now?" he asked, and there was a lost, forlorn sound to his voice. Clearly, his elevator didn't go all the way to the top floor, and I wondered what we were going to do with him.

"Not quite yet," Raphael said. "It's late right now. We'll get you on your way in the morning." I started to say something indignant, but Raphael cut me off before I got started. "We'll talk later," he said, with emphasis on the word "later." He gave me a significant look, and I understood the message: not in front of our passenger.

I didn't like it, but again I held my tongue. "So where *are* we going?" I asked instead, slumping down in my seat and hoping I wasn't about to be sick again as my stomach heaved. I was sweating and shivering at the same time.

"To Adam's house," Raphael answered. "Dominic's expecting us. They have a guest room where they can keep our friend for the night."

I turned in my seat to look at Dick, then regretted the motion when my head started throbbing even harder. He was staring straight ahead, his gaze unfocused, almost vacant. I wondered if he had brothers named Tom and Harry. I imagined some demons would have found that funny.

Obviously, Dick was a product of Raphael and Dougal's eugenics program, and obviously they'd made much more progress than Raphael had ever admitted. And since they considered intelligence a drawback in a potential host, I guess they must have been happy indeed with Dick. I bet he'd never set foot outside the laboratory until some demon had decided to make use out of him.

I wished letting Lugh take control again wouldn't

make me even sicker. Because when I got Raphael alone in a room, I'd love to have enough strength to beat the shit out of him.

We arrived at Adam and Dom's place, and we installed Dick in the guest room. The same guest room I'd stayed in a couple of times—you know, the one with the locks? I didn't think Dick was going to try to go anywhere, but I had to agree that keeping him locked in was a necessary precaution.

Afterward, we all went downstairs to the kitchen, and Dominic made a pot of extra-strong Italian coffee. It smelled heavenly, but my stomach still felt awful, and I didn't dare drink any.

Dominic wanted us to wait for Adam before I began my interrogation of Raphael, but I didn't have that kind of patience. Besides, I'd waited long enough.

"It's time to start spilling the secrets," I told Raphael. "*Now!*" He was actually uncomfortable enough to squirm, and that raised my paranoia level even higher. "What the hell is Dick? How could he heal a bullet wound to the head in ten seconds? And is Tommy the same?"

Raphael squirmed some more, then took a big sip of his coffee before straightening up in his seat and raising his head to meet my gaze.

"I suppose a demonstration will explain things a little better than words," he said. He took a deep breath, then let it out slowly. Then suddenly, there was a loud cracking sound, and Raphael let out a cry of pain.

I was on my feet before I knew it, hand grabbing for my Taser, eyes scanning the kitchen for enemies. But it was just me and Dominic and Raphael.

I opened my mouth to ask Raphael what was wrong, but the words died in my throat when I got a good look at him. My knees gave way and my ass thumped down hard on the chair.

Tommy Brewster was attractive enough in a bland sort of way, if you could get past the sullen expressions that seemed natural on his face whether he was possessed or not. His least attractive feature was his nose, which was a little too large for his face and hooked a bit at the end.

But as I watched, I heard more popping and cracking noises, and that hooked beak of his started to flatten out. Raphael was gripping the table with both hands, sweat dewing his skin as his eyes squinched shut and his teeth clenched.

It took maybe thirty seconds, but by the time Raphael let out a sigh of relief and relaxed, Tommy's nose was straight and perfectly proportioned to his face.

"Shit," Raphael said, wiping the sweat from his face, "that hurt like hell."

Dominic and I looked at one another, and I'm sure my face looked as confused and alarmed as his. Neither one of us spoke. For once in my life, I couldn't think of anything to say.

Raphael, still panting a bit from pain and effort, stared ahead at nothing as he spoke. "I told you the Houston project was working at making hosts with more malleable flesh. You saw the evidence of how much progress they've made tonight. I'd say Dick up there is from the same generation as Tommy."

I swallowed an almost absurd need to laugh. I guess my Tom, Dick, and Harry suspicion hadn't been misplaced. "But Dick is Tommy's father, so how can they be the same generation?"

"He's not Tommy's father. I suspect that Devon

Brewster is dead and that Dick—or actually, Dick's demon—used the ability I just showed you to mimic his appearance."

I shook my head, still unable to make all the pieces add up. "So Claudia's been living with an imposter and didn't notice? I mean, I know Dick is the spitting image of Devon at the moment, but . . ."

"I don't know how it was done. Tommy didn't even know Devon was an imposter, so he can't clue us in, either."

Something in his voice told me there was more. "But . . . ?"

Raphael was suddenly fascinated by his coffee cup. "But I can tell you how *I* would have pulled the trick."

"Not that you'd ever do something like that yourself," I muttered, and Raphael's lips twitched, either with a suppressed retort or a smile.

"If I wanted to have a possessed superhost impersonate someone, I'd have the demon possess the person to be replaced for a little while. Just long enough to rummage through his mind, get enough of a feel for him—and enough of his memories—to do a good impersonation."

"But then why bother with this whole replacement bit? The demon could have just stayed in Devon if he wanted to play the ultimate inside man."

Raphael gave me a look that said I was an idiot. "Let's see, I could be stuck in the body of a normal, middle-aged human being—or I could possess a superhost." He tapped his chin as if thinking deeply.

"I'm glad you're finding this amusing," I growled, but Raphael merely shrugged. I wished my stomach would settle down so I could have a cup of coffee. "How much of this did you know from the very beginning?"

"I don't really *know* anything even now. It's all conjecture."

I opened my mouth to say something scathing, then let it snap closed. Lecturing Raphael on morality just wasn't worth the effort. Strangely enough, he looked defensive anyway. Perhaps he did have a small, stunted conscience somewhere in his cold, black heart.

"If I'd thought it was important information to help us put Lugh back on the throne, I'd have told the truth." He looked back and forth between me and Dominic, I guess hoping he'd find someone who'd sympathize. He was out of luck.

"How are any of us supposed to trust you when you've lied yet again?" I asked, surprised at how calm I sounded. I felt more like I should be jumping up and down and throwing things. But somehow I was just too tired, too wrung out. And too sick. My stomach was getting increasingly unhappy again, and I suspected I'd be making a run for the bathroom in a few minutes.

Raphael picked up his coffee cup and stared into its depths. "Do I get any credit for helping you save those kids? I didn't have to do that, you know. I already had what I wanted. I already had Tommy."

Raphael's really a piece of work! This was *exactly* why he'd helped me save the children—so he could use it as evidence of what an upstanding citizen he was when he was forced to give up his current batch of secrets. I laughed a bit at the realization, though Raphael and Dominic both looked puzzled. I guess they couldn't see the humor in it.

Yes, Raphael's morality would always be in question, and I could never be sure anything he told me was the truth. But he was a powerful demon of the royal line, he was now in possession of one of his lab-bred superhosts who clearly had properties that we might find useful, and he was loyal to Lugh. For all his faults, we were stuck with him.

Sometimes, life just sucks.

Chapter 30

I was still sick as a dog the next day, and would have liked nothing more than to stay curled up in bed for the foreseeable future. Unfortunately, I was stupid enough to answer the phone when Claudia called—I'd forgotten her insistence that we would "talk tomorrow." Somehow, I ended up agreeing to meet her for lunch, although I doubted I'd be up to eating by then.

I had to bring Raphael—with his nose now shifted back to normal—to lunch with me, because I knew I'd never be able to feed Claudia the pack of lies we'd concocted. I say "we," but naturally it was Raphael who came up with the story. Although we assumed Devon was dead, we had no idea where the demons had hidden the body, so we had to let Claudia go on thinking he was on the loose somewhere, possessed by a hostile demon. I'd have preferred to have given her closure, but I honestly couldn't think of a good alternative.

I liked the story about Tommy even less. We told Claudia that when Raphael had tried to leave Tommy and transfer back to his original host, Tommy's brain had shut down, just like Jordan Maguire's. Raphael—the hero!—had quickly gone back into Tommy to save his life. And so, despite the fact that I had exorcized the demon who had originally possessed Tommy, Tommy was doomed to host a demon for the rest of his life.

"I'm so sorry," I blurted to Claudia when Raphael finished talking.

Her eyes were red-rimmed and glimmered with tears, but she managed a fragile smile. "Don't be," she said. "You did everything you could, and I'm sure Tommy's in much better hands now with your friend."

I still hadn't recovered from last night's nausea, and I almost gagged at the thought of Raphael's hands being better than *anyone's*.

"If it weren't for you," Claudia continued, "that horrible demon would still be in Tommy, and the girls and I would probably all be dead. I can't thank you enough for everything you've done for us!"

I wished the floor would swallow me. Here she was *thanking* me, when I had willingly sacrificed her son to save my brother. I sat there choking on guilt, unable to say anything, unable to meet her eyes.

"Ease up on the self-flagellation," Raphael told me when we got back into Tommy's POS car. "I didn't tell you this earlier, because I figured you wouldn't believe me, and you probably still won't. But there are a lot of cancer genes bred into this strain, and all hell would break loose in Tommy's body if he didn't have a demon in residence to keep the cancer contained. He already had a couple of tumors beginning. Too small to give him any trouble yet, but a few months down the road..."

I stared straight ahead through the windshield. "You're right. I don't believe you."

*   *   *

One week later, Lugh's council on the Mortal Plain gathered in the basement of Adam and Dominic's house. That council consisted of me, Adam, Dominic, Raphael, Andy . . . and Brian.

He and I had had a bit of a fight about my completely leaving him out of the loop when Raphael and I went on our dangerous rescue mission. Having been at the time still sick with the aftereffects of Lugh's control, I was in a weakened condition and readily agreed that I should have told Brian all. I then in a fit of recklessness invited him to be part of this royal council, or whatever the hell we really were.

I realized having him as part of the council was inevitable if he and I were going to stay together. And it seemed that, despite a whole lot of obstacles and problems that weren't going away anytime soon, we weren't ready to give up on each other yet.

A lot had happened in the week since we'd rescued the Brewster girls. The U.S. Exorcism Board had suspended me, pending an investigation into my potential mishandling of the Jordan Maguire exorcism. It was bullshit, and they knew it, but Jordan Maguire Sr. had enough money to make them dance to his twisted little song. Besides, my name had already been associated with an illegal exorcism in the past, and though the charges had been dropped, I'm sure they raised a few of the Board members' eyebrows. They were operating on the "better safe than sorry" theory.

I'd received three more death threats on my answering machine, though so far no one had attempted to make good on them.

And I'd confirmed that there was no one by the name of Barbara Paige working for the *Philadelphia*

Inquirer. I'd hoped that meant she was law enforcement of some kind—which would be bad enough, but which I could at least deal with—but Adam had done some digging and hadn't been able to find any evidence that she worked with the police or FBI.

I had an uncomfortable suspicion that I hadn't seen the last of Reporter Barbie, whoever she really was. And I *didn't* think she was in my corner. I couldn't help wondering if there was a connection between Jordan Maguire's death, the death threats on my answering machine, and the sudden appearance of Reporter Barbie on the scene. I didn't like the implications if there was.

But all of these problems paled in comparison to this very unsavory meeting of Lugh's council. Because, you see, we were about to do something that I was convinced was morally wrong. Brian wholeheartedly agreed with me, but ours were the lone voices of dissent. I don't think Andy was happy with the idea, either, but he didn't put up much of an argument. He'd been subdued and unnaturally quiet ever since he'd come back, and so far my attempts to draw him out had met with no success. When I asked him what was wrong, I was met with the most stereotypical of all male answers: "Nothing. I'm fine."

Brian and I could have stayed away, boycotted this whole thing. But the fact was there was no way we could *stop* it, and if we weren't going to stop it, then we would bear witness. So it was that we found ourselves in this basement, complicit with the other members of Lugh's council even if we weren't in agreement.

Each of us held a bloodred candle, those candles providing the only light in the room. We sat in a circle, but we didn't have to hold hands or anything.

In the center of the circle, Dick lay on his back, with his hands clasped loosely over his midsection.

The expression on his face was one of almost beatific joy, and eagerness seemed to flow out of him in waves.

I blinked away a hint of tears. Dick's eagerness didn't make this right. It hadn't taken more than about ten minutes of conversation with him to realize that by all legal definitions, he was not competent to make such a decision. We were none of us psychologists, but it didn't take a genius to figure out that Dick had the emotional and intellectual maturity of a child.

He had not been educated. He had not been taught any real social skills. He had not interacted with other, non-possessed human beings. And he'd been taught since the day he was born that he was merely an empty vessel, meant to be filled by a demon when his body was mature. Of *course* if someone asked him if he'd like to be the host of the demon Saul, he'd say yes.

I'd tried calm, rational arguments. That hadn't lasted very long before I'd transitioned to shouting and invective. But to Adam and Dom and Lugh, it seemed that they'd found an ideal host for Saul. When I'd questioned Dominic about how his morbidly masochistic former demon would treat poor, mentally challenged Dick, Dominic had dismissed my concerns.

"Saul will take good care of him," Dom had insisted, and I'd felt like slapping him.

"If Saul's such a fucking saint, then why was Lugh so worried about finding a compatible host for him?" I asked.

Dominic gave me a hard look. "Because there are a lot of people out there who have a very judgmental outlook on BDSM practices, and Saul would *not* get along well with one of them, nor would one of them be happy to host him."

"And you think *Dick* is into S&M?" I cried.

"No. I think Dick has never been taught to think of it as something sick and deviant, so it won't bother him as it would *some* people." There was no question which "some people" he meant. "And just like Saul shielded me from feeling it when things got rougher than I like, he'll shield Dick. He's really quite compassionate."

I'd managed to stop myself from arguing more, because it was clear even to a stubborn mule like me that I wasn't changing Dom's mind.

I'd assumed that to initiate the ritual, I'd be asked to let Lugh take control so he could tell Dick Saul's True Name for the incantation. Of course, my inclination was to refuse, but I didn't think Raphael or Adam would have any problem with the idea of knocking me unconscious so Lugh could take over without my permission.

But when the ritual began, it turned out my assumption had been wrong. Raphael put down his candle and broke the circle, kneeling on the floor beside Dick, then bending to whisper something in his ear. He straightened up and raised his eyebrows at Dick.

"Got it?" he asked.

Still smiling like this was the greatest day of his life, Dick nodded. Raphael returned to his place and picked up his candle. I had no idea what was going to happen next. Usually, summonings are performed only by the inner circle of the Spirit Society, so I had nothing to do with them.

I expected there to be a lot of chanting and other mumbo jumbo. After all, the Spirit Society is big on ritual and formality. Then again, we weren't the Spirit Society.

In the center of the circle, Dick began to whisper, the words so soft I couldn't make out anything except a breathy hiss. Even though I couldn't make out the words, there was a definite cadence to the sounds, and

I could tell that Dick repeated the sequence three times.

No bells clanged. No lights flashed. There was no speaking in tongues, nor any sense of a malevolent presence. It was almost anticlimactic.

After the third repetition of the chant, Dick fell silent. Seconds later, he blinked, and I could immediately see that it wasn't Dick anymore. The vapid, vacant expression had faded, and though it could have been entirely my imagination, I thought I saw a keen intelligence in those formerly dull eyes.

The demon Saul pushed himself up into a sitting position and looked around him. He grinned broadly when he saw Adam, then looked astonished when he caught sight of Dominic.

"Many things have changed since you left the Mortal Plain, my friend," Adam said. "And yes, Dom knows it's you." He put his arm around Dominic's shoulders in a gesture I couldn't help seeing as possessive.

I think Saul saw it that way, too. He raised an eyebrow, then seemed to decide to leave that puzzle for later. He continued looking around the circle, scowling when he saw me, but he clearly didn't recognize anyone else.

"Welcome back to the Mortal Plain," Raphael said, and there was a strangely ironic grin on his face.

Saul turned his attention to Raphael, looking him up and down before he shrugged. "Am I supposed to know you?"

"I look a little different than I did the last time you saw me."

Saul narrowed his eyes. "Who are you?" he demanded.

Raphael sighed. "Would it help you identify me if I

told you that I'm the one who gave your host your True Name?"

Saul scrambled to his feet, and the rest of us instinctively did the same. *Can you give me a hint at what's going on?* I asked Lugh.

I think you're about to find out, he replied grimly.

Saul stood stiffly in the center of the circle, fists clenched at his sides as he stared at Raphael. I think he'd forgotten the rest of us were there.

"Please tell me you're Lugh!" Saul demanded.

Raphael grinned, but the expression was strained. Whatever was going on, he wasn't terribly happy about it. "Would you have me lie to you?"

Saul snorted. "Why not? Lying is your most practiced skill!" He suddenly turned to face Adam, who stood almost directly behind him. "And you're allied with him?" he asked in obvious outrage. "I would never have believed—"

"Yes, I'm allied with him," Adam interrupted. "But believe it or not, *he's* allied with Lugh. It seems his allegiance with Dougal was another one of his lies."

Raphael laughed. "I never thought of it that way, but I suppose you're right." Saul didn't look any happier. "But come now!" Raphael said with patently false cheer. "Why don't you tell everyone why you hold me in such high regard? Tell them who I am to you that I know your True Name."

A premonition tingled at the edges of my mind. I'd never gotten around to asking Lugh why Saul had a True Name. He'd told me once that True Names were granted to the extraordinary. And one definition of "extraordinary" was apparently "royal."

Saul's lips twisted into a teeth-baring snarl. "You are *no one* to me!"

Raphael put on a look of mock hurt, but I was

pretty sure he was using it to camouflage a very real pain. "This would have worked so much better if I'd named you Luke," he said, then cleared his throat noisily and continued in a truly terrible Darth Vader impression. "Saul, I am your father."

Sometimes I really hate it when I'm right. "Wait a minute," I said, realizing that, despite my premonition, this revelation made no sense. I pointed what probably looked like an accusing finger at Saul.

"I exorcized you. Everyone keeps telling me I'm not powerful enough to exorcize a royal."

Saul started to answer, but Raphael cut him off. "Don't get him started talking about my shortcomings as a father," he said. "He'll go on about it all day, and it can get rather tiresome."

Saul's mother was not *a royal,* Lugh told me. *Raphael could have contributed some of his own power at Saul's conception, but he chose not to. Even so, I doubt you could have managed the exorcism if Saul had fought you. And I doubt another exorcist could have done it at all.*

It sounded like I needed to get Lugh to give me a course on Demon Reproduction 101. But now was not the time. Saul had taken a couple of steps closer to Raphael, and I didn't think it was to give him a filial hug.

"Let me get this straight," I said before things could erupt into violence. I pointed at Saul. "You hate Raphael because he's a lousy father. *I* hate Raphael because . . . well, just because he's Raphael. Brian and I are pissed off at the lot of you for letting a simple-minded innocent be possessed. Adam is pissed at me for any number of things, and the feeling is mutual. Andy is a charter member of the 'We Hate Raphael' club, and he's mad at me either for letting Raphael get to him the second time or for sacrificing Tommy Brewster to save him, or maybe both.

"And we're supposed to put all those differences aside and work together as a team to put Lugh back on the throne?" I felt one of those annoying bouts of hysterical laughter coming on, but I managed to squelch it. I shook my head. "We'll be lucky to get out of this basement without bloodshed."

The fate of the entire human race rests on the ability of this council of angry, antagonistic misfits to work together, to be honest with one another, and to watch each other's backs. I have two words for you.

We're doomed.

About the Author

Jenna Black is your typical writer. Which means she's an "experience junkie." She got her BA in physical anthropology and French from Duke University. Once upon a time, she dreamed she would be the next Jane Goodall, camping in the bush making fabulous discoveries about primate behavior. Then, during her senior year at Duke, she did some actual research in the field and made this shocking discovery: primates spend something like 80 percent of their time doing such exciting things as sleeping and eating. Concluding that this discovery was her life's work in the field of primatology, she then moved on to such varied pastimes as grooming dogs and writing technical documentation. Visit her on the Web at www.JennaBlack.com.

And be sure not to miss more heat
and hellfire in

SPEAK OF THE DEVIL

By

JENNA BLACK

The next installment in the Morgan Kingsley series

This time it's personal . . .

Hosting the king of the demons is hard enough without becoming the target of a mysterious enemy with a deadly grudge. To make things worse, Morgan must also defend herself against a lawsuit that won't die and a private investigator determined to unearth her every secret. With anonymous death threats piling up and her enemy closing in, Morgan stands to lose everything she holds dear: her reputation, her boyfriend, her freedom . . . and maybe even her life.

Coming in Fall 2009 from Dell Spectra